STEAM
THE
PIG

THE STEAM PIG

PIG

JAMES McCLURE

PANTHEON BOOKS, NEW YORK

Library of Congress Cataloging in Publication Data

McClure, James, 1939-
The steam pig.

(Pantheon international crime)
Reprint. Originally published: New York:
Harper & Row, 1972.
I. Title. II. Series.
PR9369.3.M3S8   1982   823   81-48254
ISBN 0-394-71021-5 (pbk.)   AACR2

Manufactured in the United States of America

First Pantheon Paperback Edition 1982

To Lorly

FOR AN UNDERTAKER George Henry Abbott was a sad man. He let his job get on top of him. He let it keep him awake nights. He made mistakes.

But business stayed good. It helped, having a name that had an alphabetical right to head the list of funeral directors in the Yellow Pages. And having a telephone number like 77007. Five digits—not a big city, even by South African standards, yet both populous and lethal enough to allow Mr. Abbott and his competitors little time for the morning newspaper.

Straight after breakfast he got up and opened the refrigerator door. The night before, Farthing, his young assistant, had seen to the morning job and left him the two on the right. With a sigh, he stooped and tugged at the bottom tray. It slid out silently before being arrested with a slight bump which set the toes quivering.

Mr. Abbott found the sight of them caused a strange, pleasurable tickling on the roof of his stomach. He could tell a lot from toes. These were very neat with a suggestion of intelligence more like thumbs. And very feminine.

Using the Pollock adjustable-height trolley, he transferred the tray's contents to the postmortem slab. Two deft flicks removed the sheet and a third had it folded over his arm.

This time it got Mr. Abbott in the pit of the stomach. The girl had been in the prime of life. And if there were such a thing, she was in the prime of death, too.

The startling beauty of the remains did not distress him. On the contrary, he had always held that his colleagues were being hypocritical when they declared themselves unmoved by any subject of their toil.

But he was right, damn them. Look at her. Like that poet had said: a thing of beauty was a joy forever. The perfect figure, and bones good for years yet. The navel, a dainty dish, was especially fine.

His eyes felt none of the chill of the taut white skin. His fingertips rejoiced in the spring of the thick hair. Like the toes, the fingers were exquisitely shaped and well cared for. Not a mark or blemish anywhere.

He had left the face till last. Thank God, a young face. He had had his surprises. A practiced pinch closed the mouth and showed its good humor. Above it a pert nose and alert un-plucked eyebrows. The eyes had to be blue because the hair was blond, real ash blond. Yes, they were.

Beautiful. Minutes passed.

Then resentment caught him unawares and he found himself thinking of his wife. Mrs. Priscilla Abbott, once the boss's widow, who had allowed him to put his own name up outside in the expectation this would encourage them to live happily ever after.

He just might have if there had been such a body to soothe the sour wrinkles from his mind after a late call. An urgent, life-giving body with thighs that pressed forward even in repose. Not a carrot-haired, obese form that never stirred, never uttered a sound as he tiptoed in, and had feet so cold their touch caused a spinal reflex which jerked him awake horribly.

"George!" She filled the doorway.

He gave three clumsy flicks and succeeded in covering the girl. Then he turned with a cough.

"That must be the one for the postmortem," Mrs. Abbott said. Cough.

2

"Then let Dr. Strydom do his own preparation for once and get the other one ready for three o'clock I've just had the crematorium on the line and they say it's a heavy afternoon. We can't be late again."

Cough.

"It's a Trinity job—get on with it!" Mrs. Abbott snapped and went back to man the front office.

Her spouse hurried over for the second tray.

Three o'clock and all was going smoothly. Smoothly as grand-dad on casters, Farthing observed.

Mr. Abbott frowned. Partly to discourage another labored lapse of taste, partly because he always felt uneasy when there were no hitches to confirm the part he had played in making the arrangements. Gingerly, he began to review the proceedings.

To start with, it was an Arabella funeral, all inclusive at 128 rand—or 64 pounds sterling if you were dealing with one of the old families who still called the UK "home." And had pictures of the Queen—Queen Victoria more often than not. How his mind wandered. He would pin it down with familiar fact.

Arabella was a code name used to spare relatives the added pain of mentioning money. They wandered at will around the showroom and made their choice from cards propped in little easels on each gleaming lid: Arabella, Doris, Daphne, Carson. Mrs. Abbott had chosen the names. The cost was given discreetly small but in red.

Ah, not that there had been anyone to choose in this case. Or indeed any need for a stated preference. The Arabella, being a compromise between Doris (municipal pauper) and Daphne (genteelly modest), was standard issue to members of the Trinity Burial Society.

Not that it was a burial either, but again he was right on this. An additional twenty cents on the weekly premium ensured cremation for the lonely old lady with that quite extraordinary

3

tattoo few men could have seen. Or, God forbid, a great number.

Mr. Abbott shuddered, dismissing his next thought.

Simultaneously a red light shone on the console in the crematorium superintendent's hidden cubicle. His right index finger, stiff as a baton, dropped on the button marked *Organ Finale*. His left activated the conveyor belt.

The 3 P.M. Arabella, Ref. No. A44/TBS, began its ponderous exit toward the hatch. At the last second an automatic trip parted the velvet drapes and it was gone. Then the oven door clanged faintly. Gone for good.

"Same age as me, too," Farthing muttered as the music stopped.

He added something that Mr. Abbott failed to catch as "Abide with Me" ran back at full volume to its starting point on the tape. But what he had said was more than enough.

The Reverend Wilfred Cooke, curiously subdued by having addressed a chapel empty save for the Almighty, stepped down and dried his pink palm ready for the check.

Farthing was waiting in the superintendent's office to hand it over. Then he was to see to some plaques for the Garden of Remembrance. Maxwell & Flynn were due in at half-past for a society send-off and would give him a lift back to town.

For Mr. Abbott had left very suddenly. The hearse once touched 58 mph—that was in Jacaranda Avenue.

From the street the premises of Abbott & Marcus Ltd. appeared to have little to recommend them other than an old-world matter-of-factness. But behind the coarse red-brick facade with its blue opaque windows and autumnal gold-leaf lettering, beyond the cream and brown office and showroom, was a mortuary few private concerns could equal.

It had been the realization of a dream for Franklin Marcus, the first undertaker to reach what was then a frontier town. After an initial bit of bother with the carpenter, who resented losing a lucrative sideline, he secured a military contract on the

4

eve of the first Zulu War and prospered exceedingly. Plowing back his profits, Mr. Marcus had two surgical tables shipped out and the walls of his new mortuary tiled to shoulder height. A large cold room was then added which—as he said—made the place big enough for an army.

And in his early days, Mr. Abbott had carried on the Marcus tradition by introducing a proper shadowless light and three wall cabinets of autopsy instruments. Although overt hostilities with the natives had ceased, a grossly inadequate state mortuary was often glad to have his facilities at its disposal. What was more, the state also found it expedient to have Mr. Abbott attend to the rites after postmortem and this meant a handsome retainer, plus commission. He had always been very happy about this arrangement.

Until Farthing had spoken.

Mr. Abbott swung the hearse into the yard gate and pulled up round the back beside the district surgeon's Pontiac. Damn the man—was he never late for anything? Most doctors were occasionally delayed by emergency calls, but not Dr. Christiaan Strydom. His patients either queued at stipulated times for travel shots or waited, cool and unhurried, forever if need be.

Mr. Abbott started across to the mortuary, wincing at the harsh grate of the gravel, for it betrayed the undignified speed of his approach.

In there was the girl who had made his day; the sweet enigma who teased so sweetly and whose secrets he would never know.

And in there was Strydom, reading her like a book; the rib cage split down the sternum and opened out, the organs excised and placed neatly in a row like footnotes. Poring over her as indifferent to the odor as an antiquarian searching through musty manuscript for something significant in the same old story.

Only it was the wrong book.

He slipped in one side of the double doors with their stained-glass panels, closed it carefully behind him, and edged over to

5

the slab. The district surgeon went on filling in his form with no more than a nod. They were old friends.

Mr. Abbott looked down at the toes. Clearly the label had been there all the time, for the string attaching it was deeply embedded. Worse still, there were no blots or other defacements to obscure the details entered on the card in Farthing's childish cursive. The reference number was undeniably A44/TBS. Her name was not Elizabeth Bowers but Theresa le Roux.

He coughed.

Taking it as his cue, Dr. Strydom rumbled: "Some bastard's going to pay for this, you have my word for it."

Mr. Abbott choked.

2

A SUSPECT IN the next room screamed. Not continuously, but at irregular intervals which made concentration difficult. Then the typewriter unaccountably jammed. The report was not going to be finished on time; Colonel Du Plessis had stipulated four o'clock and it was already three fifty-five with at least a page to go.

"So you can bloody well stick it, Colonel, sir," Lieutenant Tromp Kramer declared loudly. He was quite alone in the Murder Squad office.

And finally giving vent to a righteous anger. There was simply no sense in risking a hernia by hammering out the mundane events which had led to the sudden messy death of Bantu female Gertrude Mkumo. No sense at all.

Her killer, one Bantu male Johannes Nkosi, had resisted arrest just before dawn and was mostly in the intensive care unit at Peacevale Hospital. His chances of standing trial were minimal, the doctors said—which was one way of putting it. Okay, so there would be an inquest. But an inquest was nothing compared to a court case. Nobody would be interested in more than a brief statement from the witness box. Nor would there be any trouble from the families involved. Gertrude's lot were more than satisfied with the way things had gone. Shantytown folk always relished a bit of rough justice administered in this world and the forensic niceties left for the next. As for Nkosi's relatives, they had never heard of him.

Plainly a lot of totally unnecessary paper work and fiddle could be avoided by shelving the matter overnight. And the Colonel knew this only too well, the bastard. *He* had not been called out at 4 A.M.

Worse still, he would not even bother to glance through the report when he got it; if you've read one Bantu murder you've read the lot, he inevitably observed. All he wanted was the sordid particulars converted into a docket of nice clean paper which he could delicately press fore and aft with his rubber stamp. That done, he would smugly add the job to his Crimes Solved graph and get back to arse-creeping the Brigadier—yet another triumph for law and order reduced to a colonic toehold. The four o'clock deadline was quite arbitrary, a crude manifestation of incipient megalomania.

Which somehow brought the time up to a minute after the hour and the telephone rang.

Oh, Jesus, the Colonel. The voice from the carpeted office above was petulant. Kramer swung the receiver away from his ear and ran a finger down the thigh of his calendar girl. She was delightfully brown.

The shrill squeakings stopped abruptly.

Kramer responded with practiced contrition: "Sorry, sir—I'll have it with you first thing tomorrow. *Hey?*"

Something had upset the Colonel but it was nothing to do with the report, that much was obvious. Kramer grabbed a ballpoint and managed to get down three names before the line went dead. Damn, he should have asked for a recap. He had not the faintest bloody idea what was going on.

Still, he had the names. While he did not know Theresa le Roux from Eve van der Genesis, the old music hall turn of Abbott and Strydom was all too familiar. It gave more than a fair indication of where a fruitful investigation could start and about time, too.

He buzzed the duty officer, booked himself out, and left the building on foot. Georgie's place was just around the corner, behind the museum.

As Kramer turned into Ladysmith Street, he saw a taxi from the station rank draw up outside the funeral parlor. Almost immediately a great meal sack of a woman topped with ginger frizz launched herself at it from a side entrance, followed by an aging cookboy dragging two suitcases. Then Georgie emerged cautiously into the street as if expecting sniper fire, to do the soap-and-water bit with his hands.

Kramer sidestepped into a bus queue and watched the departure over the top of someone's evening newspaper.

Georgie's mute appeals were to no avail. Without sparing him a glance, Ma Abbott heaved herself aboard the taxi. It shuddered and then took off with a squeal of contempt from its tires.

Somebody had been a naughty boy again. And this time the old bitch was not going to share in the disgrace. To give her credit where it was due, her loyalty had so far been remarkable, even at the height of the Sister Constance scandal. That was when Georgie had forgotten to finish off the eyes and had displayed the nun in the chapel with a lewd wink for her mourners.

The bus had been and gone and Kramer was standing alone on the curb. Georgie had vanished. There was no more playing for time to be had—he would have to take a chance on his penchant for patterns.

The front office was empty apart from an elderly customer intent on a catalogue of ornate headstones. From the look of her, she had not a moment to lose.

Kramer went to the farthest end of the high counter and gave the service bell a pat. There was a responding clatter from somewhere offstage behind the curtains. Then nothing. Perhaps Georgie kept a cat—although Christ knew what mice would find to eat in the place.

He rang the bell again, twice.

Come to think of it, a satin-quilted deluxe model would make mice one hell of a boudoir. Maybe they came around at night

9

to sleep and have their friends in. Hmm, premature burial was a risk. No doubt that could account for the frequent preoccupation of pallbearers processing with their ears pressed against the coffin side: they were evaluating the frantic scratching sounds from within.

But it would take some cat to tweak a peephole in the curtains five feet above their hem. And to creak the floorboards so loudly in retreat. Kramer found all this instructive and reassuring. Something was definitely in the air.

An impression which was confirmed almost immediately by the arrival of Sergeant Fanie Prinsloo, who was standing in as official photographer for the week.

"Come to take my little snaps," he said cheerily, dumping an enormous gadget bag on the counter. Prinsloo could never resist bringing every damn bit of equipment with him; ordinarily he worked in Fingerprints and had to satisfy his artistic drive on weekends with a box camera.

Kramer greeted him guardedly.

"What gives, Lieutenant?" Prinsloo said after a pause.

"You try," Kramer suggested, pushing across the bell.

Prinsloo was plainly puzzled by all this standing around on ceremony. But he grinned and thumped it with his sirloin of a fist. Still nothing happened.

So Kramer sighed and Prinsloo mistook relief for agitation. Not that the sergeant was stupid, simply new to CID and as yet poorly acquainted with the men in the Murder Squad—something which Kramer intended to exploit. His ploy was to invert the unwritten law No. 178/a, which states it is an officer's prerogative to pretend ignorance in order to establish the efficiency of subordinates.

"Right, Sergeant, what were your orders?" Kramer challenged.

Orders was a rather strong word to use in the context of a routine assignment, but Prinsloo recognized the ritual and replied very properly: "I was told to report to you here and to take what pictures seemed necessary."

10

"Of?"

"Some dolly or other."

"Name?"

"Er—something Le Roux, sir."

"Theresa le Roux?" Kramer snapped, inducing the required degree of discomfiture.

Predictably, in an attempt to appease, it now all came out in a rush: "Look sir, I was in the darkroom when the chief starts yelling through the door that I'd better get down here quick because you are on your way and Doc Strydom has done a PM on the wrong body because Abbott made a balls and it's murder."

Kramer remained silent—which took some doing.

"That's all he said, sir. Plus the name. But you—"

"No need to get like that, Sarge," Kramer said soothingly. "Got to keep you new boys on your toes."

So that was it. A murder. And for once it sounded like the real thing.

Prinsloo just had time to grab his gear before Kramer disappeared through the curtains. Beyond them was the chapel, which reeked of stale water, and then a passage lined with floral tributes waiting to be distributed to the sick. Stepping carefully, they reached a door marked MORTUARY and pushed it open.

Dr. Strydom was alone. He turned sharply at the sound of the door slamming back on its spring and hurriedly waddled over.

"Ah, Lieutenant, I'm delighted to see you."

"Doctor."

"Got my little message, did you?"

"Sort of."

"Ah."

"What's been going on here, then?"

Dr. Strydom overtly looked around Kramer to see if there was anyone standing behind him.

"You've not seen Mr. Abbott? Strange, I thought he was out there. This little affair is *rather* delicate."

"Oh, yes?"

11

A deep breath, then: "In a nutshell, Lieutenant, I'm afraid there's been a bit of a muddle. Two cadavers, both female, and my official one got cremated this afternoon."

Prinsloo clucked his tongue like a wog washerwoman finding pee stains.

"Where does that leave us?" Kramer inquired coldly. He had not moved since entering.

Dr. Strydom paused to pick his words.

"You could say a lot better off—if not too much fuss is made."

Now Kramer was certain that the district surgeon had been party to the little affair, as he called it. Georgie had not accomplished it all by himself. However, that side of it could be dealt with later when the old dodderer's cooperation and self-confidence were not so essential. He shrugged negligently.

"Uhuh. Who went in the oven?"

"I took the liberty of checking while you were coming over," Dr. Strydom replied. "Some poor old dear found under a bush down near Mason's Stream where the sherry tramps hang out. Just a routine. Age? Booze? Both probably. Somebody to sign the certificate. A right tart in her day, I hear."

Kramer turned his gaze to the table.

"And this one? Another tart?"

"I very much doubt it," Dr. Strydom answered, snapping the cuffs of his rubber gloves.

"But you're sure it's murder?"

"Oh, yes! Why not see for yourself?" His tone became curiously gleeful, rather like an amateur magician's opening patter. Friends, I am about to utterly astonish you.

So the two detectives followed him over. On the way Kramer realized why the one place he hated seeing a stiff was a morgue. The trouble was the height of the table, which gave you no opportunity to adjust to the sight by degrees on the approach. You had to be on top of it before you knew what it was all about.

Where Mr. Abbott had last seen his Ophelia, Kramer now saw a life-size rag doll. Or so it seemed. Large knives, hardly scalpels, are used for opening a body. This one was now held together again by thick black thread in Dr. Strydom's erratic herringbone stitch with the surgeon's tow stuffing protruding at intervals. It was also a patchwork of bright colors—the sun having shifted across to act like a giant projector lamp behind the stained-glass windows. When Dr. Strydom switched on the main light he heightened the illusion by rendering the hues in pastel, which better suited the form, and by making the untouched head and shoulders gleam like fine porcelain. Kramer noticed that a very tiny brush had been used to paint on such long eyelashes.

And he concentrated for a while on the head. One thing was certain: he had never seen it before—that was a face you would never forget. He bent to examine the hair roots.

"Yes, it's dyed," Dr. Strydom said. "Brown eyes, you see. A common enough failing among nice young women, not only tarts."

Kramer jerked a thumb crudely.

"Well, on a rough guess, I'd say she lost her virginity about a year ago." Dr. Strydom chuckled. "But that doesn't amount to much these days either. You should see—"

"Any kids?"

"No, never."

"Disease?"

"None."

"Then the chances are she wasn't sleeping around, just having it with a steady."

"Right."

"That gives us something to go on. Recently, do you think?"

"Possibly not within twelve hours of death. Although it would depend on precautionary method preferred."

Kramer smiled wryly at the lapse into clinic jargon. The old bugger was more himself now.

"Well, Doc, what about the m.o.?"

"Like to take a guess?"

"After you've hacked her around? It looks like a Mau Mau atrocity. What did the death cert. say?"

13

"Cardiac."

"And what was it?"

"Bicycle spoke."

The words stabbed. Christ, this was really something. Bantu murdering Bantu was nothing. White murdering white was seldom any better, they just had counsel who could make a ready reckoner wring your heart. But mix Bantu and white together and you had instant headlines two inches high. It remained to be seen how much larger they could grow when it was known that a bizarre Bantu weapon had been used.

Kramer gestured impatiently for the district surgeon to turn the body on its side.

"Know what the Lieutenant's up to?" Dr. Strydom asked Prinsloo.

"He's looking for puncture marks along the spine," Prinsloo whispered, "where they put the spoke in to paralyze her—like Shoe Shoe."

Dr. Strydom smiled smugly.

"She's *dead*, not paralyzed, man. What's happened here is along the same lines but the intent is quite different. Think for a moment. When the spoke's used by the local boys they sterilize the point first with a match. Why? So there won't be any infection. So the victim will live to regret his mistakes as long as possible. Like Shoe Shoe, as you said.

"Here, however, it is used the way I saw it done thirty years ago on the Rand, in the Jo'burg townships. Not often, mind you, and it's so clever we probably missed dozens on a Monday with the weekend to clear up. Specialty of the Bantu gangs. Look . . ."

Dr. Strydom pulled the left arm away from the body and propped it at right angles on the edge of the slab. He pointed.

"Tell me what you see there," he said.

Kramer stopped. It was an armpit. A small, hairy armpit. The girl had not used a razor, unusual but without significance.

"Now look again," Dr. Strydom urged, parting the tufts with a retractor.

14

"Flea bite?"

"All quite simple if you have the stomach for it," Dr. Strydom explained. "You take your spoke, nicely sharpened up on a brick, and slide it in here between the third and fourth ribs. Your target's the aorta where it ascends from the heart."

"Yirra, you call that simple," Prinsloo scoffed.

"Oh, but it is. You just aim for the high point on the opposite shoulder. The artery is pretty tough so you know when you've hit it. An expert can do it first time, a novice may take a few shots—like trying to spear spaghetti round on a plate."

Prinsloo backed off a pace. Big and paunchy, he looked a man who enjoyed his food.

"And then?" Kramer was engrossed.

"Man, the pressure in that aorta's fantastic," Dr. Strydom continued. "I've seen blood hit the ceiling with an aneurism that burst during an op. But as you withdraw a thin thing like a bike spoke, it seals off, see? All those layers, muscles, lungs, tissue, close up. You just wrap a hankie or rag round the spoke in the armpit and that takes care of any on the way out."

Kramer straightened up, patted his pockets for cigarettes, and took one the district surgeon proffered.

"Not bad, not bad at all, doctor."

Dr. Strydom attempted modesty: "Of course I tracked it down from all the blood loose in the cavities. One can't really blame Matthews, I suppose."

"Who's that?"

"Her doctor, a GP out Morninghill way. The visible signs were identical to certain types of cardiac arrest. She had a history, I'm told."

That was a slip. In Kramer's experience death certificates never mentioned case histories. This meant that the DS must have already been in touch with Matthews. Pity, now he would have all his excuses off pat, but that was the medical brotherhood for you—more closely knit than the Mafia and often as deadly. Still, he would let that pass, too. He had one or two questions to go.

15

"How long would it have taken her to die?"

"Ten minutes, fifteen at the outside; although if the shock itself was great enough I'd say almost immediately."

"Uhuh. Scream?"

"She could've but it'd only take a pillow to muffle it. There's no facial bruising. Anyhow, with her brain starved of blood she'd be out pretty quickly."

"What about this bruising on her arm?"

"Can't be positive. Easily come by when you've been thrashing round in a convulsion."

This association of violent action with the violently inactive Miss le Roux had the subtle obscenity of a warm lavatory seat. Kramer decided he had had enough.

"She's all yours, Sergeant. When you've finished the ones for your private album, I'd like a set of six head-and-shoulders not looking too glum."

Dr. Strydom accompanied him from the room.

"Where's Abbott?" Kramer demanded in the passage.

"Here, officer," came a meek voice from the chapel. And although Ma Abbott had gone, and Farthing was out doing a country removal, he insisted on being interviewed in his showroom, which had a soundproof sliding door.

At this point Dr. Strydom took his leave, having suddenly remembered his daily appointment beside the triangle in the central prison. Those sentenced to strokes would already be lining up and waiting for him. He had to certify them fit for punishment, see the kidneys were properly protected, and keep an eye on responses. Buttocks are a common vehicle of abuse, but it is not prudent to abuse them overmuch.

"Okay, but I want the laboratory reports tonight," Kramer said, turning abruptly away. He let Abbott see to the door while he chose the big chair behind the big desk. But he did not sit in it.

This caught Mr. Abbott in a half-crouch as he was lowering himself into the sofa opposite.

Kramer smiled.

16

Then he straightened up with a little spring and went across to one of the coffins on display. He said: "Silly mistake."

"A lulu," said Kramer.

"Arabella," Mr. Abbott corrected, pointing to the easel card.

Kramer went around to inspect it. Then he leaned over to read the silver nameplate.

"False—I mean fictitious," explained Mr. Abbott.

"Uhuh."

Kramer was preoccupied with the reflection of his face in the highly polished lid. It was certainly a salutory experience to see how you would look someday. On second thoughts, though, death would not be able to make more of those sunken cheeks, deep-set eyes, and protrudent front teeth. It was a hard face, an ugly face, a face which saved you a lot of beating about the bush. Kramer winked at it with his offside eye.

Then he returned to the big chair and sat down. This time Mr. Abbott compromised by perching himself on the sofa's armrest.

"A lulu," Kramer repeated sternly. "Colonel Du Plessis doesn't know what to do with you—throw the book or pin a medal."

Mr. Abbott squirmed.

"I'm really most dreadfully sorry," he whispered.

"Save it," Kramer snapped. "I'm only interested in Le Roux."

"But what about Miss Bowers?"

"For a court to decide, if it gets that far. She wasn't much. Maybe you'll be lucky."

"Thank God."

Mr. Abbott slid down into the plush cushions.

"See it my way, Lieutenant," he pleaded. "Farthing did both removals so I had nothing personal to go on. I thought I'd looked at the labels, but we then were rushed. It never occurred to me she was on the Trinity's books."

"Why not?"

"At her age? You could almost call it morbid."

"Why?"

"You must have seen Trinity's ads, officer. They cater to the

17

elderlies and the not-so-well-off. She was young and you could tell from the toes she had money."

"Hey?"

"I know it's a bit of a cheek, but I must say I'm a bit of an expert on toes. Just the length of the nails can tell you a lot. In her case it was the toes not being all scrunched up by shoes not made exactly for her. Most shoes have quite a gap between their sizes you know, and it's only measured lengthwise."

"Come on, man, what's this all about?"

"Well, I must admit it had me puzzled at first, then it struck me: either she had her shoes made by hand, or—and this was more likely—she could afford Clarks' or some other expensive kind that come in widths as well. Most important, widths. Obviously, either way, she had money."

Kramer was in no mood to audition for Dr. Watson, but he managed to sound impressed.

"You must have spent quite a time on the body."

"Oh, yes."

"Just the toes?"

"Well . . . there were the routine checks for rings, jewelry."

"Yes?"

"Didn't find any."

"And you didn't notice on the label she was a Trinity?"

"No."

"I see," said Kramer. "So you spent most of your time on the toes. Funny that, because I think she must have been quite a dolly before your friend got his knives to her."

Mr. Abbott shifted nervously.

"In fact, I would say there's more to all this than you're telling me," Kramer added, his voice made sinister by a sudden intuitive insight.

And he watched with satisfaction as Mr. Abbott blanched. He preferred him that shade. It went better with the furnishings. It ensured that there would be no more idle chatter.

"What exactly do you want to know, Lieutenant?" Mr. Abbott managed to say at last.

18

"How come Doc Strydom didn't check out the body for himself? Is he often filleting your customers by accident?"

"Have you asked him that?"

"No, not exactly."

"Good, because I must take the blame," Mr. Abbott declared manfully. "All I said to him on the phone this morning was that there was a white female and I'd have it ready and waiting as usual."

"But he has forms to fill in, right?"

"Normally we do the names and that afterwards—together, so to speak."

"Uhuh?"

"You see, he comes in here and I provide particulars while we—"

"Yes?"

"Have a glass or two."

The poor little sod, you would have thought Ma Abbott had the room bugged from the way he dropped his voice almost to nothing for the awful revelation. Kramer tried the drawer with the key in it and scored first time.

He poured a large one for himself and another, in a glass already suspiciously fragrant, for Mr. Abbott. It was cheap medicinal brandy, no doubt a stock in trade in the event of graveside collapse. A quick calculation indicated somebody must have been spreading tales of mourners going down like ninepins out on Monument Hill. They sipped slowly and in silence.

But only for a minute.

"Let's get this straight from the start," Kramer said. "Farthing did the whatsits."

"Removals, officer. The old woman from the state morgue—Sergeant van Rensberg was up to his eyebrows after the derailment—and the girl from her home."

"Go on."

"Then he had the morning off. I was rather rushed so—"

"Yes, yes!" Kramer interrupted.

19

"What happened was we left for the crematorium before Dr. Strydom arrived."

"But there must have been forms."

"Mrs. Abbott always saw to that."

"Who had them?"

"Farthing. That was it, you see. Miss—er—she was covered up with a sheet and the Trinity doesn't allow for an inscription plate—that's an ordinary Arabella over there. Farthing just saw a coffin."

"Both women were about the same size?"

"Yes."

"There was a minister at the crematorium? Didn't he say the name?"

"I'd gone out again to park the hearse; they were expecting another right on our tail."

"And this bloke Farthing?"

"In the crematorium office still, signing the book."

"So it wasn't until you got back here you knew you had made a mistake?"

"No."

Ambiguity exercised its single virtue and a subtlety escaped Kramer. Mr. Abbott finished his glass in a gulp.

"Okay, if you weren't there at the start, were you inside at any stage?"

"The whole of the latter part."

"Ah, then can you describe any of the mourners? Anyone that struck you as—"

"There weren't any."

Kramer put his glass down. This was unexpected. According to the medical evidence, there should have been at least one. A forlorn male wondering where his next was coming from.

Mr. Abbott continued hastily: "I assure you it was advertised in the local papers as is required by Trinity under its policy, but not a soul turned up. And that's another reason I didn't expect anything was wrong: elderlies, especially the ones on Trinity's books, often have no one. That's why they join."

Now came the moment Kramer had been trying to avoid.

"Have you got Miss le Roux's papers handy?" he asked.

Mr. Abbott pointed to a ledger emblazoned *Trinity Records* beside the telephone. Kramer began to leaf slowly through it.

"I see what you mean," he murmured. "Half these old crones have got one foot and a corn plaster in it already."

Finally he reached the entry he was after and found it revealed nothing but the name, the policy number, the date and means of disposal, and the coding. He noted down the latter and then unfolded a document which had been tucked into the page.

It appeared to be the official go-ahead from the local branch of Trinity Burial Society, and there were a few details above a mass of small print about expenditure.

Name: Le Roux, Theresa
Date of birth: December 12, 1948
Race: White
Address: 223B Barnato Street, Trekkersburg
Status: Single
Occupation: Music teacher
Next of kin: None
Instructions: Disposal as convenient

Well, that solved something. Or did it? Even orphans generally have someone to weep over them. And what about the people living at 223A? And—most significantly of all—what about the pupils? A teacher dying posed parents a problem they would be only too eager to smother under a mountain of wreaths. There was the time factor, of course; the press notice had run only one day—the day of the funeral.

"No flowers?" Kramer asked.

"None," replied Mr. Abbott, pausing a moment to think visibly as he refilled his glass.

Very, very strange. For a single, unguarded moment, Kramer felt intense, almost affectionate, respect for whoever had set up this killing. For once a murderer had attempted to do a proper job. Most never bothered to give their deed any constructive thought—Nkosi had been a good example of this. With them it was a case of deplorable self-control followed by instant action with whatever weapon was handiest. Nkosi had snatched up a cane knife, slashed Gertrude thirty-two times in front of the neighbors, and then stood around wiping the blood from his hands on the seat of his trousers while the police were called. Some did try a little harder. They were usually whites or sophisticated wogs who had gone to mission schools. In either case, he was sure it was a question of reading. Do-gooders, who saw to stocking mission libraries, always seemed to have limitless private sources of secondhand Agatha Christies. This type of murderer felt a social responsibility to adopt the key role in an intricate game of skill—some would call it mischance. They were careful with alibis and fingerprints. They had answers for everything. They often took tremendous pains to eradicate the body. In the final analysis, though, they saw themselves ranged against the police—whether in the open or watching from a thicket of deceit. They knew that the very act of concealing their connection with the murder had incriminated them. They were committed to a battle of wits. Even if they succeeded in setting up a "missing person" situation, they never knew when the bugle might suddenly sound as a pet dog unearthed a delectable but forbidden bone. A perfect murder, however, owed nothing to this outlook. Its perpetrator made no attempt to disassociate himself from his deed—simply because he was totally confident his deed would never be recognized as such. He shed clues without a care because no one would ever seek them. He did not give the police any more thought than they gave an unfamiliar name in the *Gazette*'s Deaths column. His way was Nature's Way. A pedant might insist that some element of risk remained: a husband impregnating his wife could not be certain a Mongol would not result. Yet in both cases only the odds were what mattered. And the odds against having a Mongol would be considerably lower than those against a doctor doubting his own opinion on the demise of a known cardiac case—

and astronomically lower than those against a professional undertaker switching bodies in the heat of some unspeakable passion. Yet the battle had begun.

"Well, Georgie, I must say you've really pulled one out of the hat this time," Kramer remarked, affable on adrenaline.

"Thanks," Mr. Abbott muttered. He was well into his third glass and very, very much happier.

Kramer's glands had, in fact, started to cause havoc with their secretions. It was like being love-struck; he felt lighter than air, eager and ready for action. All he wanted was to go charging out and get his man. Sick. It was altogether a condition to be profoundly distrusted. So he decided to sit back, talk a little, ponder a little, be nice to Georgie, who was not bad for an English-speaking bloke.

"You see," he said, "it was a case of all or nothing with the bastard who did it. You can bet your last cent he had a lot at stake. So what does he choose? The ultimate weapon, a bloody bike spoke. Only, things have gone wrong and it's like getting caught in your own fallout. Anyone can shoot a gun, or stab with a knife, but very few can handle a spoke. That narrows it down."

"I'd say."

"Another thing: what was a white girl doing getting mixed up with Kaffir gangster tricks? That's a good one for you."

"It is indeed, marvelous."

"Go easy on that stuff, Georgie."

"Never fear, old boy, Ma's gone home to mumsywumsy. Even worse, she is. Still alive only because she doesn't want me to get my hands on her."

Kramer laughed.

"Tell you what—bring the bugger back here when you get him," Mr. Abbott offered, "I'll see to him for you."

His leer was frightening.

"Not a chance," Kramer replied, standing up. "This one's all mine. He won't know what hit him."

Mr. Abbott raised his glass to toast the sentiment.

"Just you see he doesn't get to hear of what happened today," Kramer warned softly. "This gives us a good start as long as we keep it quiet. Understand?"

"Absolutely, old boy."

Mr. Abbott's company had suddenly become tedious. Besides which, Kramer no longer felt raring to go. So he went.

3

THERE WAS STILL no one in the Murder Squad offices when he got back, but a ridiculous note had been left in the typewriter. It said that Colonel Du Plessis had an important engagement and should be contacted at Trekkersburg 21111 only if absolutely necessary. That was the Brigadier's home number. Of course—he was holding a *braaivleis* to celebrate his dragon daughter's betrothal to some fair maid of an architect. Ordinarily this would have invited a stock outburst from Kramer —what a bloody time to go stuffing yourself on barbecued sausage with an eye on the main chance. But, under the circumstances, he could not have wished for anything better. Whether something was "absolutely necessary" or not was entirely a matter of opinion. He could get on with the investigation without interference at least until morning. It was also pleasing to find the others were still out, for this meant no pressure to delegate. The case was all his—and Zondi's, when that idle Kaffir bothered to look in.

He buzzed the duty officer.

"Kramer here, just back from Abbott's place. White female Le Roux definitely murdered. Stab wounds. Suspect Bantu intruder."

The duty officer's silence was as loud as a yawn. Good; without lying he had made it sound sufficiently commonplace; after all, dozens of whites surprised burglars, to be fatally surprised in turn.

"But keep it from the press, will you, Janie?"

Captain Janie Koekemoor reassured him of this on the grounds he knew bugger all about it anyway, having just come on.

Perfect. He replaced the receiver.

Where to begin? There were already quite a number of people to see: Farthing, Dr. Matthews, the Trinity agent, and the occupants of 223A Barnato Street. He would arrange for Ma Abbott to make her statement to the local police rather than recall her; it was the least he could do.

With speed as an essential factor, the party in 223A seemed the best bet. For a start, it was likely they were Miss le Roux's landlords and that would save a bit of digging about. Kramer knew the properties down that side of Trekkersburg. Since the Act which kept most Bantu out of town overnight, many servants' quarters had been converted at considerable expense into bachelor flats. This meant 223A would probably have a key handy and he wanted to examine the murder scene as soon as possible.

Kramer paused only to scribble an offensive note to Zondi. Then he went down the back way to the car park. There was a new batch of used cars on loan from obliging dealers and he chose a beaten-up black Chrysler with three radio aerials, white-walled tires, and leopard-skin seats.

The house at 223A was exactly what he had been expecting: a blank-faced bungalow wearing its mossy roof like a cloth cap pulled low over two veranda windows. It was set only a few yards back from the pavement, to allow plenty of room behind for a sizable outbuilding.

A closer examination revealed many small signs of neglect, especially in the paintwork, and unusually heavy burglar guards over every aperture including the door, which was closed. A fortress for aged whites too nervous to have even a handyman prying around—folk who would not readily admit a stranger in the failing twilight. Well, the important thing was not to sneak up but give fair warning and let the Valentino charm do the rest.

So Kramer banged the gate and clattered the knocker as heartily as a priest. It worked. In less than a minute there was a rattle of chain, two bolts shot back, and the door opened just far enough for a gray-haired bantam of woman to poke her beak out. The reek of lavender water would have sickened a bee.

"Yes?" she demanded.

Work-worn fingers began twisting her necklace as if she meant to throttle herself at the first sign of danger. But then she belonged to a generation that believed in a fate worse than death.

"CID," Kramer announced, very civilly. He proffered his identity card. It was snatched away through the bars and the door closed.

Oh, *ja*, life was made up of waiting for the gaps between the waits. Kramer glanced about him. The veranda was bare, apart from two chairs. One was made of cane, large, easy lines, and piled with enormous cushions with a flower pattern. The other must once have stood beside a Victorian dining table. It hurt just to look at it with its impossibly upright back. Their peculiar juxtaposition suggested something. The distance between them was less than polite society permitted but greater than intimacy required. They were, in fact, just close enough for pulse-taking. So in the cane chair you would find an ailing widow wealthy enough to have a paid companion seated by her side. It was a useful insight and Kramer used it unashamedly as the door opened again.

"Yes?"

"Ah, madam, I take it you must be the householder?"

"Oh, no, sir, that's Mrs. Bezuidenhout. I'm Miss Henry." And she simpered because it was so nice to know she still had a look of gentility despite what had happened to her hands.

Kramer kept on smiling respectfully.

27

"Then I'd like a word with her, if you please," he said.

"Of course, sir."

Miss Henry's defenses were down and within seconds the guard door, too, swung wide. Kramer stepped inside.

"This way, sir."

Miss Henry led him into a living room immediately to the right. She blocked his view of the far side of the room and all he took in was a Persian cat that seemed to be comparing bald patches with the Persian rug on which it lay—both had some form of eczema.

"Here's the policeman, dearie," Miss Henry said, stepping to one side.

Facing Kramer was President Paul Kruger without his beard. It took a little longer to realize he had grown flat breasts instead.

"If it's about my Kaffir maid's poll tax, I don't want to know," barked the President.

Steady. But the likeness was incredible, even to the way Mrs. Bezuidenhout leaned forward on a silver-tipped stick. She would go a bomb in the next pageant of the Republic's forefathers, that was for certain. Just strap her in a bit and swap the full-length black dress for a shirt and tailcoat.

"I'm ninety-two, if that's what you're staring at."

"No, you reminded me of someone, madam."

"Then don't think you can get round me with that sentimental muck. I'm not your wretched mother, thank God."

"Now, dear!" Miss Henry pleaded, casting a forgive-us look at Kramer. "This is a very nice young man."

"Henry! Mind your place."

"Madam, I would like to ask you just—"

"Sit down and don't smoke."

At least she wasn't going to set the cat on him. Nasty things, skin diseases. He sat.

"It's about Trixie you've come."

"Who?"

"Trixie, Theresa, call her what you like. I did. Didn't go to the funeral, don't believe in them."

28

And Kramer was going to try and break it to her gently.

"Why should you say that, madam?"

"Obvious. Said it from the start. Something fishy about her going like that."

"Right from the start, you said it, dearie."

"But why, madam?"

"Because I know who was responsible."

"*Hey?*"

"Yes, that old fool Dr. Matthews. I wouldn't let him near a sick ox."

Kramer winced. A rookie would not have fallen for that one. And here it came, hell hath no fury like a jilted hypochondriac. He had to act fast—shock tactics.

"Miss le Roux was murdered."

Miss Henry made a passable attempt at having the vapors. It was all coming back to her now, the way a lady should act, but mainly from novels written before her time.

"Vegetarian," Mrs. Bezuidenhout sneered. "She is one, you know—part of her religion, God help us. Was that true what you said? Murdered?"

"Yes."

"How?"

"I'm not at liberty to divulge that." It was all coming back to Kramer now, too.

"Well, then, Matthews was a fool not to have noticed it. He signed the certificate."

This seemed to be her final word.

"I would appreciate any help you could give us."

"Of course," whispered Miss Henry, reviving swiftly and graciously. "We do so want to help, don't we, dearie?"

Mrs. Bezuidenhout scowled but looked interested.

"Then just tell me what you know about Miss le Roux—anything that comes into your heads."

It was like overcoming the professional reserve of two eminent behaviorists and having them expound freely on their pet subject. There seemed to be nothing they did not know about

29

Miss le Roux's eating habits, sleeping habits, washing habits, and —as Miss Henry phrased it—habit habits. Between them they must have spent months in close observation, apparently using their kitchen as a hide with its view across the lawn to the flat.

In the end, though, when the last trivial point had been made, there was not much. The trouble was it had been so largely a matter of noses pressed against glass. As with animal behaviorism, a lack of actual communication had led to somewhat superficial findings.

For Miss le Roux had kept herself very much to herself during her two years as an ideal tenant. Which was odd in a young girl perhaps, but then truly artistic people—as opposed to the rubbish at the university—were so often the retiring sort. It was something for others to respect. The trouble was there was not enough respect left in the world.

The only time any conversation occurred was when Miss le Roux appeared promptly on the first of every month to pay her rent. She would hand over the cash in a pretty pink envelope, refuse to be coaxed in off the veranda, and make exceedingly small talk while her receipt was prepared. Now and then she would ask anxiously if her pupils were not making too much noise; a recent boom in electronic organs imported from Japan had encouraged her to take on some adults for evening classes in sight reading. No, of course not, dear, we're a little bit deaf as it is. And that was all.

So they had no idea where she came from and no idea of where she went on the rare occasions she ventured out, but they did have an idea there was some terrible tragedy hidden deep in her past.

This was getting him nowhere.

"Just a minute, ladies," Kramer interrupted. "Let's just stick to the facts, shall we? You say that Miss le Roux answered an ad in the *Gazette* for this place. She had no references but you took her on because she seemed a polite girl."

"Right," growled Mrs. Bezuidenhout, peeved at being cut short.

"Okay, so she got up at eight. She did all her own housework. Her first pupils came after school, so if she went out at all it was in the morning. She gave lessons until six-thirty and occasionally after supper, which was at seven. Lights out at eleven. You say she never had friends in, but how can you be sure that those who came at night were always pupils?"

"Because for a start they weren't her type. All fortyish, smooth Johnnies, the sort who would buy themselves silly toys they wouldn't know how to work. Besides, they always had music cases with them—see?"

Miss Henry made a permission-to-speak sound. Kramer nodded encouragement.

"We could hear, too, of course," she said, "we could hear them doing their scales and making such a mess of it. Same mistakes again and again."

"She fancies she has an ear for music." Mrs. Bezuidenhout sniffed. "Deafer than I am, too."

"Did you recognize any of them?"

"We've already told you that Miss le Roux had her own entrance from the lane. Never got more than a glimpse as she opened her door, and that was from the back."

No matter, Miss le Roux would have kept records for tax purposes. He would get around to them later. Then a thought struck him.

"Did she have any around the night before she—?"

"Not been one for weeks, actually," Miss Henry said.

"Ah." Obviously electronic organs went the way of all gimmicks which threaten to delight your friends in ten easy lessons.

"She was in, though?"

"Yes."

"Can you tell me what did happen that day?"

"Ring for Rebecca," Mrs. Bezuidenhout ordered, somewhat rhetorically, for she herself raised her stick and beat on a brass spittoon.

Along the passage came a shuffle of slippers two sizes too

31

large and an elderly Zulu woman in a maid's uniform entered the room. She drew back instinctively as she saw Kramer.

"Yes, he's a policeman, you old rascal," said Mrs. Bezuidenhout. "He wants to ask you about the little missus."

The servant's fright doubled. "Rebecca take nothing in that place, baas," she said anxiously. "True's God, me not doing anything bad by that side."

Kramer greeted her courteously in Zulu: "Just tell me and the missus what happened."

Rebecca gabbled through it, using both official languages, her own kitchen Kaffir, and a pair of big rolling brown eyes.

Every Monday morning she went up very early to the cottage and, using her employer's master key, removed the dustbin for the rubbish collectors. On the previous Monday, she had gone in to find the washing-up still in the sink, and one plate of the stove red hot. The little missus had always been very clean and most particular about switching things off, so she suspected something was amiss immediately. She called out once or twice and tiptoed through the bedroom to see if in fact the little missus was at home. She was. Dead.

"Came wailing down here as if the devil himself was after her," Mrs. Bezuidenhout cut in. "Of course I didn't believe the old bag. Got Henry to take me up there. There she lay, peaceful as you could wish, but stone cold."

"And how was the room?"

"Oh, very nice and tidy," said Miss Henry. "Sheets tucked up under her chin, too, the poor thing."

So much for convulsions.

"Poison," Mrs. Bezuidenhout pronounced.

Kramer saw no need to contradict her. Instead he asked how, if Miss le Roux was so secretive, they knew which doctor to call. The question seemed to embarrass Mrs. Bezuidenhout, which was surprising in one way but not in another.

"Well, you see," Miss Henry explained, arching her voice with tact, "once upon a time Dr. Matthews used to see to Mrs. Bezuidenhout. It was when Miss le Roux first came here. She asked the name of a—er—good family doctor, nothing flashy, and we told her Dr. Matthews."

"She should have changed when I got rid of him," Mrs. Bezuidenhout said defensively. "He didn't know his job."

Which had been proved partly true, although for ninety-two Mrs. Bezuidenhout had the sort of rude health best maintained on self-administered doses of totally ineffectual patent medicine.

"Were either of you in the flat when he arrived?"

"Oh, yes!"

They would not have missed it for worlds.

"Shocking, it was." Miss Henry sighed. "He hardly looked at the poor thing. Said she was a heart case and these things were to be just expected. He signed the certificate right there on her bedside table."

"And then?"

"He asked us if we knew who to contact, you see," Miss Henry continued, reliving a glorious hour. "I said—remember, dearie? —I said the name of her lawyer was on the lease thing. I went and got it and Dr. Matthews rang him from the flat. The lawyer took a bit of time and then he told the doctor that Trixie had some sort of insurance for funerals and gave him the undertaker's name."

"Vultures were here in two twos," Mrs. Bezuidenhout muttered. "But they had to wait."

"Oh?"

"The death certificate has to be witnessed by another doctor for a cremation," Miss Henry explained kindly. "I think that's very wise, don't you?"

"Huh! Not when it's Dr. Matthews' partner; two of a kind, if you ask me," Mrs. Bezuidenhout sneered.

"Who's that then?"

"Dr. Campbell. Terrible old soak."

"Really, dearie!"

"He is. *He* didn't even bother to come right into her bedroom. Stood there in the doorway moaning about being up all night."

Kramer had overlooked the fact that a second opinion would have been compulsory, but that was a minor point and no doubt Strydom had thought so, too. Neither of the doctors seemed remotely capable of being party to an intelligent act of destruction.

"What about the flat?" he asked Mrs. Bezuidenhout.

"Her lawyer's promised to see to it and it's paid up for the month so why should I care?"

"Untouched?"

"I'm not doing his work for him, sonny."

Kramer rose.

"It is necessary that I have a look at it."

"Now?"

"Yes, and we'll probably have to trouble you again in the morning. Fingerprints, photographs."

"Well, if you have to, you have to. But see you use the side gate. I'm too old for this sort of commotion."

Something ugly shaded her bright eyes for an instant. Strange it had taken so long.

"Are we—are Miss Henry and I in any danger through what's happened?"

"No, madam, we don't think so."

"Oh."

Almost a hint of disappointment. Perhaps a less formidable son had thought the burglar guards advisable.

"I mean it's a *murder*, isn't it?" Miss Henry said. "These things are usually very personal."

"Quite right," Kramer agreed, and then cautioned them not to say a word about it. They joined the conspiracy with self-important nods.

Kramer wanted to take a second look at Miss le Roux's underwear. But he was finding Miss Henry's presence most inhibiting. In fact she was beginning to get on his nerves badly. From the

34

moment she unlocked the door to the flat, the avowed vegetarian had displayed an astonishing taste for gore. He was tired of grunting evasively as she sought to extract details of the Royal Hotel double killing. And he was tired of being asked if he had given himself to Jesus. The time had come for his Jehovah's Witness ploy.

"Oh, Christ!" he said, looking at his watch. "I'd better get a bloody move on or I'll be late for Mass."

Miss Henry shuddered away into the night.

And Kramer opened the wardrobe. Nine dresses hung from the rail, each demure and rather dull. There was also a raincoat in a severe military cut and a worn overcoat which had been altered. Nothing here to conflict with the picture the old girls had conjured up. Then he pulled out one of the drawers. In it was a large collection of what women's magazines termed "romantic undies" while refraining from specifying under what circumstances they would appear so. The colors were strong and the lace a main ingredient rather than a trimming. He thumbed through them again with the idle notion he might have missed something men's magazines called "exotic." Some of them came damn close but that was all. It worried him. Bothered him because he could not reconcile the striking contrast between the inner and outer Theresa le Roux.

Bloody hell. Nothing in the place made sense once you thought about it. He shut the wardrobe, went out into the living room for his cigarettes, and returned to lie back on the stripped mattress. The low ceiling was white and unblemished by cracks, providing a perfect surface on which to transcribe a confusion of mental jottings.

But his eyes wearied quickly of the glare and wandered to the print of Constable's *Salisbury Cathedral* which hung on the wall beyond the foot of the bed. Its qualities as a best seller were obvious; a nice, restful scene with a touch of the old spiritual uplift. Yet only two nights before, the glass over it had held the reflection of a killer getting his kicks. Oh, Jesus, this case bent the mind and his had been going flat out since before sunrise.

Presently, he fell asleep.

The face above him was black. His right fist heaved up, missed, flopped back. Somebody laughed. He knew that laugh; he had heard it where children played, where women wept, where men died, always the same depth of detached amusement. Kramer closed his eyes without troubling to focus them and felt curiously content.

Bantu Detective Sergeant Mickey Zondi sat himself primly at the dressing table. Then he opened the large manila envelope he had brought with him and shook out its contents—a batch of photographs and two laboratory reports. As a child at a mission school in Zululand, he had adapted to making do without his own textbooks. He read fast, read once, and remembered. He studied the pictures last of all, aware that Kramer was now watching him through barely parted lids.

An uncanny thing, that laugh of Zondi's—it never seemed to come from him, it was too big a sound. But it fitted. The first time he had seen Zondi was outside the magistrate's court on a Monday when it was thronged so solid with worried wives and families you had to force your way through them. Then the mob suddenly parted of its own volition and through it had come a coon version of Frank Sinatra making with the jaunty walk. The snap-brim hat, padded shoulders, and zoot suit larded with glinting thread were all secondhand ideas from a secondhand shop. The walk was pure Chicago, yet no black was permitted to see a gangster film. No, here was an original, even if someone, somewhere else, had thought of it all before. Zondi walked that way because he thought that way. And if this was fantasy, reality was only one layer down: the Walther PPK in its shoulder holster, the two eight-inch knives held by the elastic trouser tabs on either side.

"Cheeky black bastard," Kramer grunted.

Zondi tucked in the corners of a smile and went on with his

illicit scrutiny of Miss le Roux's bromide image. Even dead a white woman had laws to protect her from primitive lust.

"You want to get me into trouble, hey?"

Zondi ignored him. The photographs were sharp and expertly printed, but the lighting had been too oblique and Miss le Roux seemed to have ended up with a lot of her curves in the wrong places. Nevertheless, Zondi nodded his approval before tossing the envelope across.

"A good woman," he said. "She could have given many sons."

"Is that all you ever think about?" asked Kramer, and they both laughed. Zondi was an incorrigible pelvis man.

The laboratory reports were long, laborious, and uninspiring. Contrary to popular belief, there was not a great deal you could say about a corpse which would circumvent the ordinary processes of investigation. That Miss le Roux's blood belonged to a rare group seemed wholly irrelevant now it had gone to waste. On top of which the technician concerned was a new man, fresh from the realms of pure science and given to being scrupulously vague in the face of variables. So Kramer ignored everything except the analysis of stomach contents.

"Digestion halted after approximately four hours," Zondi quoted, noting where Kramer's finger had stopped in the margin.

"Uhuh. Which makes the time of death somewhere between eleven and midnight."

"Hard-boiled egg—see any shells, boss?"

"There's one in the kitchen. Lucky she didn't like them soft or we wouldn't have any pointers. This is interesting about the traces of drugs."

"The heart ones?"

"No, the sleeping. They had this little dolly all sorted out—and her doctor, too. The bastards."

Zondi demanded to have the whole story and he got it, right up to the poser of the panchromatic panties.

4

"SO YOU SEE," Kramer added, "there are things which just don't add up in this place. Come through and have a look yourself."

Before Zondi joined the force, he had spent a year as a houseboy. This had given him an eye for the details of a white man's abode which was as fresh and perceptive as that of an anthropologist making much of what the natives themselves never noticed. Kramer had found it invaluable more than once.

They started in the kitchen; an unremarkable room barely big enough to turn around in, which had presumably been a storeroom once.

There was a collection of invoices stuck on a nail.

"She ordered by phone, boss. Groceries, chemists, clothes from John Orr's. But mostly food."

"She didn't pay by check, you know, settled in cash," Kramer told him. "She kept her money in the post office—just over two hundred rand."

Zondi had the top off the rubbish bin. Understandably enough, Rebecca had overlooked her chore in the excitement and it was still full. An inquiring eyebrow was raised at Kramer, who grinned back.

"You've got a bloody hope," he said. "That's Kaffir work. '
The grin was returned.

"Besides, there's the eggshell on the top. Now don't tell me somebody's going to hide something in there and not break the pieces putting it all back."

Zondi went on poking in the soggy mess with the handle of a feather duster.

"Well?"

"That's a new box of washing-up powder on the windowsill, boss. When women throw away a box they never squash it down like a man would to make more room for the rest. They put it in just like that with all the air inside."

"And you can't feel one?"

"No."

"Come on, Zondi, the one over there is not all that new, you know."

"But it must be in here, boss."

Zondi picked up the pair of rubber gloves hanging over the sink and slipped them on. Then he spread a newspaper and began emptying the bin.

Miss le Roux had certainly been a young lady of regular habits. Levels of the daily round in reverse order—supper, tea, lunch, tea, housecleaning, breakfast, tea—appeared without variation, although they did become less distinct the deeper Zondi delved.

"No one's been into that lot, I can tell you for a fact," Kramer remarked, vaguely irritated.

"Quite right, boss."

Zondi rocked back on his heels and held up a crumpled cardboard container covered in tea leaves.

"Squashed flat," Kramer said.

"Folded over," Zondi said, choosing a clean sheet of newspaper to deposit it on. The carton was slippery and he had to try twice before tearing it open. Out rolled a reel of recording tape, badly damaged by flames.

39

"Jesus."

"Monday a week ago, I think," Zondi said. "After this missus's supper."

Kramer spilled some bread coupons from their box and placed the reel in it. As he did so, a number of small pieces of tape fluttered to the floor. He salvaged them. The whole thing was in bits. He sealed the box with some adhesive tape from the table drawer.

"Sergeant Prinsloo can come and take some pretty pictures of this," Zondi said with satisfaction, pointing to the mess he had made and shedding his gloves. "That is now white man's work."

For the moment Kramer was totally preoccupied with the find. He took it through into the living room and put it on the mantelpiece. He regarded it from three separate angles. He decided that he would know what it contained before the night was out. The hell with official channels.

There was a loud hiss behind him. Zondi was in the doorway, spraying himself all over with an aerosol can of air freshener.

"Finished in the kitchen, boss?" he asked blandly. He smelled pungently wholesome, like a Swedish brothel.

"I'm going to use the phone," Kramer said, making for the bedroom door. "Just you take a look at that lot on the piano meantime."

Zondi obliged. He found the entire contents of the writing bureau, plus other assorted effects, arranged neatly along the lid —but not the usual twin categories of "personal" and "business." For, as Kramer had repeatedly stressed during the briefing, there was nothing remotely personal among it all with which to begin a pile. Not a letter, a postcard, or even a snapshot.

What there was hardly made absorbing reading; two receipt books, one full and the other just begun; a ledger for tax purposes; a notebook containing pupils' names, more than a year's bills all stamped "Paid," and a reminder from a jeweler's about a repair. The collection, however, provided the first answer of

40

the day by explaining where all the flowers had gone—or many of them anyway. Miss le Roux had not taken private pupils in the ordinary sense but appeared to have had some arrangement with Saint Evelyn's School for Girls around the corner. It was a boarding establishment and a term had ended a fortnight before.

Kramer came in looking pleased with himself.

"I've got a bloke who'll look at the tape tonight," he said. "Find any trace of the adult pupils there?"

"Nothing, boss. Maybe she did not want to pay tax on the fellows."

"Could be." The thought had occurred more than once, yet it still struck Kramer as being very out of character. The records were meticulous and Miss le Roux plainly knew nothing of less hazardous tactics such as loading an expense allowance.

Zondi started switching off the lights. He was right, it was time to get going—every minute was worth double until news of the investigation broke. Kramer gathered the papers into a music case, collected the tape, and went out onto the small veranda. He just caught a glimpse of someone ducking away from Mrs. Bezuidenhout's kitchen window.

The night was wild.

Seen from the air, Trekkersburg was a green-gray mold at the bottom of an unfired bowl. Now, over the brim of blunt mountains to the west, came pouring a hot, thick wind which swirled dead leaves aloft like sediment and infused every living thing with its strange agitation. The wind did not come often, but when it did things happened.

Which suited Kramer down to the ground. He delighted in it, wondered why he had not noticed it before. Each bluster made him more impatient as Zondi fiddled with the front door, making quite certain the lock was secure. So he started alone down the short path and out through the side gate. He found himself in a small lane once used by the night-soil cart, it being a very old part of the town. The lighting was poor but he made his way down it quickly enough to have the car revving loudly by the time Zondi caught up. Then he drove off as if the leopard-skin seats had snarled.

Kramer dropped Zondi outside the city hall and headed for 49 Arcadia Avenue, where—according to the telephone directory—Dr. J. P. Matthews had his home and surgery. It was well after eleven but the man was a physician and this an emergency call. The tape expert was an amateur, a proofreader at the *Gazette*, who would not be home until 1 A.M.

Zondi had been left with instructions to find Shoe Shoe. He was to wheel him in his wheelbarrow to the corner of De Wet Street and the Parade and wait there to be picked up.

Only four years back Shoe Shoe had been an up-and-coming mobster with a pay-night protection racket just beyond Trekkersburg in the Bantu township of Peacehaven. Every Friday he had twenty men at the bus terminal who would escort breadwinners home at one rand a time. Not a vast sum but on a good night—particularly after some idiot had refused the service and was brutally reprimanded—the takings were nothing to be sniffed at.

Then he had foolishly decided to move in on the Kwela Village terminal, thinking his only competition would be from a few young toughs who stopped once they had sufficient for drink and a dolly. The thing was he had never heard of any trouble there. Why he had heard nothing was ultimately made terrifyingly clear.

Come the first Friday night, his scouts returned with a shock report: the Kwela terminal was already being worked and so subtly that the passengers were bled dry even before they reached the shadows. No one had been able to detect how it was done.

When Shoe Shoe received the news calmly, they felt bewildered and nervous. Normally he reacted to any upset with a tantrum of appalling ferocity. But these were new men, they had not known him long enough to realize that he had got

42

places by a careful study of what he reverently called Big Time.

And this was Big Time all right. It excited Shoe Shoe tremendously, making him repeat Big Time in every other sentence. It also made him determined to discover the system and apply it in Peacehaven, where a street-light project threatened to inhibit his present methods.

So he sent all his men in the following week. It was risky but worth it. Anyway, they had strict instructions to do nothing but watch. Big Time would be far too busy to notice.

Wrong again. Big Time decided to set an example—and extend its operations to Peacehaven. Which meant that when Shoe Shoe eagerly answered a knock on his door around midnight, he opened it on Big Time and bad times.

It happened very quickly. He was held down on his sagging divan and had his Palm Beach shirt ripped from tail to collar. A match flared briefly. The first prick of the spoke came near his coccyx—just his legs were to go; a minor infringement. Then the point began to tickle its way up. His arms as well. Higher still. The spinal cord was punctured.

It was a clean wound and healed in three days. The neurologist at Peacehaven Hospital found this evidence of sterile procedure even more disturbing than the impressive display of anatomical insight. He mentioned it to Dr. Strydom. The DS shrugged and said that as there was nothing the hospital could do, it was rather ridiculous admitting such cases when there were so many patients that some had to sleep under beds occupied by more serious cases.

So on the fourth day Shoe Shoe was discharged before breakfast. Two porters carried him out and set him down on the lawn a few yards from the exit gate. There he sat, with a small bandage visible through his torn shirt, until eleven o'clock, when the sun baked a thirst within him that made him call out for help.

It arrived in the form of Gershwin Mkize, following up a hot tip. Gershwin ran the beggar circus in Trekkersburg, often traveling far into the bush for his exhibits positioned strategically about the town, and he was always on the lookout for new attractions. This one needed no improvisation.

The state pension would provide half a loaf of bread a day. Gershwin could offer two loaves, a little meat, a pot of beer, and a roof—plus the comradeship of other unfortunates who, between them, could assist in intimate matters such as feeding, dressing, moving, and evacuating.

Shoe Shoe accepted without a word and seldom spoke again.

A Bantu constable, fresh from the police college, made a few ineffectual inquiries. Shoe Shoe gave him an outline, then clammed up. The constable's superiors criticized the spelling in his report and left it at that. After all, this time society had been left better off by a crime.

Now Kramer wanted him to break that silence. He did not relish the thought of working over a man four parts dead already, but he was prepared to go beyond strenuous coaxing. He knew the link was tenuous. But he also knew that Shoe Shoe must have seen his assailants and thereafter maintained a particular interest in anything concerning bicycle spokes.

Kramer turned into Arcadia Avenue and slowed down. About halfway along, his headlights glinted off a brass plate and he killed the engine to glide up on the grass verge. As he got out he noticed half a dozen cars parked outside the house on the other side. Their owners were no doubt gathered to celebrate a golden anniversary; it was that sort of neighborhood.

He took the path in four paces and rang the bell.

Dr. Matthews was in the hall balancing on one leg. By extending the other as a counterweight, he had been just able to retain his hold on the telephone receiver while using his free hand to grasp the doorknob. He grinned feebly. Just a smile in return would have been charitable.

"Police," Kramer said, and walked past into the surgery, closing the thick door behind him.

He was immediately struck by the quiet and the stink of ether. Another man whose profession demanded sound

44

proofing—and another cue to stop breathing through his nose. He went over to see if any of the windows were open behind the long, molting drapes. Not one. Not touched in fifty years if the rest of the room was anything to go by. He noted the Victorian furniture, the quilted leather, the tassels, the instruments laid out in what resembled museum cases. Across the road there was a movement in the back of one of the cars—ah, the younger generation was succumbing to the wild wind.

And Kramer turned to stare at the couch, half screened off in one corner. So this was where Miss le Roux had felt it right and proper to undress and recline. Sick. Horrible. The whole room was sick. It was certainly not the place to be told you had three months to go, taking things easy. For that you needed one of those unreal skyscraper suites with pretty receptionists to smile unwittingly at you on your way out to the lift. At the very most it was a room which should serve only for offering up afflictions of the anal region. Which seemed to be Dr. Matthews' level anyhow, so maybe he was expecting too much.

The GP was in the room without warning, moving lightly as became a fat man so daintily shod. His likeness to his mother's photograph on the desk was remarkable—except his mustache turned upwards.

"What brings you here, officer?" he said. "Don't tell me—I've made a balls and so has Strydom, but he's also getting the glory, lucky man."

He stopped and frowned.

"As a matter of fact, he was rather rude to me. I told him her history. I told him it was congenital angina. Remained quite unimpressed. *Very rude* when I said I hadn't her previous records but one has to *trust* patients, hasn't one?"

"And doctors," Kramer observed, ignoring the outstretched hand.

"Now then!" Dr. Matthews said, "May I take your coat?"

"No coat," Kramer replied.

"Of course, I've been in touch with the medical association,"

Dr. Matthews continued, unruffled. "Speaking to the secretary at his home only a moment ago. He said that off the record he was inclined to agree I'd come to a reasonable conclusion under the circumstances. One can't go ordering postmortems for everyone who pops off."

"But she was only twenty-two."

"Good God, man, she'd had cardiac irregularities since she was nine!"

"Hearsay," Kramer snapped, resorting to a bit of his own jargon. "Now just hand over that file you're waving about; I want to take a look for myself."

Dr. Matthews did so with a mildly insolent thrust and then pottered about the room, humming plump, complacent hums. Eventually, however, he came to a stop behind his desk, where he patted his pockets and took from them a stethoscope, auriscope, ophthalmoscope, and stainless steel spatula. He was like a balloonist dumping ballast in an effort to regain height. He slumped down into the swivel chair, his clothes creasing into great loose folds.

Kramer closed the file and stared across at him. Then he picked up the ophthalmoscope, switched it on, and played the tiny beam across the room until it stopped in the middle of the practitioner's pink forehead.

"You examined her thoroughly?" he asked softly.

"Naturally. Dozens of times, as you've seen—every square inch."

"With this thing?"

The spot of light dropped to bore into Dr. Matthews' right eye. He raised a protecting hand, flushing with anger.

"See here," he barked, "stop fooling about with what you don't bloody well understand. Who the hell do you think you are?"

"Lieutenant Kramer of the Murder Squad, and I have reason to believe you are lying, Dr. Matthews. This is an ophthalmoscope, an instrument used for the examination of the human eye, and yet you have Miss le Roux's eye color wrong in your records."

"What the devil do you mean?"

"It says here they were blue."

"Correct; she was blond."

"Oh, yes? I saw them in the mortuary this afternoon. They were brown."

"Brown?"

"Correct," Kramer mimicked.

Then nothing was said for some considerable time.

"I have a little theory," Kramer murmured at last, "that you never gave Miss le Roux a look-over from top to toe. From your notes it seems you concentrated your attention on an area quite unconnected with cardiac irregularities—or eye irregularities for that matter."

Dr. Matthews looked up sharply.

"Now why would you do that, doctor? Your colleague Dr. Strydom is quite certain she never suffered from any disease of that kind."

"There was not much I could do for the heart," Dr. Matthews blustered. "Just give her pills and sleeping drugs so she rested properly."

"Yes? Go on, man."

"Surely it's obvious from the file the silly little bitch was neurotic," Dr. Matthews exploded. "Open it, count how many times you see Wassermann test in it. Came in here demanding one damn near every week, for a time. Practically insisted she had the clap."

Which destroyed a very beautiful illusion. Kramer paused a moment to mourn its passing. There had been something so refreshingly healthy about Miss le Roux's previous image, both physical and spiritual. Hating Dr. Matthews a little, he pressed the attack.

"You say she was neurotic?"

"Yes."

"Yet you gave her these tests every time?"

"That's so."

"I see. How much is a Wassermann worth to you—ten, twelve rand? A nice little sideline."

"Lieutenant, take care with what you're implying. And if you knew anything about the practice of medicine at all, you would know that humoring a patient is often as important as treating them. You should have seen the girl each time I reported a negative result: she took new heart."

Kramer could not resist it. "Made you feel like Christiaan Barnard, did it?" he sneered. "Pity you aren't so handy with the transplants."

"That was a very uncalled for remark."

"Sorry," Kramer said, almost meaning it. "Let's get back to the clap. Did she ever give you any reason for her—"

"Anxieties? No. She was the kind that pays promptly and feels they have a right to use us like garage mechanics."

"But weren't you curious?"

"Not unduly; the chronically ill are apt to find some counterattraction to their main complaint elsewhere in their anatomies. Also, she was a very edgy girl. She shied away from questions. I didn't bother; I'd come across similar cases before."

"Really?"

"You'd be surprised how common they are, Lieutenant, especially among engaged girls. Little things make them suspect their future hubby is having his final fling and they get it into their sweet heads that some of this may backfire on them. After all, they say, *nice* girls don't sleep with other girls' fiancés."

"A lot they know."

"Quite, but that's the way it goes. Miss le Roux just seemed less talkative than the rest."

Suddenly Kramer felt reasonably disposed toward Dr. Matthews. He offered him a Lucky Strike, exchanged it for one without a kink in the middle, and supplied the match. The truth was they had a lot in common. They both dealt with that perverse species *homo sapiens* and both had to make what judgments they could on the evidence.

"You think she could have been going to get married?"

"Well, she didn't strike me as being a loose sort of a girl but she—"

"Yes, I know, but what about her heart? Had she a long life ahead of her?"

"No one could say. It could happen anytime—as I thought it had, you see. She could have lasted for donkeys' years."

"So you didn't warn her—I mean in case it might change her wedding plans?"

"I didn't have to; she knew already."

"Hence the Trinity Burial Society?"

"I presume so."

It fitted, but like the first pieces of blue in a jigsaw that was half sky.

"We must track down this bloke with the intimate relationship," Kramer murmured.

"Anything to go on?"

"Bugger all—no one at the funeral and no flowers."

Dr. Matthews rose with a slight smile.

"Actually I'm bloody shaken and ashamed by all this, Lieutenant."

"*Ach*, don't worry, doctor—I'm sure they won't want your scalp by the time we get to the end of this one."

"I'm not so sure. You see, I didn't fill in eye colors and that until I heard the balloon had gone up. Funny, I could have sworn—"

"Just formalities. But can I take the file along anyway?"

"Of course. Let me show you out."

Kramer stopped on the doorstep to warn Dr. Matthews that he would probably send a man around in the morning for an official statement. As they were speaking, all the cars across the road started up almost simultaneously and drove off.

"Every good party comes to an end," Kramer said.

"What party?" Dr. Matthews asked.

But it was already time to get Bob Perkins to work on the tape, so Kramer just walked off down the road.

Mrs. Perkins showed Kramer into the workroom and apologized that Bob had not finished his bath. He always bathed after work because of the ink from the proofs; they were ever such messy things.

Kramer knew that Mrs. Perkins was Bob's wife but he had never grown used to the idea. She doted on him like the pale but proud mother of a prodigy born under mysterious circumstances. They even looked alike. If they had not both been about thirty, he could well imagine her having spent years bringing him up in neat navy suits and a flutter of clean handkerchiefs.

"Please make yourself comfortable, sir," she said, unaware of the discomfiture her presence caused. "I was just going to pour out his cocoa—would you like some, too?"

"May I have coffee, please?"

"Do you think that's very wise? My Bob was telling me only the other day what awful chemicals there were in it. He knows a lot about what happens to the brain, you know."

"Black, please, if it isn't too much trouble."

"Of course not. I'll be back in a jiffy."

Mrs. Perkins bustled out, a cuddly heap of woolen night garments topped with a curly head of hair the color of a teddy bear's fur.

Kramer walked over to the wall of bookshelves. Bob Perkins should know something about the brain if he had waded through that lot: *Let Hypnosis Work for You, Amateur Hypnosis, Hypnosis and Healing Therapy, Hypnosis Through the Ages, Hypnosis.* He lost track; they were scattered all over between similarly bound books which promised, among other things, too show you *How to Make a Million* and how to *Be Master of Yourself in Seven Days.* Two of the shelves were piled with radio and electronics magazines. This was reassuring.

Bob entered carrying the tray of hot drinks and only just avoided being tripped up by Mrs. Perkins, who rushed past to clear a place on the table which was cluttered with wires and circuits.

"Ah, Lieutenant." Bob grinned. "It's good to see you again, man."

"Bobby, you must talk to him about coffee," Mrs. Perkins said earnestly. "He won't listen to me."

"Time enough; I think our friend's got other things on his mind tonight."

"Too true," Kramer agreed.

"Well, I'm not staying, so you boys can get on with it right away," Mrs. Perkins said. "I must give Bobby his welcome but that's all I can manage at this time of night."

Kramer bit hard on his lower lip.

"Good night then, dearest," said Bob, hugging her with his cheek to her bosom.

Kramer went on stirring his coffee until she had left the room. Bob failed to notice Kramer hadn't taken sugar.

"Just before we begin, Lieutenant," he said, "I want you to hear something special. No, I won't touch your tape unless you listen."

So Kramer sat back and watched him operate the controls of a large tape deck which stood against the wall. The volume came up and he heard Bob's voice saying: "What is your attitude to the pop scene, Mr. Sinatra?" The reply came unmistakably from the crooner. The recording lasted eight minutes and at the end it was plainly not a parody although the contrast of accents was most striking.

Bob laughed delightedly. "I see I've got you wondering, hey?"

And then he explained what he had done was to record a Voice of America program, make a transcript of the interviewer's questions, and then substitute his own voice, using another recorder and the master tape.

51

"Not bad, is it?" Bob concluded. "It gives the wife goose pimples."

Kramer conceded he, too, might have had goose pimples if the coffee had not been so hot—which was how he preferred it, so please don't fetch any milk.

"Okay, now what is it you've brought me?"

"This tape—open it and you'll see the problem."

Kramer liked the way Bob handled the box, setting it down first before removing the lid. He was no fool, despite his sad little tricks.

"Ah, someone's tried to put a match to this."

"Seems likely."

"Burnt a section like a slice of cake right through to the spindle. You'll lose a lot on the outer winding, I'm afraid."

"That's all right; any info you can give me is more than welcome."

"I'll do my best. I'm off tomorrow, so I can work right through."

"So you said on the phone. When do I come round?"

"Make it about nine."

"Okay."

Kramer got up to leave before any more questions were asked but did not move quickly enough.

"Where did you get it?"

"In a rubbish bin."

"I'd guessed that; it'll need some cleaner before I get started. But haven't you any idea who it belonged to?"

"It's a personal effect—the only one of its kind, or that's what I'm hoping."

"You aren't saying much, are you?"

"No. There are good reasons."

"But I bet I know where you got it all the same."

"*Ach*, never in a hundred years."

Kramer was at the door before the next sentence spun him around like a .45 slug.

"You got it from the Le Roux girl's place."

"How the Jesus do you know that?"

"It's been on page one since the first edition," Bob stuttered, shaken solid. He tugged a rolled copy of the *Gazette* out of his jacket, which lay on the chair.

Kramer snatched it. Some bastard was going to pay for this, pay through the nose and every other orifice. His eyes flashed over the headings, starting with the 72 point Caslon Bold lead banner and going in five jumps down to the 24 point Gothic Condensed five-liner over an 8 point panel:

MYSTERY DEATH OF A MYSTERY GIRL

Trekkersburg police today disclosed that a city music teacher had been found dead in her flat—and that foul play had not been ruled out.

She was Miss Theresa le Roux (24), of 223B Barnato Street, who lived on her own.

Col. Japie Du Plessis, Chief of the CID Division, told the *Gazette* last night: "The circumstances surrounding the death of Miss le Roux are giving cause for grave concern. However, we will not know what action to take until the full results of the postmortem are in our hands.

"In the meantime, a senior police officer has already begun preliminary investigations in an attempt to trace anyone who can tell us anything about her. As far as we are aware, she has no next of kin.

"May I take this opportunity of asking members of the public to come forward if they have even a small piece of information —leave it to us to decide whether or not it is important."

Col. Du Plessis added that he had every confidence that the matter would be treated with dispatch and referred to the division's high rate of success in the past.

That was all. But it was enough to make Kramer deliver a string of obscene threats which placed the entire universe in peril.

"How the hell did the press get onto this?" he demanded finally, shaking Bob by the arm.

53

"I'm not the editor," he replied, "but I seem to remember something on the social pages which might help—try four and five on a thirty-two pager."

Kramer turned to them. Christ, he should have guessed: right across the top of page four was a five-column picture taken at the Brigadier's *braaivleis* and immediately behind the old bull, as he stood with beer can raised, lurked the beaming figure of Colonel Du Plessis. What an ideal moment to take the opportunity; he was already beckoning to the reporter as the flash went off.

"Bob, you're right, man—this is the case. I thought I had a long start on the buggers but now I must have the stuff on the tape before six."

"*Six?*"

"Isn't that when the *Gazette* deliveries start?"

"Deliveries, yes, but don't forget the first edition is off the presses at ten."

"So? It's for the farming areas, isn't it?"

"We also sell a few dozen to the cinema crowds as they come out—and on the station. Some people can't resist a morning paper the night before."

"Jesus."

It was all Kramer had left in him to say. At ten he had still been taking his time in the cottage. In fact, he had not left until after eleven, because he had checked his watch just after seeing Miss Henry move away from the light. An ice cube slid slowly down his spine: all he had seen was a silhouette—back-lighting would have had the same effect whether the watcher was inside or outside the house. And another thing—those six cars outside Dr. Matthews' place in Arcadia Avenue. If you had to keep watch in what would otherwise have been a deserted street, where all the residents garaged their cars at night, it was quite an idea to invite your friends along and make a party of it. Zondi could be in danger. He had to move fast.

Bob followed him to the door, promising to do all he could but apologetically emphasizing that nine o'clock was the earliest he could expect results.

"Fine," said Kramer. "This is so buggered up now it doesn't matter that much. Thanks a lot, man."

The corner of De Wet Street and the Parade was deserted. Zondi should have been waiting there for at least an hour—the two calls had taken far longer than Kramer anticipated.

He parked the car and sat. He needed to think carefully before making his next move. It would be very rash for a white, even armed, to attempt to follow in Zondi's footsteps. On the other hand, he rebelled against the thought of calling in help. His mind reacted to the dilemma by blanking out.

He was staring across the pavement at the statue of Queen Victoria, which had presumably survived into the Republican era because it was so incredibly gross, when something stirred on the Great White Mother's lap. He saw a slim brown hand reach up for a snap-brim hat hung on the scepter. Moments later Zondi slid down and strode casually over.

"No Shoe Shoe," he said. "His wheelbarrow is round the back of the city hall but not one fellow knows where he is."

"You asked plenty?"

"Oh, yes, boss." Zondi licked his knuckles.

The wind had gone. It was very cold and very early in the morning.

"Get in, I'll take you home."

"How come? We can go out to Peacehaven, boss."

"Not tonight—I'll explain why. Move it."

As Kramer drove out to Kwela Village, he filled in on all that had happened. If that was the Colonel's attitude, then he could not expect them to miss another night's sleep.

Zondi lived with his wife and three children in a two-room concrete house which covered an area of four table-tennis tables and had a floor of stamped earth. He always had to direct Kramer to it as there were several hundred identical houses in the township. All that distinguished his home was a short path edged with upturned condensed milk cans too rusty to catch the car's headlights.

"Go for Gershwin Mkize in the morning," Kramer instructed him after they had stopped. "He should know where his merchandise has got to. Maybe Shoe Shoe's sick. I've got to see the Colonel and Mr. Perkins, then I'll be in the market square if you're not back in the office by ten."

"Right, boss, see you."

Kramer waited with his lights on the door so Zondi would not fumble the key, and then started off down the hill into town again.

Lucky man; that wife of Zondi's was a good woman with a fine wide pelvis. Kramer caught himself wondering if it was not time he got lucky; he liked the idea of a loyal woman and he liked children. But no, he was a man of principle. It was not fair taking on such a responsibility in his job—you never knew when you might end up grinning at Strydom with your stomach. Anyway, he had found himself a widow with four kids. She would love a surprise guest.

5

FOR THE SECOND time running, Kramer awoke startled and lashing out. He was being kneed in the groin.

"Hey, watch what you're doing!" someone yelled.

He pulled the sheet off his face. A delighted boy of five was advancing up him on all fours.

"Good morning, Uncle Trompie," the child said, grinning at his mother, who stood by the wardrobe.

"You nearly took poor Piet's head off," chided the Widow Fourie.

"I don't mind, Ma," Piet said generously.

And the noise brought his siblings scrambling into the room to bounce on their Uncle Trompie. They were all older and that much bonier, but Kramer would have willingly put up with it for longer than their mother.

"What's all this?" she demanded. "Out you go and let your ma dress in peace. She'll be late for work in a minute."

"How long is a minute, Uncle Trompie?" asked Marie, the eldest, who knew anyway.

"Out!" shouted Widow Fourie.

"Hold it," said Kramer, sitting up and reaching for his cigarettes. He had bought them from a machine and there was some change slipped into the cellophane wrapping. He added it to what was in his trousers pocket.

"Yes?" Marie moved eagerly forward.

"If *you* can tell me how long a minute is, then all of you can have a fizzy drink down at the Greek shop; it'll be open by now."

"Sixty!"

"Seconds! Right first time—now you lot get out of here and don't come back till you're burping."

The flat emptied like a greyhound trap.

"You spoil them, Trompie."

"I spoil myself."

Unwarily, the Widow Fourie had wandered too close in a search for her stockings. One hand was all Kramer needed for the wrist lock which brought her tumbling on top of him.

"Hey! You bloody police think you can do what you like!"

"Don't you like it then?"

She giggled and nuzzled.

"I've been late twice through you."

"I'll give you a lift."

"That's lovely," she said as she went under.

Lust was a many-splendored thing, Kramer decided, as he watched the enchanting ritual of a full-bodied woman jigging her way back into a tight corset. Pure lust that was, none of your permissive society muck the government banned from the newsstands. He had seen a *Playboy* magazine once in the Vice Squad's office and it left him thinking of dogs watering lamp-posts to excite other dogs they would never know. Filthy, degrading muck. But real lust—

"Isn't it about time you started thinking about getting up?"

"Uhuh."

"Just because you're mad at the Colonel doesn't mean I've got to be late for work, after all. Marie will have to give the kids their breakfasts as it is."

"Uhuh."

"Come on, Trompie; there's a razor I use for my legs in the bathroom."

With a groan, Kramer staggered out of bed and went through into the bathroom. The Widow Fourie threw his underpants in after him and was gratified to hear the sound of the washbasin taps running. She hooked up her bra and looked around for her stockings again.

"Seen my nylons?" she called.

Kramer appeared in the doorway, scrubbing his chin with a bar of laundry soap in a final bid to get a good lather. He had his underpants over one shoulder.

"What color are they?"

"Pink," she answered, hurriedly pulling on her spare overall—she would never have time to change in the locker room at Woolworth's.

"Pink," Kramer repeated. "That's not for stockings."

"Fat lot you know. We're all wearing them in haberdashery; the counter's so high the customers can't see."

And then the thought struck him. Kramer dropped both soap and underwear in his rush across the room. The Widow Fourie glanced up irritably.

"Come on," said Kramer. "Undo your buttons."

"Keep your hands off me, they're wet!" she protested. "Have you gone crazy, Trompie?"

"Undo them!"

She looked frightened, which he regretted, but the matter was too important to waste words.

"This must be how they see you," she said softly as her fingers worked down the row of large white buttons on the plain blue uniform. "Please don't do it again, that thing with your mouth."

Kramer was not listening. He was intent on examining her undergarments as they appeared longitudinally in the gap. The low bra was a brilliant red, trimmed with a black lace frill with a dot sewn into it. The corset was scarlet with a bold pattern in deep crimson. The panties were an odd pair in poster green, cut very high at the hip and embroidered on the more substantial areas with yellow roses.

The Widow Fourie was standing stiffly as if she expected to be touched where her flesh would crawl.

"Relax," mumbled Kramer, finding a smile. "I just wanted a look."

"Oh, yes?"

She began rebuttoning. Her expression was grim and obviously her mind made up.

"I think we must have a talk in the car."

"Tell me something: why do you wear those things? It's very important."

Now she was completely taken aback.

"What do you mean?"

"Why such fancy stuff? Why not the ordinary white you see in the showwindows?"

"I dunno. I suppose it's because I have to wear this uniform all day long."

"Go on."

Kramer scooped the stockings off the floor right at her feet and handed them over.

"Oh, ta. Well, all the assistants at Woolworth's wear the same one and it's a horrible blue. Drab, I call it."

"Yes?"

"*Ach*, work it out for yourself, man."

"You tell me."

"If you wear the bright undies you like, then—even though no one can see them—you're still different. That's it: I put them on because they make me feel more the person I really am."

Bull's-eye.

The stocking on her left leg had got itself twisted. Kramer gave her his arm as she hopped over to sit on the bed while adjusting it.

"So what would you say about a dolly of twenty-two who is her own boss, can do what she likes, but goes around in drab frocks with a rainbow underneath?"

"I'd think there was still something forcing her to."

"Forcing her?"

"Of course. What woman wants to give the wrong impression of herself?"

"True."

Flattered now by the rapt attention being paid to her every word, the Widow Fourie added: "What *I* say, and I've told the manager this umpteen times, I say that a little color cannot hurt anybody."

It seemed, however, that Miss le Roux had feared it might. Hurt her very badly. And as she had been, it was something else to think about. But not now.

"I'll shave at the office," Kramer said, dragging on his clothes. He was dressed before the Widow Fourie had found her other shoe. He scrounged it from under the bed, slipped it on her foot, and said: "Okay, Cinderella, the Pumpkinmobile is downstairs waiting."

She found herself laughing fondly as they reached the passage to the lift.

"You're a nasty bit of work, Trompie Kramer," the Widow Fourie said. "But come around again soon, hey? The kids like you."

"Poor little bastards," he chuckled—and ducked.

The way Mrs. Perkins looked at Kramer when she opened her door made him uncomfortable. So did the dried lather, which felt like localized rigor mortis.

"My Bob's been up all night," she said reproachfully. "I had no idea."

"I'm sorry, but I'll see he is looked after properly."

"It's not that. It's his health. He isn't very strong, you know. Asthma."

That figured. It also accounted for the yoga books.

"I'm sorry," Kramer said again. "It's just he was the only man who could do the job."

"Oh?"

"Yes, your Bob's a very clever bloke," he confided, gaining his

61

entrance and starting off down the corridor to the workroom.

"Lieutenant?"

"Yes?"

"Er—have you had breakfast?"

"Well . . ."

"You poor thing, you can't have had a wink either—I'll bring you an egg and some toast."

Guilt was not Kramer's favorite emotion. And he felt very bad when he opened the workroom door to find Bob on the floor in the lotus position, his eyes closed.

But the bulky lad was on his feet in an instant.

"Got it all ready for you, Lieutenant," he said cheerfully. "Excuse the socks."

"Good man. Anything interesting?"

"Very, very peculiar. I thought I had it and then I didn't. Let me show you. You see I carefully spliced in some clean tape exactly the length of each burnt piece. This meant I could play it although there were silences in between."

"Yes, that's clear enough."

"I'll put it on then."

The threading took a little longer than before, then sound came from the amplifier. It was piano music. A few bars. Silence. More music. Silence. The tune changed but remained very basic, real beginner's stuff. Silence.

These continual interruptions worked on Kramer's nerves.

"How many more numbers like this?"

"They stay simple right to the end."

"Which is?"

"The tape is an hour altogether."

"Hell, somebody must have been keen."

"What do you make of it?"

"I can't bloody well concentrate with all these breaks in it, man. Sorry."

"Nor could I—that's why I made this other tape from it, leaving out all the joining pieces and bringing it into one. It's still a bit of an earache, but easier to follow."

62

The reel was already in position on a second tape deck. Bob switched over to it.

Kramer listened for the first ninety seconds and then had enough.

"Okay, thanks, Bob," he said.

"I think you should listen to a bit more than that, Lieutenant."

"No, I've heard what I want to. Is it double track?"

"Yes, a few Christmas carols and endless 'Greensleeves.'"

"That's it then, isn't it? Miss le Roux was a music teacher and sometimes they use recorders to help their pupils to check their own playing. There were five mistakes just in that little bit."

"And the way the rhythm stays virtually the same, too, whatever the tune. A heavy-handed amateur dee-da, dee-da, dee-da."

"Exactly."

"Well, I'll go along with you on that, Lieutenant—but only so far."

"Why, man?"

"Because that's what I thought until I'd let the tape run on a bit."

Kramer pressed the on switch himself.

"So?"

"Sssh, there's one now."

The playing suddenly stopped. There was silence. A prolonged silence just like those caused by the burnt sections. And then on again, from the same point in the score.

"We were getting our silences mixed up," smiled Bob happily. "That silence was *recorded.*"

Kramer frowned.

"So what? You heard the wrong note—they stopped and started again. It's what would happen during a music lesson."

"Then why don't we hear the voices? Surely the teacher would have been saying something in that pause? It can't have taken that long for the pupil just to go back one fingering."

Which was true. And suddenly something began niggling in

a corner of Kramer's mind, but for the moment he could not recall what it was.

There was a knock at the door and Bob sprang up to allow in Mrs. Perkins with a breakfast tray. The egg was wearing a balaclava helmet.

"Ta very much," Kramer said, taking the tray on his knees. "Very kind of you."

"Has my Bob been a help then?"

"You've said it," Kramer replied, the entire yolk in his mouth already.

"Not really, dear. All I've done is set the Lieutenant a real poser that I can't begin to make head or tail of."

Kramer started on the toast and Mrs. Perkins stared at him with morbid fascination; he was not eating at all but refueling like some voracious robot. The huge mug of black coffee could have been a half pint of high-test from the way it went down.

"Joking apart," Bob said, eager to distract his spouse, "does this get you any further?"

Kramer wiped his lips on the paper napkin so thoughtfully provided, swallowed a belch, and stood up.

"Yes, it does and I'm very grateful, man," he said. "I haven't had time to think about it properly but I'm certain it'll help a lot. There'll be a check coming your way as soon as I see the boss at ten."

"It's almost that now," Mrs. Perkins said.

"God!" Kramer exclaimed, forgetting himself. "Bob, I must be going."

Colonel Du Plessis was scratching his backside at the window when Kramer burst in without knocking.

"Good morning, Lieutenant," he said without turning around. "I have been waiting for a full report. You have it in writing, I hope?"

"The hell with that; I'm interested in *printed* reports."

Colonel Du Plessis sidled over to his chair beneath the large

64

portrait of the President. He held his hands to his small paunch and watched Kramer slyly out of the corner of his eyes.

"*Ach*, don't be so liverish, hey? It should be me this morning; my stomach is really in a terrible state."

He was an old woman and no mistake. He had the face of one, the stature of one, and the voice of one. When he handed you a docket across his desk, you expected to find weak tea and scones balanced on it. Yet he had the reputation of being one of the meanest, toughest men on the force. This was due largely to an unpredictable rage as shocking as having grandmother come for you with her crochet hook.

And he had an old woman's guile as well.

"The Brigadier was very pleased to hear I had put you in charge of this case."

"In charge? Don't make me laugh. I didn't decide to bugger up the thing just to get your name in the paper."

The Colonel tutted.

"Let me finish first, hey? The Brigadier said to me, he said: 'That's one of our best blokes, Japie, see you give him all the help he needs.' In fact, he asked me to make a press statement —knowing you were up against no-next-of-kin troubles."

"Crap."

That should have done it. That should have brought the bastard leaping over his blotter. Kramer had waited a long time to provoke him into a charge of striking a fellow officer; now that he had the perfect excuse for his own behavior, nothing happened. Like they said, the bitch was unpredictable.

"Please sit down, Lieutenant, Good. I've just been chatting to your little Bantu sergeant. He had a lot to tell me, all very interesting. A little worrying, too."

So that was it. He now knew far more than Dr. Strydom had managed to babble over the telephone. And if Zondi had done his job properly, the Colonel was browning his trousers at the thought of what the Brigadier would do if he got to know how seriously the *Gazette* story had affected the investigation. The

Brigadier had plainly never said anything about the press—he hated them.

"You're worried, Colonel?" Kramer echoed innocently.

"Tell me, Lieutenant, how does a white girl, a teacher, get mixed up with Kaffirs who use the spoke? I can't see it happening."

"Not Zulus either. Dr. Strydom says he's only seen it done on the Rand this way."

"And Zondi says she's been in Barnato Street for two years."

Then Kramer had an inspiration. "Who says she had to be mixed up with Kaffirs at all? These killers aren't always in gangs —some work free-lance. All you need is a contact and the right kind of money."

It was not really an inspired thought—simply a repressed one, surfacing. Why his brain had sought to shield from it was obvious: it made him sick to the stomach.

"God in heaven," the Colonel whispered. "You mean some *white* fixed this one up?"

"I'm just guessing, but it makes better sense."

"God in heaven."

They sat in silence. Kramer turned the idea over and over with a stick. It was ugly, it was revolting, it was unprecedented that a white murderer should get a black to do his dirty work. But it had a curious logic.

"Cost one hell of a packet," the Colonel said at last. "If the killer came down from the Rand, you'd have to get him a forged pass or he might be picked up by the vans for vagrancy."

Typically, he had chosen the point of least importance.

"Money's nothing. Maybe he's moved down here on his own and taken a job as a houseboy. Things might have got too hot on the Rand; we'd better put through a Telex to Jo'burg and see if they have any leads."

"I'll see to that."

"It's the contact that is the trouble. A Kaffir wouldn't think of doing this job for a white unless he trusted him completely, knew him better than his own brother. But how? Where would they meet? Somebody would notice them together—the Special Branch are always on the lookout."

"Maybe they could help us."

"No, we're not dealing with fools."

"What about a middleman then? A black who fixes the deal independently?"

"The same goes for him. It could be a trap and he would be an accessory. Trust. Trust who?"

"What about this bloke Zondi says she was going to marry?"

"Oh, him. Yes, he's our best bet so far—if he exists."

"What do you mean?"

"Right now he's just a medical theory, but I'll look into it."

"And Shoe Shoe?"

"Another theory, but it looks like we've moved out of his class. I'd better get round to the market square and call Zondi off."

Kramer stood up and the Colonel accompanied him to the door.

On the way over, he said: "So you've found another excuse to have your Bantu pal along with you, hey?"

"It's as much a Bantu case as white!" Kramer flared back.

"Easy, man, easy, I'm just pointing out that this trust you're talking about can build up in certain situations, properly controlled of course."

He should not have qualified his remark; now Kramer was no longer defensive but angry.

"Look, if you're not happy with the way I work, then let's go and sort this one out with the Brigadier."

Beautifully done, a phantom toe cap right in the old crone's scrotum.

"Please, Lieutenant, there's no need for that. Both of us know you—er—are best as a team. You missed my meaning."

"So my work is all right?"

"Yes, yes, of course."

"And I'm in charge of this case?"

"Completely in charge."

"Right; then I don't want any follow-ups in the *Gazette*, understand?"

"Should I tell them it was a false alarm?"

"Tell them if they print *anything* you'll want to see the editor."

"Fine; much better idea."

"Also, I'm not writing a report on this case until it is finished and over."

"You just get going, my boy, be your own boss. I've got a lot of interest in your success."

"I bet you have," said Kramer, closing the door behind him.

Shoe Shoe was still missing.

Zondi completed his ninth circuit of the city hall and halted at the main entrance. The other beggars were around as usual, but he ignored them. He was going to ask his questions at the top.

So he crossed over De Wet Street and entered the courthouse gardens where the glimpse of a yellow Dodge drawing up at a side gate made him hasten toward a vantage point under A Court's windows. But no one left the sedan, as it was not yet one o'clock. Time to smoke a Texan.

At one the sun had passed its zenith and then the true afternoon began. As the shadow of the city hall began to edge out over the pavement, the halt and maim left the civic portico and took up fresh positions. The spear of shade cast by the steepled clock tower switched sides and advanced on the other flank. At five it would slit into the General Post Office and people would pour out, cover the pavements, eddy into the gutters, and finally trickle away. But right now there was no rush. The heat was terrific.

And the yellow Dodge roared away down the Parade, leaving Gershwin Mkize to come lazily up the wide gravel path. The brown lawn on either side of him was so dry that the grasshoppers made tiny puffs of dust as they landed and took off. Their incessant movement contrasted strongly with the still forms of

Bantu office messengers who lay sprawled during the lunch break with yesterday's bread and yesterday's papers. But it found an echo in the curious spring of Gershwin's gait—which Kramer had once said was the result of going with a dirty woman. He certainly looked a type who would take on anything, with his thin lips, toffee-colored skin, and straightened hair.

Gershwin stopped and leaned against a palm tree. It was on a slight mound that enabled him to see over the traffic. The ringmaster had come to make his daily inspection.

Zondi remained where he was, about fifteen feet directly behind Gershwin, and smiled with satisfaction. It was always advisable to approach a man like Gershwin from the rear, whatever your motive. If it was hate, then, with his bodyguards waiting with the Dodge in the Market Square, your friends could lay odds. If it was just a few questions you wanted to ask, then men of his kind had no more sensitive area than the back—a slight touch there unsettled them, made them garrulous.

Gershwin began to show signs of irritation. His thumbnail worked on the bark of the palm tree, fidgeting the fibers away, and his two-tone shoe tapped smartly. Then out came the yellow handkerchief. He used it on his face like a powder puff before giving it a twist up each nostril. He snorted.

And snorted again, in surprise. Zondi had flicked the stub of his Texan so that it struck the sweat patch in the yellow suit between the shoulder blades. Before he could turn, Zondi was at his ear.

"What's the trouble—is Arm Chop swallowing his pennies again?"

"Ah, Detective Sergeant Mickey Zondi," said Gershwin without a sideways glance. "Arm Chop he a good boy now, spend short time in lavatories. My thoughts are for this new fellow by the phone box. He not look too damn happy."

It was part of Gershwin's vanity that he would rather speak bad English than Zulu, his mother tongue.

"Why not?" Zondi's tone was light, bantering. "His first week

69

in the big city? I bet when you spoke to him about it, the wax turned to honey in his ears. Look here, you said, you're not useless after all. Your brothers cannot come in to find work because they have no passes, but the police will not mind if you don't have one—they leave your kind alone. All you have to do is show your legs to the Europeans and they will give you money that you can send home to your mother—and your brothers."

"Too true," agreed Gershwin, supremely amiable.

Zondi switched to Zulu: "But now he knows. He wants his brothers to carry him away. But they have no passes."

"Later he will get more for his families," Gershwin said, sticking to English. "I'm telling you this one took much petrol to find, he stays far in the mountains. Much, much petrol—much money."

"Have a Texan."

Gershwin nipped one from the packet and dropped it in his eagerness to whip out a flashy gas lighter.

"Hell, no, have another," said Zondi in English again, catching him by the shoulder as he bent to retrieve it. Gershwin nodded—then, noticing a quick movement, used his heel to grind the tobacco into the ground. A black urchin, who made his living by rolling smokes out of stubs, slunk back onto the courthouse veranda.

Zondi made Gershwin take his light off a match. That was for the kid.

"But business stays good, does it, Gershwin? I see there are two other new ones besides the boy."

Gershwin took care to exhale into Zondi's face. He did not blink.

"So so, Mr. Zondi."

"How many altogether?"

"Ten, maybe twelve."

"And is Shoe Shoe still your number one?"

"Number one topside."

70

There was a slight hesitation before the affirmation of Shoe Shoe's status.

"But he has not been living down at your place in Trichaard Street for nearly a month now."

That was the way; play it down, play it cool.

"Silly fellow that, Shoe Shoe. I telling him it best place but he like to sleep in the market too much."

"Why so?"

"He no like the other unfortunatelies. Say he different from them. Say he was not born to shame mother."

"Who looks after him, then?"

"I pay boys."

"With his rent money?"

"I must not be out of my pocket because he is funny chap, Mr. Zondi."

"That boy over there, is he one who helps?"

"Any boys. My driver finds them."

"So Shoe Shoe just says he isn't coming back to Trichaard Street one night?"

"I telling you."

"Why so suddenly? He had been there four years—yes?"

Gershwin's thumbnail went to work on the bark again. He was digging quite a hole in it.

"That's right," he said, very bored.

"And suddenly last night he leaves the market, too. Without his barrow."

"Ah, now I know your troubles, Mr. Zondi! But nobody steal Shoe Shoe, you know. Police not to worry."

Gershwin was grinning from one small ear to the other.

"No?"

"He fear a spell from the others, they jealous. He take taxi up mountains to look for witch doctor."

"When?"

"Saturday before yesterday."

"By himself?"

71

"Shoe Shoe save much money—not one family to him, you see—but why pay for two?"

"Do you know which taxi?"

"Parrot taxi cheapest."

He meant pirate—and knew no inquiry was ever likely to succeed in that direction.

"There's a whole row of witch doctors in Brandsma Street, Gershwin."

"Those with shops no good; all same like white doctors. Shoe Shoe come back by and by."

Gershwin's grin had fixed, hooked back on his eyeteeth. His disclosure was in no way absurd, it all tied together nicely. If anything could make a Zulu—even as handicapped as Shoe Shoe—head for the bush, it was the dread of having had a curse on him. Such spells could only be dealt with in a secret place.

It seemed that Gershwin held a winning hand. So Zondi played the joker. He tipped his Texans out, so they showered down at his feet, and beckoned the scavenger over. Then he walked briskly away, turning once to enjoy the conflict on Gershwin's face that finally lost him his composure. The kick was a second too late—the boy and the jackpot had disappeared into the shimmering air.

KRAMER WAS SEATED at the wheel of a taxi in the Market
Square, an old sock drawn over the *For Hire* bracket. The
owner was away drinking his health in a nearby bar.

He had chosen the taxi because the rank was close to the
flower stalls and he wanted to keep an eye on the yellow Dodge.
There had been nothing rewarding so far. Gershwin's stooge
was leaning listlessly on the hood, exhausted by writing some
very elementary words in the dust on the back window. The
driver was asleep.

Which, by a process of association, made Kramer aware that
he was suffering a hangover from some dream which had
plagued him until little Piet came in. There was a little of it left,
like a heel tap at the bottom of his skull. He could still taste the
cloying sweetness of it. Gradually a few images re-formed in his
mind's eye. Theresa le Roux had been warm from her brow to
the trim of her ankles. Under the blue gums by a slow brown
river, with Christmas beetles shrilling in the bush beyond, she
had reached out for him. The little gray dress had slipped off on
its own. The hooks on her purple bra had parted at a touch. But
as her round breasts sprang free, Dr. Strydom's stitching had
come undone and they had flopped into his lap.

He flinched. It was high time he got his thinking straight
about Miss le Roux.

But at that moment he spotted Zondi making his way toward him through the flower stalls—and between them stood the Dodge. A robust housewife beckoned for a Bantu to take some oranges to the car park which lay farther back. Zondi barged the other contenders aside and shouldered the bag, effectively masking his face with it as he passed the stooge.

He dumped the bag not far from the taxi rank, accepted a coin with a humble smile, and approached on the stooge's blind side. Kramer raised a hand to call him over, to tell him it was not worth it, then changed his mind. It could be amusing to see what happened next.

Almost to order, two Cape colored tarts began a slanging match a few feet on the far side of the Dodge. The stooge slouched over and a small crowd of idlers gleefully gathered. Cheers woke the driver, who got out to join his colleague. The obscenities were riveting, but Zondi hesitated. The men in yellow were still too close to the car.

Then an Indian road sweeper stopped his handcart beside Zondi. He obviously wanted to exchange droll remarks but found instead he was tucking the housewife's coin into his turban and watching in some bewilderment as Zondi advanced on the mob with the hired broom.

Kramer switched on the taxi's engine just in case. You never knew with Zondi. It could turn into a very unpleasant situation.

Zondi walked swiftly up behind the stooge and driver, stopped a yard short, aimed the broom handle between them, and lunged with all his weight. He caught the bigger tart 'twixt buttocks—it was like being goosed by an ostrich. She reacted on reflex with a practiced and devastating backhander. The buckle on her bag ripped across the stooge's face even before her head could turn. And then the driver got his. They screamed and went for her. The other tart gave the rallying cry to every colored within half a mile and the fight was on.

It was all action.

Except over on the near side of the Dodge. There Zondi was displaying an almost supercilious calm as he opened the doors

to examine the interior. He went over every inch of the uphol-
stery, pried into every stub-filled cranny, tipped up the ash-
trays, which were empty. Something in the glove compartment
finally caught his eye. He carefully closed the doors before
crouching to inspect the underside of the vehicle.

He came up smiling just as the market master arrived on the
scene blowing frantically on a police whistle. It was definitely
a situation in which you went by priorities. Kramer abandoned
the taxi to its driver, and the fracas to an Indian constable
wobbling up on his bicycle. Zondi had a lead.

7

THE JAZZY CHRYSLER had been exchanged for Kramer's personal sedan, an enormous Chevrolet flat enough for a helicopter pad, which was parked half a block away in Library Lane.

Zondi got in behind the wheel and Kramer tossed across the ignition key. He was pleased to have him drive; the glare had produced a stabbing headache.

The Chev nosed its way out of the back streets and then headed north, picking up speed. Zondi had said not a word, but that was his way. Kramer wondered instead what he had done with his sunglasses. He closed his eyes.

But only for a second. Zondi was going it like a Free State farmer on his way to a Rugby international.

They were straddling the center line at close on sixty along one of the old streets calculated to take no more than three ox wagons abreast. An oncoming bus lost its bluster, chickened out, and nearly stamped on a Mini Minor in its rush for the curb. A sports car tried to hide under a five-ton lorry. A jaywalker paled, panicked, prayed, but was left virtually untouched, staring down at his opened fly in disbelief.

"Must get the right wing mirror adjusted," Kramer said. Zondi remained preoccupied.

Up through the oldest part of town, with its jacaranda avenues and corrugated iron roofs and orange brick, past the squat prison, under the railway bridge and out onto the dual carriageway—no quarter was given or asked.

Normally a good passenger, Kramer was relieved that the road would narrow again in less than three miles for the climb up the escarpment. In fact the fast section lasted only as long as the length of Peacehaven. It took the vulnerable white motorist through as quickly as possible, reducing the shacks and shanties to a colorful blur, and provided an excellent surface for the deployment of military vehicles in the event of a civil disturbance.

But Zondi was not going the full distance anyway, it seemed. He braked into the next curve, changed down and was in second by the time the turnoff broke clean in the straight. The car plunged down the dirt road and churned a high wake of red dust toward the old experimental farm which lay a mile or so beyond the last mud houses.

Kramer remembered the place well. A year back there had been a culpable homicide there; one laborer had stabbed another in the neck with a penknife in a fight over an apple. But there was no one there now; the hybrids had failed and the government had decided to cut its losses. The few buildings had been bulldozed in case homeless families took them over.

The Chev's sump clanged on a rock as it topped the last rise and slithered down into the overgrown yard. Kramer was about to suggest a quick check for oil leaks when he noticed a car had flattened a path through the weeds. He kept silent as Zondi took it.

The trail ended a scant fifty yards farther on at the start of another dirt road. Zondi continued along it without hesitation. On either side were vast untidy plots which retained their look of scientific symmetry only because each was given up exclusively to one variety of cereal—and weed killer was still doing its work.

Some forgotten fertilizer was not doing badly either, from the look of an immense field of Kaffir corn coming up on the right. It was extraordinarily high and had a most curious reddish hue.

Car tracks extended into it for about ten yards.

Zondi stopped and switched off. It was deathly quiet. So quiet that when Zondi reached out and pulled a corn stalk, Kramer heard the squeal as it left its tight sheath of leaves.

The hybrid was distinctive. No wonder the peasant farmer's son had so readily recognized a sample caught in the Dodge's substructure.

Zondi pressed the glove compartment catch and it clattered open. Kramer saw the thin film of pink powder which lay over the road maps. Peacehaven dust could penetrate anything, even spectacle cases. This was not remarkable in itself.

"I see, so the Dodge had been cleaned inside except for in there. That's why you looked—"

There was no point in talking to himself. Zondi was already making off across the field. He did not go far.

As Kramer approached there was a sudden buzz like a bullet, so immediate and menacing that his fists clenched. Then a spangled pall rose above the Kaffir corn, dithered a brighter blue against the sky, and disintegrated into zipping threads of belligerent flies.

Five paces on sat Shoe Shoe, exactly where he had been left. Only now he appeared to be twice his normal size. Since dawn the sun had been urging life and growth in all living things. Shoe Shoe was dead; but millions of bacteria were multiplying and feeding in their host, breaking wind millions of tiny times and filling his body with gases which distended him horribly.

Even so, the stink was not that bad and both Kramer and Zondi had seen it all before. This enabled them to ignore nature's remorseless processes and search for any sign that man had played his sinister part. There was none. It was a natural death.

That was if you ignored the fact that someone had taken a man, paralyzed from the neck down, and dumped him out of sight and earshot in a deserted area surrounded by *Keep Out* signs. The sun and the ants and the beetles—even the bluebottles—had simply done as ordained.

And while they toiled, Shoe Shoe must have broken his silence.

Kramer replaced the handset of the dashboard radio and accepted Zondi's offer of chocolate.

"Bloody hungry," he said. "What's the time?"

"Three."

"The meat wagon's coming; Dr. Strydom has one call to make on the way—police widow, or something. We should get back to town by four."

"Why didn't you put out an alert for Mkize, boss?"

"Gershwin? Because I want you to have him, my friend."

Zondi gave a grunt of deep satisfaction.

"That's the way we are playing this one, man, by ourselves. I told the Colonel and he's dead scared about the tip-off he gave the killer."

"Better not make any slipups though."

"*Ach*, I'll just blame my Kaffir."

They laughed. The sound reached a crow about to settle in the Kaffir corn and it flapped resignedly away again. Overhead larger birds with hooked beaks kept to their stacking column.

"Shoe Shoe's still got his eyes," Kramer remarked.

"Them flying up there? They are worried; they wait for Shoe Shoe to lie down. He does not look dead enough for them."

"What about the crow then?"

"Oh, he just another damn fool black bastard."

"Watch it. How long have they waited, do you think?"

"Since Shoe Shoe come here—one, maybe two days. You can see he was in the sun a long time."

"And Gershwin said that he had gone to the mountains on Saturday. Funny that he only became important to us three days after Dr. Strydom found the spoke wound. You could say this is a fluke."

"Boss?"

"Yes, has nothing to do with the Le Roux case. This is just a little private affair of Gershwin's. No one was ever meant to know about the girl—why look for trouble by chopping a witness in advance who would never be called anyway?"

Zondi spread out the chocolate wrapping and licked it clean. Then he made a small silver ball of it which he flicked at a passing butterfly. It missed.

"Not a witness, boss," he said. "Informer."

"Hey? Shoe Shoe was your mate but he never told you a damn thing."

"Perhaps if he heard what they were going to do to the little missus."

"Warn us, you mean? Why should he?"

"Oh, no, boss—wait until afterwards. Then he would come by and offer information if we kept him in a safe place. He would just stay there until they were hanged. I think he would like that very much, boss."

Kramer lit a Lucky Strike in slow motion.

"But it wouldn't be the same mob, would it? This spoke man was from Jo'burg."

"That's what Dr. Strydom says; maybe Shoe Shoe know different."

"And even if he didn't, it would be a spoke man and that's what really mattered to him?"

"Yes, boss."

"And he would get Gershwin, too?"

"It seems like it, boss."

Zondi borrowed the Lucky Strike to light his Texan off it. His expression was slightly sulky.

"*Ach*, it's good thinking, Zondi, man—but why didn't Shoe Shoe pull this one when they first got him four years ago? Why wait all this time?"

"Because they did not *kill* him, boss," Zondi reminded Kramer, as tactfully as possible. "The most for assault would be fifteen years inside and then they would come back for him. Or maybe their friends would do it meantime."

Kramer sat up. "Friends? Then this time he had to put *everyone* in the bag to make it safe!"

"That's right, boss. Your white fellow, too."

Jesus, with stakes that high it was a wonder they had been so confident that the exposure treatment would work. Zondi read his gaze out of the window.

"They probably left a man here to watch that Shoe Shoe died without any trouble," he said.

"Okay, so you win. And if it hadn't been for Kaffir corn under the Dodge, we'd really have been buggered. Never even begun."

The meat wagon arrived as if making deliveries in a district ravaged by rabid dogs. Every week Sergeant van Rensberg handled on average a dozen bodies mangled in road accidents and his frenzied motoring was some sort of inverted reaction. As Kramer had once remarked, you could only feel safe with Van Rensberg if you were already on one of the two trays under the curious pitched roof which covered the back of the Ford pickup.

The mortuary sergeant came coughing and hawking out of his dust cloud, trying to find a handkerchief. He was a colossal man. The combination of banana fingers and thighs that stretched trousers taut made the search quite something.

Kramer cuffed the grin off Zondi's face and then the pair of them got out, averting their eyes.

Van Rensberg reached them, turned his broad back on Zondi, and saluted Kramer. A very excellent salute that should have been available for all recruits to study. A textbook salute slow enough for Kramer to note the wide gleam down Van Rensberg's right forearm. So he had not found what he sought after all.

"Hear you've got a real farty one for me, sir."

"Sorry, Sergeant. He's been out in the sun for a day or so."

"That's all right, sir—I'll get your Bantu to put him on the tray."

Kramer glanced over his shoulder.

"Sergeant Zondi's not a big man."

"*Ach*, he can roll him, sir."

"Fine, but just wait for the doctor first, hey?"

"Okay, sir."

It was a long wait. Kramer and Zondi spent it on the humdrum of investigation; measuring the distance between the road and the body, calculating the wheelbase of the car which had left the tracks, making rough sketches and compiling notes. Van Rensberg followed them about, talking with inordinate nostalgia of his days on the beat down in Durban where, it appeared, he had done little else than solve famous cases. It soon became obvious that a flash of executive genius had given him the dead for company.

Dr. Strydom stepped out to a warm welcome from him.

"So we meet again, doc."

"You'd think once a day was enough, Sergeant. What is it this time, Lieutenant?"

"Bantu male, a cripple."

"Oh?"

"Your old friend Shoe Shoe."

"What has he been up to?"

"Nothing. For too long."

"I must see this."

And away he trotted, blinding himself by pulling the rubber apron over his head and nearly falling right over the corpse. He took a long look.

"It's not often these things affect me, but I must say, Lieutenant, this really gets my goat. It's the most bloody inhuman—"

Obscenities failed him.

"I'd say the girl had it easy by comparison," Kramer murmured.

"Too right you are. Quick and clean. Nothing in this axilla but bugs."

"What?"

"Armpit," Van Rensberg explained smugly. That was another thing about him: he had all the irritating traits of medicine's sucker fish.

"Fetch the tray, Sergeant van Rensberg," Kramer ordered.

82

"Come," Van Rensberg ordered Zondi.

"Yes, there's not much more I could tell you now," Dr. Strydom said. "I think you're right, it's exposure. I'll do a check for poison and anything else I think of. No bruises, of course, no need to be."

"The important thing is: how long?"

"Oh, at least three full days out here. Today's Wednesday—make it Saturday."

Zondi slouched up, dragging the tray behind him.

"Are we finished now, doctor?"

"He's all yours, Van Rensberg. I've just got an internal check to do tomorrow."

"Right you are, doctor. Hear that, Zondi? You can use your foot to push him over. Just lay the tray alongside—like so. Now shove hard, man."

Shoe Shoe went over slowly with a long belch like a reveler leaving his bench for the straw. A group of startled dung beetles, suddenly exposed in the middle of a round damp patch on the ground, scuttled for cover.

Kramer felt suddenly much happier about missing his lunch; one of the beetles had gone up his trousers leg.

"Shall we leave it to the experts?" Dr. Strydom suggested.

"Fine," Kramer replied, stamping the intruder free on the way back to the road.

"By the way, were the lab reports satisfactory on the girl, Lieutenant?"

"Not bad."

"And you've seen Matthews?"

"Yes, we had our little talk. Quite a good bloke actually. Careless."

"We all are sometime or another."

"No, I mean he even had her eye color down wrong in his file —which he only bothered to fill in after you rang."

"They're brown."

"Yes, but he swears they're blue. Although I bet he never looked before yesterday."

"How extraordinary! Old Georgie Abbott does, too."

Kramer stopped short.

"It's more than that then, it's bloody peculiar. Now I just took a look through the slits and saw brown—did you open them properly?"

"Yes, in the prescribed manner."

"Which is?"

"Are you doubting my word, Lieutenant?"

"No, man, don't get in a knot. I just wanted to know."

"Like this then; fingertips on the temples, thumbs facing in on the eyelids, a gentle push up."

"I see."

"Where does that get you?"

"Nowhere; I'm sorry."

"It's all right, man."

Kramer kicked at a stone.

"How about that stained glass of Georgie's? Could that have affected observation?"

"The examination light was on. I don't know; it might, I suppose. But isn't this a rather trivial point?"

"Yes, but strange."

"Let's have another look, shall we? I've got time before punishment."

"What's it, four o'clock?"

"Twenty past."

"That's pushing it. Like you said, it's a small point."

"Please yourself."

Kramer helped him off with the apron as Zondi came over smelling his hands gingerly.

"Perhaps you have some tissues in your bag for my sergeant," Kramer asked.

Dr. Strydom looked a little surprised but began to rummage about.

"He's driving my car, you see."

"Ah, of course. What about some TCP? That should do the trick. And spirits to dry it off."

84

"Ta," Kramer said, leaving the effusive thanks to a dutiful Zondi.

Then the meat wagon took a short leap at them. Van Rensberg leaned across the front seat and bawled his farewells over and under the roar of the engine. Kramer caught a line about working office hours and returned the salute. That got rid of him. Off he hurtled, clearing the traffic for them all the way back into Trekkersburg.

"I'll take you up on that offer, doctor," Kramer said suddenly. "Come on, Zondi, don't bugger about, man. It'll stop you picking your nose."

They detoured to pass the Market Square, with Dr. Strydom still tailing them, and confirmed that the yellow Dodge had left it.

"This shouldn't take long but I want to see Farthing if I can," Kramer explained. "So I want you to leave the car with me and get down to Trichaard Street on foot. Don't do too much or get too close. You could ask Maisy if Gershwin's mob have been in for extra booze lately."

"Okay, boss."

"If I finish early, then I'll drive down Trichaard Street once, fast, and you meet me in Buller's Walk."

"Got it."

"And if not, then come back to the office by seven."

"Yes, boss."

Zondi got out at the next traffic light and Kramer drove the rest of the way cursing himself for not thinking of radioing headquarters earlier and asking them to warn Mr. Abbott they were coming.

But there he was, scrubbing away at his palm in the yard doorway to the mortuary. He looked somewhat perplexed by the sudden arrival of the law. And a little concerned. Poor Georgie.

"Well, what can I do for you this time?" he asked.

"Tell me the color of Miss le Roux's eyes."

"Hey? Blue, of course,"

"Why 'of course'?"

"Because her hair's such a lovely blond."

It was not very pleasant when a man in his profession spoke of the dead in the present tense. It could be just a slip of the tongue though, just as thinking a blonde had blue eyes could be a mere slip of the mind.

"Thank you, Georgie. Now our friend Dr. Strydom would like another look at the person in question."

"Certainly, certainly, come through, gentlemen. Please don't mind the mess."

The mess he referred to was a very orderly arrangement comprising a trolley of embalming instruments, two arterial drains on stands, and an enamel bucket of viscera. At the center of them a small, shriveled man of about eighty lay on the table with his shroud pulled up.

"Nice neat sutures," Dr. Strydom said, casting a professional glance over Mr. Abbott's work.

"He's an American," Mr. Abbott confided in almost a whisper. "Poor chap only just got off the ship for a tour. Stroke. I've got to have him on a plane in Durban tomorrow early."

That explained the extra care taken with the sutures—it was a matter of national pride.

"Won't keep you long," Dr. Strydom said, pulling out Miss le Roux's tray. "Can we have a bit of extra light here, do you think?"

He waited until Mr. Abbott had supplied it before he drew back the sheet.

"Christ, what's happened to her face?" Kramer said.

"Nothing to worry about, just a touch of mottling," Mr. Abbott assured him. "I can get rid of it quite easily with talc."

"I haven't come to bloody take her out," Kramer responded.

"Steady, man," Dr. Strydom cautioned. "We've had a bad day, Georgie—a bloater out on the veld."

"I understand."

Nevertheless, he backed away hurt.

"Now let's see the eyes," Kramer snapped.

Dr. Strydom placed a hand on either side of the face and pushed up on the eyelids with his thumbs. The irises were brown, deep brown, with no little flecks of hazel or yellow.

"You pressed down very hard," Kramer muttered.

"One doesn't have to be gentle! Besides, they're apt to be a bit sticky."

"I thought you needed pennies . . . ?"

"Not always. Depends."

Kramer took a deep breath.

"Can I have a go?"

"Georgie, get us some more gloves, will you?"

Kramer and Mr. Abbott made their peace as they struggled with the gloves, which were a size too small. Then Kramer adopted exactly the same procedure as Dr. Strydom.

God, her head felt hard. The lids, however, moved easily, like grape skins. His stomach knotted.

"Well?" There was more than a hint of challenge in Dr. Strydom's tone.

"Just a minute."

Using his fingertips now, which were much more sensitive than the edge of his thumbs, Kramer felt all the way up each lid to the edge of the eyesocket.

"Doctor, do you have little lumps up here?" he asked very quietly.

"Tear glands. No, not there—closer to the nose."

"Here is where I mean."

"I shouldn't think so."

"Feel for yourself."

Dr. Strydom reached out with confidence and drew back again, plainly shaken.

"I'd like to take a look underneath if I may?"

"You may," replied Kramer, doing what the Widow Fourie hated him to do with his mouth. He shuddered involuntarily as he removed the borrowed gloves.

Mr. Abbott brought a small tray over from one of the wall

87

cabinets and Dr. Strydom shakily selected a slender probe. Kramer looked away and studied the American visitor's face; he had a mustache just like Wyatt Earp's.

"Here, Lieutenant."

Dr. Strydom's voice was barely audible. In his hand lay two tiny glass dishes. And they were a deep blue, except for a circle in the middle which was clear.

"Contact lenses!" exclaimed Mr. Abbott. "My goodness, they don't half give us trouble."

"I—I must have shoved them up there—pushed a little too hard, perhaps—they were sort of wedged—probably slipped up before my thumbs reached them—there's this bend where the eyeball presses against the bone, the superior fornix I—"

"Forget it," Kramer said.

"Please, Lieutenant, allow me to explain."

"Look, doctor, I've got what I wanted now so I don't give a stuff about your excuses."

Then the dizzy pleasure of having a hunch come off softened him.

"We all make mistakes, you said so yourself."

"But what will the Colonel say?"

"None of his bloody business, don't you worry."

"I appreciate this."

"You'd better."

"If there's anything I—"

"Yes, tell me who makes these things around here."

Dr. Strydom gulped.

Then Mr. Abbott spoke up on his friend's behalf; he owed him a favor: "The wife wears contacts herself. There's a specialist who does them, Mr. Trudeau."

"Hey?"

"It's a French name, but he lives in Trekkersburg."

"Where?"

"He might still be in his office," Dr. Strydom said. "Let me try and track him down for you. I know the ropes."

Dr. Strydom was gone for three minutes. He came back looking glum.

"Not in his rooms and not at home," he reported. "His wife says he isn't on call, so she hasn't any way of contacting him. But she is expecting him home for dinner at eight."

"Address?"

"Forty-seven Benjamin Drive, Greenside."

Dr. Strydom was now very much on the ball and determined to stay there.

Kramer wrote it down.

"Good," he said.

Mr. Abbott cleared his throat. "Care for a sundowner, Lieutenant?"

"I suppose you boys are going to have one?"

"I *need* one." Dr. Strydom laughed, showing he was still smarting over his clumsiness.

"Let's go," Kramer said, and they trooped through to the showroom, took their glasses, and sat in a ruminative silence broken only when Farthing phoned to say he would be late.

Dr. Strydom left at five to five for the prison but Kramer stayed on. Georgie had been out and bought a really good brandy now the hellcat was away. There was nothing for him to do that he could not do right there until seven o'clock. And that was think.

Think about Miss le Roux. Order the facts and analyze them. Georgie would not interrupt because Georgie was far too intent on savoring each sip.

But before he could begin, the known was again overwhelmed and brushed aside by the unknown—like the tape and the contacts. Yes, those blue lenses suggested something far more significant than dowdy frocks over naughty panties. He wished he could see the damned specialist right away.

Kramer took out the stray card on which he had written the man's address and glanced at it idly. He was looking at the other side—at the jeweler's reminder to Miss le Roux. God, he had forgotten clean about it.

What the article was he had no idea, for it simply stated: "Adjustment." Jewelry: that rang a bell. Of course; Georgie said she had none when he looked her over. Not even a ring. Which was very odd because even nuns wore rings. Wait a minute, maybe you could call making a ring larger or smaller *adjusting* it. Every Afrikaner knew English was a hell of a language.

"Hey, Georgie, have you ever heard about adjusting a ring?"

"Is this a funny story?" Mr. Abbott asked hopefully.

"No, a straight question. Can you or can't you?"

"Quite all right, I should say."

"Good."

"That's all?"

"Well, what sort of ring would you have adjusted?"

"We pass a lot on to relatives, they have them changed to fit."

"Of course."

"And—"

"Yes?"

"I was just going to say, engagement rings. Sometimes they are bought by the chap in another town or something."

Mr. Abbott was gratified, if startled, to note the effect his words of wisdom had upon Kramer.

"Christ, that's it! He doesn't live here!"

And Kramer was gone.

The prissy little man behind the clock counter was not at all eager to serve a customer who pushed aside the boy as he was closing the doors on the many strokes of five-thirty.

Kramer put down the card and asked: "Please let me have this."

"Hmmm, you're not Miss le Roux," sniffed the assistant.

"No, but—"

"You understand we can't have just anybody walking off with expensive goods for the price of the repair work. Have you a note from this lady?"

"No."

"Then I can't let you have it."

"Come on, please, it's late."

"If you don't mind me saying so, *sir*, that could be one of the oldest dodges in the book."

"What?"

"Coming rushing in here at closing time and hoping to catch the assistant off his guard."

Kramer had purposefully refrained from identifying himself. Whenever he came across this sort of sniveling misery, he made it his job to make him even more miserable. Safeguarding property was one thing—being bloody rude was another. He was never in too much of a hurry for an object lesson.

"You'll pay for that remark."

"Oh, I'm sure I will. Now get out."

"Or you'll call the police?"

"Yes."

The assistant snatched up the card as Kramer undid his jacket button and leaned across.

"Now, little man, tell me very politely what you see in there."

The assistant had no need to be told where to look. As the jacket fell open his eyes had fixed on the .38 Smith & Wesson stuck in the waistband. He clutched the counter and his heart went tock-tock. Then he began to sway.

"What seems to be the trouble, Finstock?"

Kramer turned and smiled affably at a portly old gentleman approaching in pinstripes.

"Careful, he's got a gun, Mr. Williams!" warned Finstock, scurrying to his side.

Mr. Williams put his keys behind his back and looked very solemn.

"He has, I saw it in his trousers!"

"Good evening, sir, I'm from the CID—here's my warrant card."

Mr. Williams read it from where he was standing and then turned to Finstock.

"Your nerves again, I suppose, Finstock? That will be all for today."

"Funny bloke," Kramer said a moment later.

"Very, very trying at times," agreed Mr. Williams. "I've been meaning to speak to him. Now, officer, can I be of any assistance?"

"Yes, it's some repair work. Your man insisted I produce a letter from the lady but she is unfortunately dead."

"Bless my soul, the poor creature. But have you the card?"

"I think it's been dropped behind the counter. Yes, here it is."

"Extraordinary! If you will just come down to the strongroom, you can have it immediately. I lock up this sort of thing at night."

Kramer followed him with a secret grin, elated by his corrective training and by the prospect of getting the ring. What a lead if the design was unusual.

"Here we are," Mr. Williams said, pointing into a shallow box holding an assortment of labeled articles.

Kramer reached out.

"No, not the ring."

"Hey?"

"Number four one nine."

"This?"

"No, officer, that very nice little locket."

It was a nice little locket. A beautiful little locket. A little locket that sprang open to reveal two heart-shaped photographs. One portrait was of Miss le Roux—and the other was not.

8

ZONDI WAS HAVING his problems. Ordinarily there was nothing to a surveillance job in Trichaard Street. The Group Areas Act had placed it within Trekkersburg's sole nonwhite zone, which meant it did the job of ten streets elsewhere in the town. So there were always plenty of people about from sunrise until curfew, shortly before midnight, and plenty of them with nothing to do either except stand around. It was easy to remain unnoticed. You could submerge yourself in a jostling crowd around the game played with Coke bottle tops. Or you could sit on the curb and shuffle your feet in the gutter with the others who never earned a glance from passersby. You just took off your tie, turned your jacket inside out to show the satin lining like a farmboy, and went to work. It was a cinch, especially after twilight.

Unless it rained. It was now coming down all right. In torrents which sluiced the pavements clean of orange peel and turned the potholes into ponds. For two days a blazing sky had been sucking up every particle of moisture from the land to gorge its clouds until they had grown fat and heavy—it was as though an avenging claw had slashed their bellies open, for the drops were warm and as blinding as blood.

There was the sound of calico ripping and then a bolt of

lightning caught Zondi, crouched in a shop front, in its flash. A curtain opened and closed like a shutter.

He started running. He hurdled the puddles. He slithered on the melon rind. He crashed through the door.

The thunderclap itself caught up with him as a tall Indian in a fez snatched up a knife and backed toward the cash register. His customer shrieked, tripping on her sari.

"Police!" Zondi barked.

The storekeeper recognized him and lowered his right hand. "Shut up, Mary!"

Every Indian woman was Coolie Mary. She did.

"Who's that in your room upstairs?" Zondi demanded, crossing the floor. "Don't waste time, Gogol."

"Moosa."

"You're telling me the truth?"

"You can go look."

Then Gogol shrugged indifference, picked up a cabbage, and began trimming its stalk. Zondi kicked the knife out of his grasp.

"Listen to me, churra, it had better be Moosa—you hear?"

"Come," Gogol mumbled.

Zondi followed him out into the hallway cluttered with fruit crates where the smell of curry was like a cushion against the face. The stairs were uncarpeted. The landing had a square of linoleum worn badly one way but not the other. They walked across the brighter pattern.

"In here," Gogol said, opening the door.

A middle-aged Indian rose as far as he could—without his special shoes he came up to Zondi's shoulder. He was already in his pajamas.

"Sergeant Zondi, what a pleasure." He beamed.

"Sit, curry-guts—you, too."

Always a man to oblige, Moosa sat. Gogol, his appointed patron, perched scowling on a shoe locker. The Muslims always looked after their own, unlike the Hindus who made up most of the Indian population, and you never saw a Muslim trader go

94

down for good. Moosa had served six months for receiving stolen goods after a trial which had cost him every cent his general dealer's store was worth. When he came out, Gogol brought him home, gave him a room, and waited for him to reinstate himself. This was beginning to take an unnecessarily long time. Gogol had put it around that Moosa was quite happy to lie and stare at his bleached pinups of Jane Russell and do nothing. The Muslim community was sympathetic but pointed out what a shock prison could be for a man of Moosa's cultivation. It had, however, also agreed to share some of the expense even though Gogol was unmarried.

Lightning flashed again; this time the thunder was hard on its heels. Moosa flinched.

"What's wrong? Are you frightened?"

"I've never liked violence; you know that, Sergeant."

Zondi caught the allusion and smiled meanly.

"Still say those radios were planted, Moosa?"

"I do."

Zondi looked into the cupboard, inspected the wall decorations.

"Who was it, you said? It's a long time since I was in Housebreaking."

"Gershwin Mkize."

Zondi stared right through Miss Russell and went on staring until his eyes lost their focus. Then he snapped his fingers.

"Of course, I'd forgotten."

"So you would have, Sergeant. All water under the bridge."

"Not your bridge," Gogol muttered.

"What was that?"

"Nothing, Sergeant. My landlord and provider can be a little sour at times, may Allah reward him."

"The shop door is still open," Gogol retorted. "I could be losing everything in the till while you jabber-jabber your nonsense."

"You had a customer."

"She's gone a long time, you bet, Zondi."

"Please, Gogol! Remember who this African gentleman represents."

"You get out," Zondi said softly. "You go down and you lock up and you stay there."

Gogol slunk out, his tail between his teeth.

"Yes, that's enough of this rubbish talk, Moosa. I want to know who was in this room when the storm began."

"Just me."

"If you're lying . . ."

"In the name of Allah—"

"I said no—"

"There was nobody but me here. I implore you."

"What were you doing?"

"Listening to Springbok Radio."

"In a storm? With lightning?"

"Oh, it crackles a bit but I—"

Zondi reached out to touch the small wireless. It was cold. Moosa hunched himself up in the corner, brushing brilliantine from his gleaming hair over a favorite picture of a little white girl and two golden spaniels.

"We are going to have to talk some more," Zondi said, barely parting his lips.

Moosa watched with growing apprehension as Zondi removed his jacket. The sight brought a tic to his right eye. He began breathing through his mouth.

"That's better," remarked Zondi, slipping the jacket on again with the lining on the right side. He knotted his tie in the small mirror decorated with rose tranfers. Then he sat down and put his feet up on Moosa's lap.

"Talk," he said. "Tell me why you, who are so afraid of lightning, were watching me through the window."

"Was that—?"

Zondi shook his head dolefully.

"Yes, it was you, Sergeant, I won't pretend I did not know."

"You had been watching long?"

"Yes, but it was not until the flash that I saw who it was. It is very dark tonight."

"But why watch, Moosa? What is there to see?"

"Things."

"Like?"

"I was waiting for someone."

"Who?"

"Gershwin."

"More."

"Gogol wants to know why I don't go out. Would you if you had that monster right next door by the school? Yes, you would, you are different to me. I am not a man of action. I am a—"

"But you watch him."

"I can't help it. It is like you would watch a snake. A mamba. I can't keep my eyes off him. Someday I will know."

"What?"

"Why he did that thing to me."

"That was the weak part of your story, wasn't it, Moosa?"

"But he *told* me he did it! Told me straight out. And he laughed right in my face."

Moosa was getting himself quite worked up again. Zondi stood up and peered between the curtains.

"Why were you waiting, though? What have you heard?"

Moosa giggled softly.

"There was talk in the shop today."

"Yes?"

"Gogol told me. He said there was talk that Gershwin was in trouble. With you people."

"And?"

"The Dodge has not been back all day, not once."

He giggled again.

"Then I must speak with Gogol."

"That's all he knows. People do not like to be heard talking about Gershwin today."

Zondi had found this out for himself.

"This is bad."

"If you ask me, Sergeant, you had better start looking for him on the Lesotholand border."

"Or Swaziland. It's close, too."

"True. It's just that maybe once a month a car comes by here for Gershwin with Lesotho plates on it."

Zondi took it as calmly as he could: Lesotho—a state without apartheid, in which all races could learn to trust one another, and the cradle of the spoke man.

But all the same, his smile instantly transformed their relationship.

"You're a bright boy, Moosa. Who comes in this car?"

"I've never seen properly, he drives it round the back."

"A white man?"

Moosa was politely astonished.

"I'd have noticed *that*, Sergeant!"

Still, it was good enough for Zondi to leave immediately and sprint all the way back to CID headquarters. He was late as it was.

It must have been the hundredth time Kramer had looked at the wall clock. He started on the pile of overseas photographic magazines again.

Exasperation made turning each page no more than an exercise in self-control for nothing registered. He had been forced to wait for more than an hour for Sergeant Prinsloo to get back from the scene of a payroll robbery. And now the man had been in the darkroom for nearly twenty minutes without even getting through on the intercom. On top of which, Zondi was overdue and he wanted to get out to Trudeau's place right on eight.

The darkroom door slid open and Sergeant Prinsloo came across, wiping his hands on a towel. He saw Kramer had stopped at a page which had been windowed by the censor's scissors.

"Yes, makes me bloody mad, that does," Prinsloo said. "Okay, so we don't want nudes all over the place making trouble—but

I wanted to read that piece on the back about fine-grain developers."

Kramer nearly hit him.

"Sorry, Lieutenant, nothing to offer you," he went on, dipping into his apron pocket and taking out the second heart-shaped portrait. "This print is all shot to hell. I thought maybe there was some detail in it I could bring out, even by just holding a lamp behind it, but there's nothing. It's flat and that's all there is to it."

"That took you till now?"

"*Ach*, no. I copied this and blew up some big contrasty prints."

"What the hell for?"

Sergeant Prinsloo reddened. He threw the locket picture down in front of Kramer.

"I had to bloody try something. Look at it! All gray tones. A nearly black blob in the middle. Light little blobs in the background, blurring together. Grain like beach sand. It's a proper balls-up."

And so it was. Kramer had just hoped it could be made to reveal something of what was presumably a man standing near a hedge with the sun behind him. The face was so dark you could not even make out the line of the nose.

"Useless; don't know why she didn't throw the bloody thing away with everything else," Kramer muttered, hinting an apology.

"Not useless."

"How come?"

"You look in a snapshot album sometime," Prinsloo said. "Half the pictures are as bad as that one. There's Uncle Frikkie, they say, and all you see is a doughnut in a beach hat. You *see* when something is new, after that you *recognize*. Like it jogs the memory, makes a picture inside your head. And not just photos; it happens with me with my pa's walking stick."

Kramer suddenly saw the real significance of the picture: it was wholly intimate yet totally unrevealing. He was certain now that Miss le Roux had been a girl with a past which she took pains to hide.

The lenses increased in importance.

Zondi met him on the stairs but Kramer shouted angrily and ran on ahead, refusing to listen until they were in the car headed for Greenside. Then he listened very carefully, saying nothing about having his orders disregarded. Zondi's chief virtue was arrogance.

The fragrance of furniture polish put Kramer at his ease in such unfamiliarly elegant surroundings. His grandmother, too, had believed furniture should be groomed daily until it shone like a racehorse's flanks. Of course you had to have furniture like that which surrounded him to make it worthwhile. It was all imbuya or stinkwood from the Knysna forests and the designs solid Early Cape.

Kramer's appreciation of the room ended at this point. He liked paintings to have lots of thorn trees in them and not just one big thorn. He also preferred even a tasteful vase of plastic flowers to an old wine bottle with dead grass stuck in it at all angles.

Mr. Trudeau stepped warily across the waxed parquet flooring with a drink for him. Kramer took it and went on looking out over Trekkersburg through the picture window. The storm had passed and it was a fine moonlight night. He saw the glint of a large swimming pool below on the lawn.

"Like it, Lieutenant? We do. Wonderful view; all those lights like necklaces on black velvet, or so Susan always says."

"It's a nice house," said Kramer.

"You think so? We're pleased with it. Got ourselves an excellent cookboy now—he was the gardener before, funnily enough. Wouldn't live anywhere else in the world."

"Very nice," said Kramer, downing his brandy in one.

"Thought you chaps—er—didn't on duty?"

"We don't."

"Ah, I see. Well, what has brought you careering out here then? Susan says it sounded important."

Kramer told him and Mr. Trudeau's whiskey-and-soda voice went flat.

"Murdered, you say?"

"Yes; I'm afraid I cannot divulge any details at this stage."

"No, no, quite right. You just want me to say what I can about the contacts. You've got them on you?"

Kramer handed over the envelope.

"Good Lord, these are unusual little chappies."

"Why so surprised, sir?"

"Never thought I'd come across a pair outside a film studio. You see, they are simply cosmetic cornea lenses, no optical qualities at all. Worn just for effect."

"Never medically?"

"Well, we do have a version of this type of thing for certain conditions involving hypersensitivity, but these aren't them."

"I see, sir. Where would someone get a pair like this?"

"Overseas, I should think. The States, Germany—possibly London. Did she travel much?"

"Not in the Republic?"

"No demand I've ever heard of before. It would be possible to send the prescription over, I suppose."

"This would have to be done by an eye specialist like your-self?"

"Oh, no. Any proficient optician can take a cast of the eyeball —a little local anesthetic and there's nothing to it."

"In Trekkersburg?"

"Quite possibly. Yes, I don't see why not."

"Any names spring to mind, sir?"

The specialist became wary—professional ethics and all that.

"Sorry, Lieutenant, not one, I'm afraid."

"Can you tell me any more about these then?"

"Hmm. Hand-painted, of course—you can see how it's done, just leaving the pupil area translucent. The pupil's quite small,

101

actually, showing it was made for use in bright sunlight. That's the trouble with these things; doesn't allow the wearer's eyes to adapt to conditions. You'd need a hole about four units larger in poor light."

"Like a cat's eyes get bigger?"

"That sort of thing, Lieutenant."

"And what would they cost—a lot?"

"Around fifty guineas. Perhaps fractionally more, what with postage and so on."

"Nothing else?"

"What more can I say? If it wasn't for the painted iris they would be the same as any other contact. They have their advantages and disadvantages. Some people take to them, some don't."

"Oh?"

"I mean some eyes get so irritated, the things have to be discarded. While with others, after a little practice they can be worn for up to eight hours a day—even longer."

"Very interesting."

"Oh, yes, practice is most important. Everyone has tears streaming down their face to begin with. The old eye thinks it has a foreign body to dislodge. Some learn, others don't."

He was beginning to repeat himself—and this was what Kramer had hoped for: some sign he had come off guard again.

"No doubt science will find a way round it sooner or later, sir. Just one other thing: have you a patient called Theresa le Roux?"

He lobbed the name carelessly across. Mr. Trudeau met it with a smashing backhander.

"Don't try that sort of trick with me, Kramer. There's a good fellow."

"Have you?"

"No."

"You're very certain."

"Yes."

"Le Roux's not an uncommon name—you must have a lot of patients on your books."

"Hardly rare, as you point out. It was my mother's maiden name; I have always been particularly sensitive to it."

"So I see," Kramer said, thanked him, and left through the French windows.

Zondi had gone to sleep in the car.

First things first. There was an old wog saying that it was better to fill your belly with the meat of bush pig before seeking out the buck whose droppings were dry. They would start by running Gershwin Mkize to the ground.

Kramer had rejected Zondi's suggestion that they radio headquarters and initiate the search right away. He wanted to see to it himself—that way it would be done properly, or, more exactly, his way. Give the Colonel half a chance and the Republic would be roadblocks from Skeleton Coast to Maputoland. He had a somewhat more subtle plan in mind. Of course he had lost an hour but that could not matter much.

Anyway, they were already back at the central police station and making for the charge office to get the name of the duty officer.

They went in on the white side and the place seemed deserted. So Kramer looked around the high partition plastered with Wanted notices and bilharzia warnings and found Sergeant Grobbelaar leaning on the nonwhite counter, reading a newspaper. He ignored their arrival and went on sucking his pencil over the children's crossword.

"Bloody English," he said suddenly, scoring the puzzle across. Every time he patted the blond crown of his crew-cut head like that, Kramer expected it to bounce like a tennis ball. He wished it would. He hated the slob's guts.

"Busy, Grobbelaar?"

"Always. How's it, Friday?"

Zondi looked away.

"Not so busy you can't listen to serials on Springbok, hey?"

The transitor set was poorly concealed between the files above the fireplace.

"What do you want, man?"

Some of the blokes in uniform were like this. They resented the CID so strongly that it was as if they believed all that pulp in their lockers about randy blondes and racing cars. They overlooked the long hours which made a two-to-ten shift sound like a sinecure for pensioners. And they overlooked the fact that most of them had attempted to join the CID, only to fail on probation. Sergeant Grobbelaar was a case in point. He had panicked when a manacled suspect had tried to escape from the interview room. The bullet had put him back into blue.

"The duty officer—who is it tonight?"

"Captain Johns."

"Then ring him."

"He won't like this; he's got a cold and he's still staying in the Buttery. He was going to bed early."

"Ring him. Now."

The idea amused Kramer not a little. The Buttery was a private hotel over a restaurant right in the center of town; it took commercial travelers and served business lunches, but its main income came from a twitter of decrepit widows who sat until all hours in the lobby watching life go by and waiting for the worms. They would get one hell of a kick out of Captain Johns shambling to the guests' telephone box in his raincoat, hiding his face in a handful of tissues.

Grobbelaar turned from the phone: "It's engaged."

"Then hold on."

Kramer spun the newspaper around. It was the *Daily Post*, once the Colonists' weekly source of government news and now an evening rag not worth putting in the cat's sandbox. He checked the headlines carefully. Good, the Colonel had resisted temptation. Not a line about the case. He glanced over the inside pages, stopping at the sports section. Then he thought of the Stop Press on the back. He flipped the *Post* over and grinned.

Zondi moved to his side.

"Look at that, man!"

Zondi looked and saw a small item which read:

MARKET RIOT

Fifteen nonwhites arrested in Trekkersburg market at noon following fracas. Policeman injured.

"You can try yourself," growled Grobbelaar, dropping the receiver with a clatter. He was plainly annoyed at being excluded from the merriment.

"Give me the OB," Kramer said.

Grobbelaar made no move toward the Occurrence Book, which lay on the table with the typewriter.

"What you want to know?"

"This business in the market—did you see who they got?"

"*Ach*, no, a lot of coons. Khumalo booked them."

"Where's he?"

"Khumalo!" Grobbelaar yelled.

The door to the veranda opened and Bantu Constable Khumalo put his head in.

"Yes, my Sergeant?"

"Come, CID wants to speak to you."

"Suh, I have got five prisoners for the train out here."

Kramer held up his hand.

"Just tell me, Khumalo, who did you book from the market?"

"All rubbish."

"*Who?* You bloody baboon!"

"Lily Francis, Bob Jafini, Trueman Sithole, Gershwin Mkize, Banana—"

"OB—make it quick this time."

Grobbelaar could not help himself. The Occurrence Book slammed down in front of Kramer, open at the right place.

"By the bottom here," Zondi said, "it says the Dodge was taken to the pound."

Kramer read down to the entry, through the list of names. Then he looked up at Grobbelaar, who was trying to do the same upside down.

"Get me this man Mkize."

"Khumalo is busy," Grobbelaar replied. "Get him yourself." But he wisely threw the cell keys to Zondi.

Then, after a moment more of Grobbelaar's company, Kramer decided to leave, too. He caught up with Zondi in the long corridor leading to the yard. It was unlit but its gloss-painted walls reflected the orange tungsten glow at the far end like a flare path. Their footfalls locked and echoed off the high ceiling. The headquarters had been built in the days of the old mounted police and the architect had apparently made whimsical allowance for a platoon to gallop through with lances elevated.

The young Bantu constable over on duty outside the cell block greeted them with the heartiness of a secret sleeper. He twisted the master light switch in the wall niche, took the keys, and swung open the steel door. Then came the customary pause before stepping in out of the fresh air. Actually Kramer never found the odor within wholly unpleasant; the blend of vomit, urine, and carbolic formed a nostalgic reminder of a certain nurse's uniform often used as a pillow.

The three cells on the left had the extra bolts and padlocks which had become mandatory on the doors of political detainees since the Goldberg escape. No sound came from behind them.

Across the way were three others reserved for whites. The constable stopped at the second of these and grinned, poking his thumb at the inspection flap. Kramer pushed it aside and looked in.

A disheveled man of around forty was sprawled on his coir mattress on the floor, moaning and cursing drunkenly. His belt had been confiscated and his trousers were down to his grazed knees.

"Black whore," the prisoner pronounced with startling clarity.

The constable giggled, his eyes searching for approval. Presumably Grobbelaar had spent a hilarious half hour there earlier on.

"Love you, black whore, I love you," sobbed the fool, rolling over to muffle his agony in the soiled ticking.

"Him contradict Immorality Act," the constable needlessly explained. And he laughed elaborately the way Grobbelaar did, heaving his shoulders as if to dislodge an errant coathanger.

Kramer's fists bunched. So Zondi performed a sly act of charity by grinding his heel into one polished toecap.

The prisoner was being sick. Kramer looked back at him. He knew the man from somewhere. That was it: the railway ticket office. He was the clerk who never had to look things up. The one who always said he wished he were going with you and sounded good company. No more of that now for the rest of his life. No one would want to be seen with him ever again, certainly not in a public place like a buffet car. Fifty to one it had not been a prostitute either; more probably another of the big, fat, ample ones with gentle faces all mothers were meant to have. If he was a bachelor it might not be so bad. He could have the money for top counsel and get off lightly. But even if the case was withdrawn after a remand in the morning, it would have smashed him for good. Stupid bastard.

"Gershwin Mkize," Kramer said, letting the flap drop.

This surprised the constable. He dithered a moment before taking the cork off the tip of his spear and leading the way around the corner to the general nonwhite cell.

There were sounds of stirring within and the constable shouted that everyone should lie down and keep still. Then he undid the lock silently and stepped back. With a practiced ease he used his spear to lift the latch as he jumped forward, kicking the door open.

There were over thirty prisoners in the cell and about half of them were sitting up blinking blearily in the light. One old lag, thinking it was morning, had already rolled up his grass mat. A slobbering snore was the only sound.

The constable stepped aside, pointing. His gesture was hardly necessary. Gershwin, the stooge, and the driver, all in their yellow suits, stood out against the far wall like three traffic signs against a gray sky.

Kramer noticed several things immediately: that they were only feigning sleep, that Gershwin reclined on five mats while four youngsters nearby lay on the bare concrete, and the stooge and the driver, both bloodstained, had decided three extra mats befitted their station.

"Clear them," Kramer ordered, nodding at the prisoners who lay between him and Gershwin.

Zondi motioned the constable to stand by the door with his spear and then dragged the intervening forms to one side. Small as he was, he had the strength of a stevedore—or perhaps it was just a knack.

Kramer stopped a foot from the pile of mats.

"Gershwin."

The stooge fluttered an eye.

"Gershwin Mkize."

There was a murmur of excitement among the other prisoners. The constable stamped for silence.

"It's time to go, Gershwin."

This brought the driver scrambling to his feet. Kramer elbowed him sharply, deep in the belly.

"Where to?" inquired Gershwin, as his henchman sank gasping beside him.

The stooge screwed his eyes up tight as if he dreamed of impalement.

"Ah, never you mind," Kramer replied quietly.

"No, thank you, boss."

108

"Hey?"

"I've got number one Jewboy lawyer. He say Gershwin—"

"Sam Safrinsky? You're going to need an advocate for the Supreme Court, not a solicitor."

"Supreme? For a little trouble like this one? Mr. Safrinsky he say I've got a good alibi, I just coming down by market side to look for Dodge and—"

Gershwin had noticed Zondi's expression. So had some others and they had turned away.

"So Sam says it's all right," said Kramer. "But does Sam know also about Shoe Shoe?"

Gershwin's lip curled. He stared back at Kramer without blinking. Then he looked down at what Zondi dropped on his knees. It was a head of red Kaffir corn.

"There's more," Kramer said. "And it's stuck under the Dodge that the traffic cops are keeping nice and safe for us."

"My turn?" Zondi asked.

"No, I think Mr. Mkize wants to go with us now. Actually, I'd thought of a little ride out to the kids' paddling pond in Wilderness Park."

Gershwin jerked upright.

"It gets around, doesn't it?" Kramer chuckled to Zondi. "Funny thing is that only the people we want to believe it ever do. The magistrates hear about the park and just shake their heads. What liars these black buggers are."

"And it's not raining now, boss."

Zondi came close to looking mischievous.

"On second thoughts, perhaps just a little chat in the office. What do you say, Gershwin?"

Gershwin got up with difficulty—his legs were not themselves—and presented his wrists.

"No cuffs," Kramer said. "You haven't far to go."

Zondi took an elbow to guide him.

"Constable! Take these two canaries and put them in separate cells."

"Yes, Lieutenant!"

"And no mats—you understand?"

"Suh!"

Kramer watched the constable carry out his orders; it was never safe for a policeman to be left on his own in the block. It was all done with surprising efficiency. Kramer was about to leave when a thought struck him.

"And, constable, take the buckets out of those cells—we don't want the bastards being too comfortable."

Shoe Shoe had had to sit in it, right up to the end.

IT WAS ONE hell of a night.

Gershwin Mkize's final words were: "The steam pig . . ." Then he slumped, fell face first to the floor, and lay very still with his arse in the air.

Kramer and Zondi remained seated, staring at it dully. They thought they had broken the bastard. They thought they had taken him to the edge and dropped him over. Perhaps they had. But the posture seemed to proclaim an insolence that ended things the way they had begun.

Kramer raised a foot. Gershwin was just out of reach. His foot flopped. Zondi did not even make the attempt. They were both exhausted. Pooped.

Sure, it was all over—only Kramer's body needed time to adjust to the idea. It was still running rough on a too-rich mixture of hot blood and gland juice. His face was flushed, his left temple pulsed quick as a toad's throat, and his stomach hurt. His bladder, too, was under stress. One false move and he would be walking with his knees pressed together.

Outside it was morning.

One of those edge-to-edge mornings that make milkmen feel superior as they skim off its cream while the white boss sleeps.

By now, however, pint bottles stood half-empty among the cereal packets and Trekkersburg was hurrying along to keep

111

the economy going boom boom boom. In the street, cars, lorries, buses, and motorcycles had regressed to an assembly-line crawl; nose to tail, never quite going, never quite stopping, but getting someplace. Then right beneath the window, which was still covered by the slat blind, a giggle of secretaries paused to wait for a friend.

Kramer felt he must take a look; he suddenly craved their shower-fresh skins and crisp cotton blouses and sticky pink lipsticks. It was a mistake.

The sun speared him in the eyeballs. They bled red, robbing him of all but a glimpse of the girls as they tiptapped off with the latecomer. And worse: when he turned around he discovered that the light was the kind that turns a party's gay litter into a squalid mess come dawn. This had been no party, but what the day did to his office was intolerable.

Every sordid item now declared itself in stark relief against its own sharp shadow; the coffee cups, the hose pipe, the crumpled packets, the wet towels, the plastic duck. The floor was a mess from smoking—and so was the air. Only the stench did not show up, although it was a close thing.

Then a passing schoolboy whistled across to a classmate and Kramer wondered at himself. It had been like this before and would be again. In a few minutes a fatigue party would be brought up from the cells. The scuff marks and cigarette smudges would disappear as completely from the parquet flooring as Gershwin's thin bile. The towels would go down to the canteen and the duck and the rest of the stuff back into the cupboard. By nine the room—with its four cream walls, brown woodwork, two chairs and a desk—would be unremarkable as ever.

Which was the way he wanted to feel.

"Zondi, I've got to go, man."

"Boss."

"Send down for Khumalo to help you get this crap bag charged with Shoe Shoe's murder on Saturday last. You said you've already charged the other two?"

"Straight away after I saw them at four."

"Fine. Tell the prosecutor—think it'll be Mr. Oosthuizen this morning—that I want a week's remand. He'll fix it up. After that, you go home. I'll ring the township manager if I need you before then; otherwise six on the dot outside here."

Zondi nodded and reached for the telephone.

All the way down the passage Kramer kept his mind off his bladder. He did not want to give it any excuse for overexcitement. He made the white tiled wall just in time and was marveling at one of life's elementary pleasures when Sergeant Willie van Niekerk emerged from the cubicle behind him. He was the first Murder Squad man Kramer had seen in two days.

"Morning, Lieutenant," Van Niekerk murmured with his customary civility, turning on the tap at the basin. There was no soap but he had brought his own in an envelope.

"How's things?" Kramer asked, eyeing the Lifebuoy.

"*Ach*, so so. Can't grumble—got my reports finished last night. All up to date."

"Oh, yes? Looking for work, are you?"

"Like the soap, sir?"

"Ta. I've got a nice little lot lined up for someone who knows what he's doing."

"Really? The case Colonel Dupe keeps starting to talk about?"

"What does he say?"

"Nothing. That's why I'm interested."

"*Ja*, that's the one."

Van Niekerk appeared to be examining his pen sketch of a mustache in the mirror but he was keeping the edge of an eye on Kramer.

"But haven't you got someone working on that one already, sir?"

Kramer smelled tact.

"I've got a coon. He's no bloody good for what I want done."

"Which is?"

"Statements, phone inquiries, paper work."

"I could take a look at it, sir."

Kramer handed back the soap, unused.

"Then let's go up to the main office for a minute, Willie."

The minute lasted one hour and some seconds. By the end of it, Van Niekerk knew all he needed.

And Kramer was on his way home. Home sweet home being a room in the house of a retired headmaster. Perhaps, strictly speaking, it was more than simply a room, for it opened out onto its own enclosed veranda covered in granadilla vines. There was space enough for quite a bit of furniture and not a few callers. Kramer preferred to live without either. He settled for a divan, a small wardrobe, and a cardboard carton in which he kept his laundry lists and private papers. He had long since secretly conceded that he shared, in part, the philosophy of the Kalahari Bushmen. These hunters believed that shelter and clothing should be no more elaborate than circumstances demanded—a man's duty was to invest his labors in his belly so to labor again. And that was how Kramer spent his money. Whenever possible, he would glut himself on steaks rich and various and as rare as a welder's thumb.

His living arrangements did, however, have one disadvantage which a savage might laugh off but which distressed him in the mornings: he had to share a bathroom with the landlord, Mr. Dickerson, and his lady.

Kramer braked hard. The traffic lights outside the Rugby ground had beaten him to it. He sat back in the bucket seat of his own little Ford.

And in a moment of total recall he felt the pinch of the narrow, cold bath on his shoulders. Then the icy droplets falling from the washing festooned above it on a rack. The old dear's underwear would dry in ten minutes out in the sun. Oh, no, she feared the sight of it might incite the garden boy. It was no good speaking to her about it either. She would only ask again why the law required bikini girls on cinema posters to have decent dresses painted over them. There was no answer to that.

The lights changed.

As if to demonstrate that such feats of memory were not necessarily an act of will, his brain made manifest what really had caused him to balk at the thought of a bath before ten o'clock: the smell.

Mr. and Mrs. Dickerson were of age and disposition well known for its morbid preoccupation with bowel movements. The windowsill, the shelf above the washbasin, and the medicine cabinet itself bore weighty testimony to this. There were patent pills, powders, and potions by the score, promising everything from gentle relief to an event not far short of common assault. Each label presumed the sufferer need search no further, but Mr. and Mrs. Dickerson preferred to approach their problem with at least an open mind—and as some might the blending of an elixir. Every evening they met to discuss a fresh formula in laboratory whispers, gulp down the ingredients, and retire with expressions of hopeful anticipation.

Unhappily, the test bench was also in the bathroom. Not any amount of lace trimming around the seat lid could disguise the fact twelve hours later. Not with the window nailed shut for fear of tempting the garden boy.

And after all Kramer had been through, it was just too much. His mind relented and it was like finding a full bottle among the empties: he realized it was Thursday—and the Widow Fourie always had Thursdays off.

Kramer gave the Ford its head and took the first turning left. Hibiscus Court's basement car park swallowed him up just four blocks later.

The Widow Fourie answered his second knock, a little sleepy but in her housecoat.

"Where are the kids?"

"Out with Elizabeth. They've gone down to the swings."

"Who?"

"Oh, just my new Kaffir maid. Sonja got her for me—she's very clean."

Kramer smiled wryly.

115

"Come on in, Trompie, people can see me."

He stepped inside and leaned back on the door to close it. The click cocked his nervous system.

The Widow Fourie walked toward the bedroom. Then, noticing that Kramer was not following her, she turned and allowed her housecoat to swirl open. She had nothing on underneath.

Kramer approached her. She closed her eyes and he kissed her. Then he covered her nakedness.

"Got any Lifebuoy?" he asked.

The Widow Fourie blinked.

"Could ask you the same thing." She smirked, but regretted it instantly. "Hey, no you don't! You stay right here. There's your chair. I'll get the water running."

But Kramer was afraid to sit. He stayed standing until she returned to undress him, very gently. It was a mother's touch.

"That's not Lifebuoy," Kramer protested as he was led into the sun-bright bathroom. "I'll come out of here smelling like a bloody poof."

The Widow Fourie responded by sprinkling another handful of crystals into the already murky water. She knew how he liked them.

The first thing he did once he was in the water was to grab a plastic toy and hurl it into the corridor.

"Man, you're in a funny mood," sighed the Widow Fourie. "Annie loves her duck. Don't you remember bringing it to her?"

"So?"

"Now look here, Trompie—"

"More hot, please."

He forgot the duck and concentrated on the cabin cruiser. It was a good wide bath and by moving his arms skillfully it was possible to create a current that sucked the boat all the way from the plug. On his third attempt it went aground on the weed-locked shores of his chest.

"You're just a big kid," the Widow Fourie muttered, tying her belt tight like apron strings. "I suppose you want chips with your eggs?"

He was asleep.

And he stayed asleep until she tried to change the water, which had become surprisingly chill for such a hot day.

"No, leave it," he said. It was like a Cape stream in spring.

So the Widow Fourie perched on the wash basket and lit two Luckies. Kramer dried a hand and took one. He began to talk.

Eventually the Widow Fourie asked: "What was this Gershwin like when he confessed? Was he all relieved like they are in plays on the radio?"

"Oh, *ja*. All off his chest. One big smile."

"I can never understand that. It seems so stupid. I mean, now you're going to hang him."

"So? What is everyone afraid of? What they don't know. Now he knows. Simple."

"Still, it must be hard getting it out of a Kaffir like him."

"True."

"Zondi has their mind, of course."

The cabin cruiser sank beneath his fist.

"True, too."

Bubbles came up in a thin stream.

"Why so quiet all of a sudden?"

"Nothing."

"Can't you see a connection between these two cases—is that what's troubling you?"

"Naturally, we wasted a whole night on it. I tell you it's quite straightforward. Gershwin killed Shoe Shoe for some damn fool reason, you know what these wogs are, and now he's trying to make a good story for the court. They always do, even if they know they're going to hang."

"You mean this thing about getting a message from an unknown gang to kill his bloke or else?"

"Yes, it's either that line or the one about spirits whispering evil things in their ears. What made it sound wrong at the start

117

was he didn't know the gang's name. We just didn't give him a chance to make one up, that's all."

"Oh, I don't know, Trompie, he could have heard something somewhere."

"A whisper, you mean? Okay, so there's a gang that makes small fry like Gershwin jump to attention and mess themselves. Let's say the same lot's behind Miss Whatsit's murder. Is it likely that an outfit that uses a hired pro would delegate a job to a fumbler like Gershwin?"

"Thought you said you were impressed by his m.o.? It was a fluke you found Shoe Shoe's body so fast. It could have been there years and then do you think anyone would have bothered to even ask Gershwin about it? Not a chance. You didn't do anything when he was stabbed. And that's another point; if Shoe Shoe was found dead in an ordinary way, surely the chances would be that someone would look for a spoke hole?"

"That's my girlie, but it wasn't a fluke that we got on to Shoe Shoe—it was a logical progression from the Le Roux murder. Zondi just followed it up."

"Ah, but they didn't expect that to be discovered in the first place, did they? There's your fluke."

Kramer began to soap his hair.

"Have it your way," he said. "But this is all theory. The only link it suggests is that a gang with a name we don't know is going about knocking off white girls and black beggars. Take it from there, if you can."

The Widow Fourie went out and returned with a fresh packet of Luckies. Kramer had slid down to rinse his hair and so only his nose, mouth, and kneecaps were above water level. It startled her mildly when the lips parted to speak.

"I know for a fact that Gershwin Mkize murdered Shoe Shoe," the lips intoned slowly, "and I know for a fact that even if what Gershwin said was true, there is nothing more he can tell us."

It was strangely impressive, rather like a scene from some

118

ancient legend about a sub-aqua oracle. The Widow Fourie stood fascinated.

But Kramer said nothing more. He surfaced with a great splash and grabbed for a towel. The Widow Fourie handed him one absently.

"What about Shoe Shoe, though?" she asked. "Surely *he* would know—you'd have thought he'd have said something when they were doing that to him."

"According to Gershwin he had a hell of a lot to say—but it was all nonsense. He must have cracked with the shock. Can't say I'm surprised; it was the second time for him."

"What sort of nonsense?"

"Just gibberish and it didn't help matters that Gershwin tried to put it all into bloody English as usual. We pushed him hard on this but got nowhere. In fact Gershwin was beginning to go a bit himself by then and you couldn't really tell one lot from another. Stuff about people who tipped him—Shoe Shoe, I mean—and those that didn't and councillors and the mayor's car and all the important things he knew about important people watching from in front of the city hall all day. *Ach*, I can't be bothered. We didn't even try to write it down in the end, just let him run on until he keeled over."

"Do you remember any of it?"

"No. I tell you most of it was real rubbish."

"Oh, just try to remember one thing. I think you're so lucky to have an interesting job like yours is."

Kramer could see he had made her day. Come to think of it, it was high time he made her. So, simply to sustain the mood, he said: "The last thing he said was 'the steam pig.'"

"The Steam Pig," she repeated slowly.

Kramer looked up from her legs.

"Come again?"

She was puzzled.

"The Steam Pig—the same as you said it."

"No, it wasn't!"

119

"For God's sake, Trompie, there's no need to snap like that over a little thing."

The Widow Fourie had reached the door before Kramer could speak again.

"You see," he said quietly, "you say it like it's the *name* of something."

She turned and understood. And shivered.

Van Niekerk had made a most satisfactory start. For years he had gone about with a platoon of ballpoint pens ranged at the ready in his breast pocket. One wrote in mauve ink, the others in red, black, green, and the conventional blue. The thing was that he seldom felt justified in using them all in a single engagement, but this time he had.

And nobody could dispute how much such diversity had helped to clarify the complicated case sheet he had drawn up from his notes. Colonel Du Plessis, who had wandered in to ask casually after the Lieutenant, had done him the honor of staring at the finished job for fully five minutes.

He was alone again now, having moved into the Lieutenant's delightfully spick-and-span office with all the paraphernalia he could possibly imagine his duties would require. He had pinned a large street map of Trekkersburg on the wall and marked various pertinent addresses with colored drawing pins. He had spread the crime sheet on a card table borrowed from the sergeants' mess. And he had placed the sparse collection of reports in a yellow basket labeled *Priority*.

Which somehow forced him to read them all again even though they contained very little information. The one from Fingerprints on the cottage was a complete waste of time.

So he picked up two lists prepared from the Yellow Pages and debated whether to begin on the dispensing opticians or the electronic organ retailers.

A spin of a coin decided him on the latter. Soon he was copying down immense lists of improbable names read over to him, somewhat irritably in most cases, from invoice books. As the traders pointed out, this check failed to take into account the cash sales; but his reply to this was to the effect that the class of person he was interested in would hardly be likely to indulge in such vulgarity. This was also the reason he gave himself for omitting the two large cash-and-carry bazaars in the main street. The old women in Barnato Street had been most emphatic that the men they had seen going for lessons had been well-dressed, prosperous-looking types.

As it was, Van Niekerk lost a lot of his early enthusiasm when he totted up the results and found he would have to check out 173 names. They could wait. The opticians might provide an immediate lead.

But an hour later, and with two names still to contact, he was looking exceedingly sourly at Kramer's name scrawled on the telephone directory cover. The opticians had been astounded by his inquiry—some had had to have the whole thing explained twice to them. Cosmetic contacts were definitely still a thing of the future in Trekkersburg, if not the entire Republic, and most of them doubted very much if they would ever catch on. He shuddered at the thought of going on to make a list of possibilities in Durban.

Thankfully the coffee arrived just then and, combined with a dozen brisk push-ups, restored something of his former vigor.

In fact he was actually reaching for the telephone again when Mr. Abbott came through.

The undertaker had asked specifically to be connected to Lieutenant Kramer's office, so he wasted no time on formalities. He spoke briefly in a hurried whisper and rang off.

Van Niekerk shook his head sharply to clear it. Then he looked down at his shorthand note of the message:

"Got someone in the parlor asking questions about the deceased girl. Come quick. Not sure I'll be able to keep them without a fuss."

The mild-mannered coordinator took his cue. He was up and away and streaking for the street before it occurred to him to call the Lieutenant. But then this was a matter of extreme urgency and everyone knew how difficult it was at times to contact him. He could be anywhere.

Kramer was four blocks away in the cells of the Trekkersburg Magistrate's Court, talking to Pop van Hoff, the sergeant in charge.

"Anything for you, Trompie old son," Pop was saying, keeping an eye on the Bantu prisoners tiptoeing up to the tap outside his office door to fill tins with drinking water.

"Hey, Johannes, you old skelm," Pop bawled. "Don't tell me you've been at the *ntombis* again?"

A lanky prisoner looked up from the tap and smiled bashfully.

"Greetings, my father," he said respectfully in Zulu.

Pop waved an affable paw.

"Just one of my old friends," he explained to Kramer. "I tease him about the girls, say he's a rapist—he thinks it's helluva funny."

Kramer glanced at the man.

"What is he then?" he asked.

"Buggered if I know, but he does it often enough. Now who was it you wanted in the end cell by himself?"

"Gershwin Mkize—he's just been remanded."

"Of course—Mr. Banana. I've got names for them all, you know. You see he—"

"Wears yellow. Will you get it moving, Pop?"

The sergeant took it good-humoredly and waddled out into the hall bawling orders. His staff shepherded all the stray prisoners into their cells and took a yellow figure into one in the far corner.

Zondi came in through the grille from the court corridor and joined Kramer.

"Nice timing," Kramer remarked. "He'll have a week now to become a pretty boy again before he comes up in front of a court. But why wasn't the remand earlier?"

"Big roundup last night for pass offenders. I gave your note to Mr. Oosthuizen and he put Gershwin through in between cases."

"Uhuh. Sam Safrinsky turn up to represent him?"

"Not a chance, boss."

Pop returned to greet Zondi warmly.

"Hello, Cheeky," he said. "Is this the way you want it?"

"Too quiet," Zondi observed.

"He's right," Kramer agreed.

"Damn right," Pop echoed. "You never know who you've got in here these days. Come on, you lot, I want to hear you talking."

His staff took up the cry, translated it, and immediately there was a babble of voices. After half a minute or so, it settled down.

"Fine," Kramer said, and he and Zondi walked shoulder to shoulder down to the end cell.

Pop retired to where he could overhear nothing incriminating and joked with Ephraim, another old favorite. They enjoyed some good laughs.

Kramer had the broad piece of tape ready in his hand before they entered the cell—the gauze which had kept it sterile was back in Pop's wastepaper basket. And he applied it to Gershwin's mouth before he could utter a single whimper.

They closed the door.

"Listen to me, Gershwin," Kramer said. "I have come here this morning to ask you one question. When I take that plaster off I want just to hear your answer—nothing else."

Gershwin nodded vigorously, clasping his handcuffed hands before him.

"No, we haven't time to have a rehearsal," Kramer went on. "Or to talk all day, too. Sergeant Zondi and I are going to give you half of something; if you lie, we'll let you have the other half later."

Gershwin cringed, trying to protect his head.

"First, the question," Kramer went on. "Last night you used the words 'the steam pig.' What we want to know is: was this some nonsense of yours—or was it something that Shoe Shoe said?"

Gershwin was mouthing frantically as Zondi took up his position behind him.

They concentrated on the soft parts of the body, the areas where there was no backing of bone to fracture or aggravate capillary damage through excessive resilience. One soft part was particularly favored for its extreme sensitivity and relative isolation from vital organs.

They did it all with the fingers, never with the fist.

She kept her eyes on him all the time, which made Van Niekerk feel even more of a fool when he had to replace his revolver in its holster before leaving.

And she had such frightened eyes, that poor little old lady perched on the edge of the sofa in Mr. Abbott's showroom. Small wonder when you considered the way he had come in off the street.

Mr. Abbott was hovering about waiting for him at the front counter.

"Any good?" he asked.

"I want words with you," Van Niekerk growled. "What the hell do you mean making phone calls like that and having me think you had a bloody tiger around here?"

"Steady on. I said nothing about tigers."

"You said you 'couldn't keep them' without a fuss—what was I to think?"

"But you always fuss old ladies if you spring things on them. I didn't want her upset. This *is* a business, after all! I thought you'd know how to handle it better than I."

There was quite a considerable pause.

"Thanks anyway," Van Niekerk conceded. "It could have been something big. You never know."

And with that he left Mr. Abbott to console the old dear and send her on her way.

Van Niekerk was still smarting when he reached the office

and found the Lieutenant and Zondi there making a mess of his crime sheet by writing in some nonsense all over the place.

"What's all this?" he said, as brusquely as he dared.

"That's what they're saying down in Housebreaking," Kramer chuckled. "Fanie Prinsloo swears you were touching thirty by the time you passed their window."

"I mean this 'steam pig' business," Van Niekerk muttered.

"Oh, that? Well, it just could be a lead."

"Really?"

Kramer nodded. Now it was plain why he was in such unusual spirits.

"We've just paid a little call on our friend Gershwin Mkize," Kramer explained. "We wanted to check on something he said last night, these three words."

"And?"

"It seems that Shoe Shoe used them not once but often after realizing why he was out there playing scarecrow. In fact he kept saying to Mkize it was because of the Steam Pig that he was being done in."

"He shout it many times," Zondi quoted from his notebook. "He says all this trouble is trouble from the Steam Pig. It is a bad thing. It make even the white baas much frightened. He hear white baas telling friend that the Steam Pig will mean the end of his days."

"Christ."

"Yes, the link, Willie. These cases are definitely connected."

"Did this Mkize say under whose orders?"

"He still says he didn't know then. But thinking about it now he wonders if the Steam Pig wasn't behind it."

"So it's a gang, Lieutenant?"

"Seems like it. Or somebody running a mob. What else could it be?"

"Dunno. But I've never heard of it."

"You shouldn't have if it's any good."

"True."

"All the same, I want checks made. Zondi here will go round

his informers. But I want you to be careful, hey? We don't want to give any warnings."

"Okay, boss."

"You, Willie, you're to check the name out in Records—see even if you can find some bunch with the same initials."

"Just two things, sir: why didn't Gershwin come out with this before—"

"Because he thought it was rubbish."

"And did he say what white men were heard talking?"

"No; Gershwin just imagined that Shoe Shoe overheard things said from where he sat at the side of the city hall steps. He must have, come to think of it—it's the sort of place that people speak their minds, especially coming away from meetings when they've had to bottle it all up."

"You're saying that Shoe Shoe got this off city councillors and that, are you, sir?"

"No, I'm not, just giving an example—be sensible, man. I'm talking about what *Gershwin* thought. Shoe Shoe could have picked it up round the back in his wheelbarrow—the car park's right by his sleeping place."

"Europeans often say private things in front of Bantu," Zondi chipped in. "They do not expect men like Shoe Shoe can speak their language either."

Kramer suddenly realized that he had spoken critically to Van Niekerk in front of Zondi. He hastened to make amends.

"Tell me, old mate," he said, "where were you off in such a hurry to? Get a hot tip on the geegees?"

He knew Van Niekerk's weakness, but it misfired. The man squirmed and frowned for a reply.

"I've just had an idea, sir," he said with recruitlike eagerness. "This 'expression,' for want of a better word, is in English. Now I know there is an English saying 'pig iron'—do you think that 'steam pig' is another of these sayings?"

"It's worth a check," Kramer agreed. "Now come on, man, what has been happening round here?"

"Well, to cut a long story short, I did get a tip-off, sir, but from

Georgie Abbott. He rang to say somebody was on his premises asking after Miss le Roux."

"For God's sake, man! Why didn't you say so in the first place? I'll see them right away."

Van Niekerk swallowed hard.

"I let her go, sir."

Only Zondi's presence saved Van Niekerk from castration. Anything less drastic held no interest for Kramer, so he simply asked: "Why?"

"Because—because there wasn't much to it, sir. She said that she was a dressmaker, that she had made two or three frocks for Miss le Roux about two years ago. She remembered her because she was such a nice, polite young lady."

"Why wasn't she at the funeral?"

"She didn't know her that well, sir. She says she thought she'd be sort of intruding."

"Into what? Did she know if the girl had a family?"

"I asked her that, sir. She said there had never been any mention of one but she had the impression her customer came from somewhere in the Cape."

"If she knew all this, why didn't she come to us then?"

"That was it, sir. She said she didn't know about the report in the *Gazette*. She was quite surprised when I told her."

"Then what in God's name was she doing in Abbott's place?"

"Well, she said she was just passing and had seen the funeral notice and couldn't help wondering why a young girl like that had passed away so sudden. Those are her words, sir—they're here in my notebook."

"Go on, Willie."

The familiarity heartened Van Niekerk.

"So she just nipped in and tried to chat up Georgie. You know what old women are."

"She was an old woman then?"

"Oh, yes, a nice old girl—about sixty-five, you know."

"Uhuh. Tell me, did she seem at all—er—frightened of speaking to you? Why do you hesitate?"

127

"Because it's difficult to say. People are funny when they talk to police. I'd say no more nervous than usual."

"Good. Then it seems you did a very good job. But I'd still like a word with her; might be something else I could get."

"Of course, sir. She gave me her name and address. A Mrs. Johnson. Gladys Johnson."

"Fine—and where does she live?"

"One six nine Biddulph Street."

Van Niekerk crossed confidently to the map and ran his finger along Biddulph Street to where 169 was marked. Zondi took one glance and discreetly left the room.

For, according to the map, Mrs. Gladys Johnson was the old woman who lived in a shoe factory.

As it happened, there was no need for Kramer to say anything. Van Niekerk said it all, out loud to himself, over and over again.

"So she lied to you," Kramer interrupted.

"The bitch."

"Cut it out now, Sergeant. I want to get after her while there's a chance. She didn't lie to you anyway, she lied to us— the force. Why?"

This stopped Van Niekerk from taking ridiculous punches at the wall.

"Well, because she was trying to hide something. Cover up a connection with the girl."

"Right. What gets me is this address she cooked up. How did she come out with it? Did she stutter or anything?"

Van Niekerk closed his eyes.

"No, it was pat enough. First the number. I wrote it down. Then the street."

"Biddulph Street. She knew the name but not much else about it."

"Most probably the first one that came to mind, sir."

"Or the only one she knew in Trekkersburg. Funny choice, I must say."

"You mean she could be a stranger here?"

"Yes, I do and that's what makes me feel we'll have to move fast on this one even if she isn't too good on her legs."

"We could put out a radio call to all the vans."

Kramer was in half a mind to do just that but the other half rebelled.

"How long is it since you left her at Abbott's?"

"About ten, maybe fifteen minutes."

"Not so long I can't chance a call to him first then," Kramer replied and began dialing the funeral parlor. "He might have picked up something."

Mr. Abbott racked his brains. No, he didn't ask her about where she lived. Never thought to. Kramer urged him to remember everything which had happened after Van Niekerk left. Negative. Wait a minute, though; now he came to think of it he had seen her from his doorstep stop to ask the newsboy at the corner something.

"Get going and ask him what she wanted," Kramer ordered.

Van Niekerk suddenly clicked his fingers, took out one of the reports, and typed out a short list from it on pink paper.

"Yes?" Kramer said as the other receiver was picked up again. "She asked the way to Biddulph Street? Boy, this is a lulu. Ta."

He went over to the map.

"I've got it!" he exploded suddenly. "The Biddulph Street out-of-town bus terminal! Why the Jesus didn't we think of it before? It fits."

"I'll say. Shall I come with you, sir?"

"Best you stay here to liaise with Zondi if he comes through."

"Then maybe you'd like to take this with you, sir?"

Kramer took the pink slip and looked blankly at the figures on it.

"Vital statistics," Van Niekerk explained. "What every dressmaker should know."

There were other times when he excelled himself.

Zondi had bought an ice cream for the urchin who had finally admitted, amid the jeers of his companions, to having looked after Shoe Shoe over the weeks before his disappearance. And Zondi had bought himself one, too.

They sat together behind the war memorial and talked between licks. It had been a shameful confession, for even the most wretched Zulu hates to have it known he has had to accept women's work, but a Vanilla Glory brought total absolution.

"So old Shoe Shoe said he was going to get you some shoes, did he?" Zondi asked idly.

"No, uncle; proper boots he said."

"And this was good?"

"I could find work then."

Zondi winked. The child laughed. Of course he did not mean it. They were playing The Game.

"When was he going to get these boots then?"

"Oh, when he was rich like a white man."

"And all white men are rich?"

"Yes."

The small pink tongue took off just a wetness of cream each time.

"And how would he become rich? He could not work."

"Ah, perhaps not, but that Shoe Shoe was a clever one. He could get rich by just saying words—he told me so."

Zondi frowned in pantomime disbelief.

"True's God! I never lie to policemen."

They both laughed.

"Did he say who he would speak these words to?"

Small bony shoulders shrugged.

"He never said, but I know."

"Oh, yes?"

"This very small sucker is nearly finished."

"Look in your pocket."

"Hau!"

"Yes, so you see you are not the only one who is clever with pockets, little *tsotsi*."

"All right, I'll tell you. The white men, of course—who else can make you as rich as they are?"

He had a point there.

Zondi caught sight of Kramer's car flashing by and jumped up. Too late—it was a foolish notion anyway.

What the young scruff had had to say was interesting but did not really lead them any further. Nor had what he discovered from his chief informers. While they all readily agreed there was definitely always room for a new gang on top, not one of them had ever heard of the Steam Pig.

The bus terminal in Biddulph Street was practically deserted.

After a quick look around, Kramer went to the supervisor's office to learn that most buses left on the hour. It was just after one.

"And I can't honestly say if there was or wasn't an old lady in a black cotton dress and a flowery hat on any of them," the supervisor said. "You could ask the ticket staff."

The ticket staff referred him to the ticket collectors and then he interviewed the Bantu porters who loaded the luggage. No one would commit themselves—the fact that Mrs. Johnson was also carrying a large yellow tartan bag should have been a clincher but it was not.

Kramer began bitterly to regret he had not brought Van Niekerk with him. Suddenly the description seemed so inadequate.

He dithered on the forecourt, fighting the logic which would drive him ultimately to calling in help. God, he abhorred the thought. The Colonel would love it.

Then an idea struck him. He went back to the supervisor's office and asked if he could borrow one of the girl clerks for five minutes.

She giggled nauseatingly when he asked her to search the women's lavatories but she went. And came giggling her failure to discover any little old ladies—although she had spied what she was certain were an old gentleman's boots under the door of one cubicle. Kramer dismissed her without thanks.

This was it. He would have to go back to the car and put out a general call. He also had a list of the buses which had left at one and headquarters could arrange for checks to be made along their routes and at their destination.

Kramer cut diagonally across the nonwhite area of the terminal, which was crowded as always, and got into his car at the curb. He switched on the radio. There was someone on the air calling for an ambulance, which gave the message priority.

Oh, well, another minute or two could not hurt, it was such a balls-up already. Pity about that lavatory idea getting nowhere. He had liked that one. Just look at the mob around the black bogs.

"Jesus!"

A little old lady was making her way from the entrance marked NON-WHITE FEMALES. She walked unsteadily, tacking into the breeze which bellied out her black dress and made the sad roses bob on her hat. She came to rest not fifteen yards away with a bump of her yellow tartan bag against the back of a bench.

Kramer was at her side in seconds. He took her thin arm in two hands like a rudder and was steering her to the Chev before she recovered from her surprise.

"What's happening? Where are you taking me?"

"Not far, madam. Just to this car."

"But who are you?"

"A policeman."

"But what have I done?"

"Contravened a municipal bylaw for one," Kramer answered. "Get inside, please."

He depressed the hidden lock and then closed the door firmly. He went around and slid into the driving seat.

"What bylaw are you talking about?"

"Mrs. Johnson, is it?"

"Y-yes."

"That was pretty clever of you, Mrs. Johnson, hiding from me over there. How did you know what I was?"

"Hiding? Where?"

"In the nonwhite lavatory."

"Is that what you think I was doing?"

And she began to laugh, not for long but it was horrible. It surprised him.

Mrs. Johnson dug deep into her bag, extracted a crumpled tissue, and dabbed her nose with it.

"Do you really think I'd go into one of those awful places if I didn't have to?"

Surprise was one thing, shock was another. It was such a rare experience for Kramer that he gaped like a cartoon character. The effect was very comical but Mrs. Johnson did not smile.

"I suppose I could get away with it," Mrs. Johnson added softly, "but it just isn't worth the risk."

"No," Kramer said, automatically.

His mind was battling to regain its equilibrium. So the old woman was a colored, a person of mixed race. This took a lot of adjusting to—she certainly did not look like one. Or sound like one. Still stranger things happened.

"Look at me," Kramer ordered.

Mrs. Johnson turned her head toward him slowly. He noticed she was trembling. How much older she suddenly seemed.

Kramer started at the top. The hat was limp black straw, decked in velvet roses which had long since abandoned any pretensions to natural representation. The hair beneath was very white, very fine, and curiously free of any kinking. The face was broad but not remarkably so. What was striking was the mute pain which showed in the deep brown eyes—the white of which had none of the usual yellow cast—and in the lines cut deep about the kindly mouth. By contrast, the neck was swan smooth. The hands, clasped tight in the black lap, were strong yet delicate, with a faint cornflake mottling on the back. The feet were small, too.

It was plain that her colored blood confined itself to the arterial system. And that Mrs. Johnson must have been a rare find for Mr. Johnson.

"You're frightened," Kramer said.

Mrs. Johnson nodded, maintaining her elusive dignity with difficulty.

"Why?"

"I don't want any trouble."

"Well, if you go around telling lies, then you've got to expect it, ma."

She nodded again, vaguely.

"Haven't you got another tissue?"

Mrs. Johnson rummaged obediently in her bag, tipping it up so as to reach to the bottom. A newspaper clipping fluttered out onto the seat between them.

Kramer tweaked it up and held it so that she could read the headline: MYSTERY DEATH OF A MYSTERY GIRL.

"See what I mean?" he said. "You told one of my men that you had no idea Miss le Roux was the subject of an inquiry."

"He wouldn't tell me what sort of inquiry."

"Never you mind. You also said that you lived here in Biddulph Street."

"I'm sorry, sir."

"Sorry? Who sent you?"

Mrs. Johnson frowned.

"Nobody sent me. I just came."

"From?"

"Durban."

"Why?"

"I told the other policeman."

"That you were a dressmaker and all that rubbish?"

"I am one."

"And you knew Miss le Roux personally?"

"She was once a customer."

"So she used to live in Durban?"

"Yes."

Kramer stared hard and long at Mrs. Johnson. She moved uncomfortably, but kept her chin firm.

"All right then, ma—why did you come?"

"Something just made me. She was a lovely girl, Miss le Roux. It seemed so terrible, something happening to her like that. I read about the foul play thing and it all preyed on my mind so I couldn't think straight. She had such a lovely skin."

"What the hell's that got to do with it?" Kramer snapped, losing patience.

"I—I don't know, sir. It's just what kept going through my mind."

"Why did you lie to the sergeant?"

"Because I was afraid of telling the truth to him, sir, being . . . A colored person hasn't the right to go poking their noses into things."

Mrs. Johnson seemed altogether too conscious of her race. This, and the other unsatisfactory aspects of her story, had Kramer wondering if he had not been right after all—she had taken refuge in a nonwhite bog to evade him.

"Have you got any papers on you to prove what you are and where you live?" he asked.

"No, sir, I haven't. I'm sorry."

Kramer frowned. But he was not altogether displeased. Mrs. Johnson was the first strong link they had had with Miss le Roux and there was obviously a great deal they could learn from her. The main problem, however, was the time factor. From the moment this press report had been published, a race had begun. Every hour that passed was an hour to the killers' advantage. The way things were going, it would take until nightfall to extract what Mrs. Johnson really had to say. Pity she was so old and frail.

Kramer knew what sort of mood he was in. There were days when he thoroughly enjoyed a long symphonic interrogation, with its different movements, its moments of sweet counterpoint, and that final triumphant surge to the climax. And then there were days when all he wanted was the truth and nothing but the truth, the way the judges got it. Gershwin knew what he meant.

And Mrs. Johnson seemed to have sensed something of it, too. She had pulled her bag up protectively before her and was regarding the silent figure beside her with mounting anxiety.

Suddenly Kramer's face lit up with an inspired idea.

"The body has not yet been formally identified," he said. "You say you know a Miss le Roux—let's see if it is the same one."

After a long pause, the old woman nodded once.

Kramer flicked on the radio. Central Control answered almost immediately.

"Lieutenant Kramer here. I want an urgent message phoned through to Abbott's funeral parlor. Message to read: Prepare Le Roux for formal identification in ten minutes. Request slab is used. And tell them it came from me. Okay?"

Central Control acknowledged and went off the air.

A formal identification was routine, no shock tactics involved there. But using the slab instead of the tray would allow the full extent of Dr. Strydom's ministrations to be abruptly displayed under the merciless light. It would shock all right.

Farthing took the call from Central Control, as Mr. Abbott was at his Rotary luncheon. It made him very indignant.

So indignant, in fact, that he put his feet back on the desktop and resolved to do nothing about it until *his* lunch hour was over. After all, it was not as if he was idling his time away: studying was no easy matter when you worked on a round-the-clock basis. Life was often as trying now as it had been when he was a male nurse.

Besides which, his manual had just arrived from the British Institute of Embalmers and the chapter on bacteriology was utterly absorbing. He would have to warn the boss about the risks they were taking with some of their hospital jobs.

Then his conscience began to get the better of him, so he skipped quickly to the section on surgical reconstruction for a glance at the illustrations. They were beautiful.

"Well, well, well," he said to himself as he strolled down to the mortuary. "So they said you would never do it, with your education, Nurse Farthing. We'll see."

He had just opened the refrigerator when Kramer entered the room, escorting Mrs. Johnson.

Kramer did not like what he saw. He did not like having his orders disobeyed and he did not like the look of this young man. He was too young and too intimate in the way his gaze touched you.

Then things went totally out of control.

Farthing pulled out the tray. Mrs. Johnson moved with astonishing speed across to him. Farthing drew the sheet gently off the head. Mrs. Johnson sighed very softly.

It was the look on her face that kept Kramer standing where he was. He was aware that he had seen it somewhere else on someone else but he could not make the connection; a curious resignation that hinted at things so profound it hollowed your belly.

Farthing saw she was trying to ask him something.

"Yes, dearie?" he prompted.

"Was she—was she *marked* in any way?"

The question had Kramer across the room in two bounds. He grabbed her.

"Why do you ask that?" he demanded.

Mrs. Johnson shook herself free, anger putting color in her cheeks.

"I've already told you that, young man—she had lovely skin."

Kramer was suddenly aware that she, too, had lovely skin, now there was a flush to give it life.

And he noticed something else that stopped his breathing.

When seen together, the girl on the tray and the old woman standing beside it were, not in general but in detail, uncannily alike.

"You're her mother?"

The reply was proud: "I am."

Farthing waited, then replaced the sheet.

"She was not marked, Mrs. Johnson," Kramer said softly.

Gogol was not pleased to see Zondi again but Moosa was.

He said that Thursday was quite the worst day of his week. It attracted far too many raucous people and noisy lorries to Trichaard Street—why, he could not imagine. Ordinarily he could tolerate the odd hoot of a car horn or a peddler's cry, but on Thursdays it was all too distracting for him to continue his third careful reading of Chamber's Encyclopaedia, prewar edition. Although he had reached *Ichthyology* and was eagerly anticipating picking holes in *Islam* again, he sensibly opted for a pile of undemanding American comics on Thursdays.

"Why not go out?" Zondi asked.

Moosa took sudden umbrage that one of Gogol's fruit flies should dare to invade his sanctuary. He zapped it with Batman.

So Zondi just went ahead and disclosed the fate of Gershwin Mkize and his two henchmen. They were behind bars and this time for good.

"Damn," Moosa groaned, looking very sorry for himself. "Damn and blastings. Have you told Gogol yet?"

"He doesn't like Kaffirs in his store who aren't there to spend their money."

Moosa sighed.

"A hard man, Sergeant," he said. "A very hard man."

Zondi allowed him to dwell silently on the ruthless nature of the greengrocer. And then he observed philosophically: "There is work and there is work."

"What do you mean, Sergeant?"

"That there are many different things a man may do to earn his money."

"Huh, money! That's all that Gogol thinks is important. I tell him one, two hundred times, education is what makes a man. He just rubs his thumb."

"Hau!"

"Yes, that's the truth of it. He's so mean that the other night I took one little bag of peanuts off the shelf downstairs and he wrote that down in his book, too."

"So he is expecting you to pay him back then?"

This made Moosa laugh like a clown, one of the sad ones.

"But does it matter where the money comes from, Moosa?"

The Indian looked sideways at Zondi.

"I'm not mixed up in anything," he said darkly—and showed his hurt when Zondi chuckled.

"You're a man of education, right, Moosa?"

"I apply myself to my studies."

"You have a quick eye and a good ear? You can think intelligently?"

"I have always done so."

"Good. Then would you like a job where you decide your own hours—even what you're going to do?"

"This is very interesting, I must say, Sergeant. What is it?"

"Ah, let us test your powers!" Zondi replied. "You guess."

Moosa spent some time on it. Then he got it in a flash when Zondi took two rand notes from his wallet and pushed them into the row of encyclopedias.

"It's good money and no tax either," Zondi coaxed.

"Too damn dangerous. I'm a man of intellect, not a man of action, Sergeant—thanks all the same."

"Rubbish, Moosa, you can take your time. Surely you don't think a man with your mind is going to be outwitted by the types we're interested in?"

Moosa shrugged.

"It happened once," he said, flattered but wary.

"And couldn't happen again, not with all the reading you say you've done. How about it? You could even have a little revenge if we can fix it."

Moosa waddled over and examined the notes.

"But what are these for?" he asked.

"The tip-off about the Lesotho car."

140

"Did that help you then?"

"Not so far—we need more about it and quickly. So you can call our small gift an advance if you like."

While he was talking, Zondi took out a paperback and admired its cover.

"James Bond," Moosa said. "Have you read any? Beautiful writing."

"I've heard of him," Zondi replied, casually handing the volume over.

Moosa took a long look at the blonde in Bond's arms.

"Well, I must get back now," Zondi said from the doorway. "We're in a big hurry on this one. Maybe you could go out for a look this afternoon, Moosa?"

The reek of the flowers was overpowering. It began to sicken Kramer as he sat, ankle deep in bouquets and tributes, at Mrs. Johnson's side in the storeroom and waited for her to stop weeping.

So he decided to go through and have a belated interview with Farthing. He might even take a statement.

"Is she comfy in there?" Farthing asked as he approached the counter. "I was *so* surprised when you said the showroom wouldn't do. She doesn't look it, does she?"

"Name?" Kramer asked gruffly.

"Jonathan Farthing."

"Address?"

"I live here; I've a little flat round the back."

"You took the girl from the cottage in Barnato Street?"

"I did the removal, yes."

"By yourself?"

"We've got one of these clever newfangled things with wheels on and handles."

"I see. What can you remember of the occasion?"

"Just it was very straightforward. Bundled her in and shot back here."

"You don't seem to take your profession very seriously."

"Frankly, Lieutenant, I'm not very interested in that side of things. I'm more—"

"*I'm* not interested, Mr. Farthing. Tell me what you saw at the cottage."

"Well, it was all very tasteful, wasn't it? Lovely curtains in the bedroom; I've been trying to find some of that material ever since."

Kramer sighed and hoped his breath was bad.

"So sorry, I'm sure. The girl? It struck me she was very peaceful; the bedclothes were not disturbed or anything, apart from what the doctors had moved. Oh, yes, I'd almost forgotten—I switched off her bedside lamp."

"Still burning?"

"Yes, but it was the only one. After that I noticed whether the others were out."

"You didn't leave any fingerprints—how was that?"

"The little difference between the old and the new schools, you might say. I always wear gloves."

"Uhuh."

Kramer closed his notebook.

"That seems to be all, Mr. Farthing. But tell me one thing: why didn't you fix up Miss le Roux yourself and not leave it to Mr. Abbott?"

"Oh, there's no hurry once they're in the fridge. Besides which—"

"What?"

"I personally prefer—not to do females."

"And Mr. Abbott?"

But just then three off-duty postmen of roughly the same height arrived to change into their pallbearer suits and earn an afternoon's beer money. They apologized on behalf of the other corner, who could not come as he had the hiccups.

Kramer left Farthing panicking quietly at the thought of finding a replacement, and went back down the passage to see how Mrs. Johnson was getting on. He found her sitting up very straight, her eyes dry and her hat off.

142

"Somebody killed my little girl," she said as he entered.

"Yes, they did. Now, are you going to help us find out who?"

"If I can."

"Thank you, Mrs. Johnson."

"The name is really Francis, sir. Johnson was my maiden name."

"But Gladys stays the same?"

"Yes, sir."

"Okay, Gladys, that's the style. Was your daughter trying for white?"

Mrs. Francis smiled wanly.

"She was trying for white, as they say."

"She made a good job of it," Kramer remarked. "There wasn't a trace of her past anywhere in her flat. A spy couldn't have done better. The only thing I found was one tiny photograph."

"Oh? Where was that?"

"In a heart-shaped locket."

She bit her lip.

"That was Mr. Francis, her dad."

"Look, Gladys, maybe it would be better if we went back right to the very beginning."

"Must we?"

"It could help me a lot in understanding."

This obviously appealed to her.

Kramer sat down on the other chair that Farthing had provided from the chapel and prepared to write.

"You were born in the Cape?"

Her scornful laugh brought his head up sharply in surprise.

"Why do you people always think coloreds are all born in the Cape?"

Again, that curious overreaction on her part.

"Where then?"

"Durban."

"And—?"

Kramer's ballpoint hovered, ready to set the date down. But the pad slid unheeded from his knee a moment later.

"And I was born white," Mrs. Francis said. "We were all born white. The whole family. And we lived white, too."

OVER THE YEARS Kramer had taken down a great variety of formal statements. They had ranged from long, rambling allegations about neighbors' dogs to short, pitiful admissions by parents who had failed to keep a proper eye on baby in his bath. More than once he had snatched his tiny cramped words from a dying breath.

This should have prepared him to function professionally under any circumstances but he abandoned the idea after the first ten pages. He just let Mrs. Francis talk and jotted down what he could. His brain was bruised from doing somersaults; it needed a rest.

Not that he got it.

"We moved into a flat behind the Esplanade about a year after we got married," Mrs. Francis explained. "Palm Court it was called—one of those skyscraper things with sea sand all over the verandas at the back. Always lots of children around, noisy but nice.

"Tessa was our first. She was a good baby even if she cried a lot at nights. Pat said, 'No more,' what with him just working on the buses, you see. Leon—he happened to us, if you know what I mean, and somehow we still managed.

"Up till their teens, that was. Then they started wanting all sorts of things. It was Tessa, really. She had such a gift for music, we had to get her a piano. That's when I started dressmaking to help with the extras.

"Well, Tessa went from strength to strength with her playing. Her teacher, a Mrs. Clarke, came up to me in town one day and said it was time our Tessa got herself another teacher.

"I was shocked. I asked, why on earth? What had Tessa done? This Mrs. Clarke laughed and said, didn't I know? Tessa had passed so many of her Royal College certificates she was now as well qualified as she was!"

"You mean she could teach music?" Kramer asked.

"Yes, that was it. Mrs. Clarke, the dear old thing, had taken Tessa right up to where she was. She couldn't take her further, could she? So anyway I told Tessa what had happened and she said the best person was some Belgian or other in the orchestra —municipal, I mean.

"The next day we went along to see him and he said all right if we could pay the fees. They were steep, I can tell you.

"Pat and I talked it over and we decided we must give her the opportunity. I would take in more work, sack the girl, and Pat would try for overtime."

"And you did that?"

"Yes. Then Lenny—Leon—started to give us trouble."

"Oh?"

"It wasn't serious, not then. You see, he wanted to be a pilot but his math was terrible. He asked his dad if he could have extra lessons, and he said yes. Tessa was having them, wasn't she?"

"Was he jealous of his sister?"

Mrs. Francis hesitated.

"He said cruel things at times but brothers and sisters are like that."

Kramer underlined the word "jealous" three times.

"Go on—what happened? Did he pass?"

"He never got the chance."

"Why? What school was he at?"

"Durban High. But that's got nothing to do with it. Pat got

146

sick with all the long hours he was working and not getting the proper food either, he was in such a rush. I nagged at him until he went to Addington and the doctors there said it was TB."

Mrs. Francis stopped talking abruptly. Fearful that she would not carry on, Kramer broke off a carnation and handed it to her.

"Nice smell," he said.

"Funny, that," Mrs. Francis murmured. "It was always carnations in the hospital—I suppose it was because of all those Indian kids selling them outside.

"What was I saying? Oh, yes. Well, Pat went in for what they call observation and the next thing I knew was they sent us a card saying he had been transferred to another hospital. I remember reading it and running in to our neighbors to ask if I could use the phone."

"But why?"

"I thought there had been a mistake. I said to the girl at Addington that I wanted to know where my husband was. She asked for my name and then she was away from the phone for a long time. When she came back she asked if I hadn't been sent a card. That's why I was ringing, I said—the card said Pat had been sent to a *native* hospital."

There was nowhere Kramer could look except straight at her.

"By this time my neighbor was getting all excited, she was right next to me, you see, and she grabbed away the phone and started to give the girl a bit of her mind.

"All of a sudden she stopped talking. She went as white as a sheet and put the thing down. 'What's happened?' I asked her. I was crying by then—I don't know why. She started to cry, too. It was terrible, the two of us in the hall like that. Every time I asked her what they had said, she just shook her head.

"Then her man came home and he asked her. She said that—"

"Yes?"

Mrs. Francis regained control of herself.

"While Pat was in hospital the doctors had noticed some-

147

thing. I don't know what, I'll never know. But what happened was that he had been reclassified Colored."

Kramer knew something of what she felt—it had happened to a school friend of his. Quite a bombshell. But laws were laws, so he put an official edge to his voice.

"You were later informed of this through the proper channels?"

"Yes, sir."

"Did you go before the classification board?"

"Me and the children did. We were reclassified, too."

"What about your husband?"

"He killed himself in the hospital with a rubber bandage."

There was a perfunctory rap on the door and Farthing trotted in.

"Sorry to disturb," he said, scooping up the flowers. "The old man's back if you want to see him, Lieutenant."

Kramer shook his head and waited for the silly bugger to get the hell out again.

"You know that neighbor?" Mrs. Francis asked. "She never spoke to me again, she didn't. We were coloreds now.

"Oh, well, then we packed up our things and went out to live in Claremont. Everyone there was very nice to us except the usual one or two. I managed to keep on my old customers—I didn't tell them, you see—and found some new ones."

"But wasn't there anything about this in the papers?"

"A little piece, months after, when there was the inquest on Pat. Not so you'd notice it."

That would be right. The press did not attend inquests but picked up their stories when the records were filed at the attorney general's office.

"And what about the children?"

She drew her fingertips hard down her cheeks.

"It was terrible. I did everything I could but it didn't work.

"They had to leave their schools for a start. That didn't matter so much to Tessa, she had her music, but Lenny had still a way to go."

148

"They have schools in Claremont."

"He wanted to be a pilot, though. Job reservation broke his spirit."

This line did not ring true to Mrs. Francis's way of talking—or thinking. She was bitter but not political. It sounded very much like the sort of thing a Jew lawyer would say.

"Lenny got into trouble, did he?"

"How do you know that, sir?"

"Never you mind. Just tell me about it."

"He stole from people on the beachfront—in a gang that would go down from Claremont. They didn't catch the others, just him. I told the magistrate all about it and so did Mr. Golder. That magistrate! He said he would be lenient but he sent Lenny to a reformatory."

"Well, he could have been given cuts, too," Kramer objected.

"Yes, sir, I suppose that's true."

"Of course it is. But what happened to Tessa meantime? Did she go on with her lessons?"

"That bloody Belgian really had me fooled!"

The sudden, totally unexpected profanity was a tonic for both of them. Mrs. Francis even managed a smile which did not mean anything else. Kramer leaned forward.

"I suppose if it hadn't been for him, then none of this would ever have happened."

"Then I must know."

She nodded.

"You will understand, sir, it is very difficult to say these things when your daughter . . ."

He waited.

"I went to this man and said that Tessa could not come anymore because there was not enough money. He was very shocked, he said, that such a thing should happen. And then he said that he would give Tessa her lessons for nothing. I knew that like most foreigners he was a liberal but this seemed to be too much to ask. Then he told me it was his duty as a musician not to neglect a talent like Tessa's. He even said there were

149

things more important than money. I've thought about that often. Oh, yes, more important to him, maybe."

Kramer experienced an insight which made him cringe. Peculiarly uncomfortable. The old girl really had an odd effect on him.

"I see. How did you find out?"

"The Belgian's wife told me. She said if it happened again she would report them both to the police. And she would, too, I know the type."

"And so?"

"It was up to me, wasn't it? I got Tessa alone that same night and came right out with it. You should have been there. It was terrible. She wasn't my Tessa anymore."

"What did she say, Gladys?"

"I don't know really. That she didn't care—that nothing mattered anymore. She would sleep with any man if it got her what she wanted. Her life was ruined, she could never have the nice things she had always hoped for. She cursed me for bearing her even."

"That was nasty."

"Do you know something, sir? That's when I started to understand what she was saying. I had made Tessa, I made her with a weak heart. All this life she was talking about could stop at any time; the doctors had said so."

"You can't blame yourself for that."

"Have you any children?"

Kramer shook his head.

"Then some other day you may understand. So when my neighbor made a joke about us trying for white, I suddenly saw here a chance for Tessa."

"What did she think of the idea?"

"She jumped at it. She was more my girlie again and talked about all the nice things she would buy to put around her. I promised her that she need never fear me getting in touch with her or anything."

150

"That must have been hard for you."

"No. I thought it would give her what I owed her. It was my sacrifice."

"What then?"

"Tessa just went. Two years ago. I didn't ask her where."

"And Lenny? What did he say to all this?"

"He was still in the reformatory at the time. I told him when he got back and he was angry. He said he would kill her for leaving me."

That could have been awkward but Kramer said lightly: "So old Lenny has a temper, has he?"

"You've never heard the like of it! I don't know where he gets it from either; my Pat was the quietest of men. But he loved his old mum, you see, and didn't think it right what Tessa had done. Not until I told him about the other thing."

"How did he take that?"

"For a long time he was as quiet as can be. Then he came to me in the kitchen and said perhaps it was best she had gone. There had been enough disgrace in the family."

Kramer was stiff having sat for so long. He stood up and stretched and slumped down again with an encouraging smile.

"Better finish it now, Gladys. Now we've got so far. Tell me, how did you know that Theresa le Roux was your daughter?"

Mrs. Francis smiled crookedly.

"Because I chose the name for her, sir. It was the one thing I asked of her. I wanted to know in case anything happened, in case she became famous."

"And you read it in the *Gazette*?"

"No, I don't get a paper. It was Lenny who came round to tell me."

"Had he left home then, too?"

"He wasn't trying for white as well, if that's what you think."

"I don't."

"Lenny's a good boy, sir. But he is a young man and it is right he should have his own place."

"Of course."

"Well, as I was saying, Lenny came round to me two days ago —Tuesday—and told me about the funeral notice. I asked him to drive me up here straight away so I could go to it, but he said no."

"Why was that?"

"Because he said it could mean trouble for us if anyone found out. I said, what could the police do to us? But he said it was best not to, even if it was hard. I knew he was thinking of his job."

"Oh? Where does he work?"

"I don't know exactly—he's never told me. You see, sir, I think he is a little ashamed of it; a colored person's job somewhere. That's why I never asked him straight out. He has his rights like his sis—must you hear all this?"

"Just tell me the rest quickly, Gladys."

"Yes, sir. All right. Lenny said not to fret too much because he would make sure there were some flowers from me at the crematorium. He could leave them there without a card and nobody would know. He's a good boy to his mother. Anyway, he left and I went by myself to the church where the nuns are."

Kramer took the press clipping out and put it on her lap.

"Did they show you this, too?"

She picked it up slowly.

"I haven't seen Lenny again so far," she said. "No, what happened was this. Yesterday morning I suddenly wanted to have the paper with the funeral thing in it. I wanted something I could *see*, if you understand.

"I asked in town where I could buy the Trekkersburg paper and they said at the station. My mind was in such a whirl, you see, that I didn't think that the funeral was already over and there would be nothing in it. Then I noticed this."

"It must have been quite a shock. Did you try to contact Lenny?"

"No, sir. He would never let me come here but I had to find out. Besides, I don't know where he lives."

So that was it. She had made another sacrifice, given him his privacy, too. Both the little bastards had abandoned her.

"Lenny is going to be really cross when he hears what's happened now," Mrs. Francis added quietly.

Moosa had been pacing up and down his room for more than an hour. At least that was all Gogol could conclude from the heavy thumping sounds overhead. He stood behind his till and stared fascinated at the ceiling. It showed no movement but one of the neon strips had developed a stutter with the vibrations. Altogether it was quite extraordinary—the old devil was normally so lazy he kept a chamber pot in the closet.

A customer slipped into the shop, a white youth in a T-shirt, jeans, and expensive suede shoes. Gogol ignored him.

"I'd like these grapes, please."

"One pound—two pounds?"

"One."

He did not want grapes, Gogol knew that. Still, he might as well go through it—every little helped.

The grapes were dumped into the dirty scale pan, weighed, tipped into a brown paper bag.

"Anything else, sir?"

The old ritual. Gogol realized the youth resented his look of disdain, but no doubt it was preferable to the recriminatory expression of a druggist's assistant.

"Two, please."

Gogol reached under the till, palmed a couple of packets of rubber prophylactics, and popped them in with the grapes.

"One rand fifty, sir."

The youth paid without demur.

It amused Gogol to watch him head for his sleek sports car on the other side of Trichaard Street and make a mess of his takeoff. They were always so nervous.

The thumpings had stopped.

Gogol turned from the shop window just in time to see Moosa, all dressed up to the nines, lifting a bag of peanuts from the spike. He must have come downstairs on tiptoe like the Phantom Avenger.

"Hold it!"

Gogol snapped his fingers and extended his right hand. To his immense surprise, Moosa put a rand note into it.

"On account," Moosa said airily. Then he walked to the shop door and opened it.

"Where the hell you think you're going?" Gogol asked.

"Out on a little business," Moosa replied. "I'm going to see a man about a car."

Of all the bloody cheek.

Kramer had one thing on his mind when he arrived back at his office with Mrs. Francis: he was hungry. So ravenously hungry that the void had squeezed its way right up his gullet and was now fingering the little button that makes you retch. It reminded him of his childhood and that was intolerable.

As was the sight of Van Niekerk tidying up the remains of a late lunch eaten at the desk off a large white table napkin. The sergeant's wife was obviously an excellent provider. In the center of the cloth was a pint-size Thermos flask with splashes of gravy on its wide rim. Around it were gathered a number of translucent plastic containers, very like those used for cultures, each containing a scrap of lettuce or some other organic residue.

"All you need now is a ruddy microscope and you'll really be set up," Kramer grunted.

"Pardon, sir?"

"This all you've got to do—eat?"

"It's after two, sir. I've been busy and I've got something for you."

"Not now. Where's Zondi?"

"Oh, he's back. Just fetching my coffee."

"Right."

Kramer turned to Mrs. Francis, who had been doing her best to remain hidden from Van Niekerk behind his back.

"I'll take you down to an office where you can be alone for a while," he said. "The Bantu sergeant will bring you something to eat."

He escorted her to a vacant interrogation room, switched on the light, and left her to her thoughts. None of which could have been too pleasant.

Zondi had taken care to slop a good deal of coffee into Van Niekerk's saucer. And so he was standing, poker-faced but happy, listening to the recipient's plaintive grumblings when Kramer spotted him.

"Food!"

"Yes, boss?"

"Go round to the Greek's tearoom and fetch me one big curry with double rice."

He handed Zondi his change.

"And while you're there, get a pie for yourself and the old woman."

"Thank you, boss. Coffee, too?"

"I'm not drinking the muck from the canteen at this time of the day. Make it two pots of tea as well, hey?"

Van Niekerk watched Zondi's exit with some satisfaction and then went on packing his lunch things away in an airline bag.

"You've been there?" Kramer asked, pointing to the sticker which read *New York*.

"No, you buy them like this," Van Niekerk explained.

"Uhuh."

"Do you want to hear now what I've picked up, sir?"

"Okay, go ahead."

Van Niekerk rose from behind the desk and gestured at his vacated chair.

"You'll be needing it for your lunch," he said.

Kramer murmured his thanks, and sat down.

Assured now that he had Kramer's full attention, Van Niekerk flipped open his notebook.

"I did these calls in alphabetical order, sir, as I took them from the directory. The last one of all was to Messrs Webber and

155

Swart in Buchan Street. I spoke to Mr. Webber himself and he told me he had prescribed a pair of contact lenses such as I described."

"Make them himself, did he?"

"No, sir, he sent to Germany for them."

"I see. Go on. Did the girl buy them from him?"

"The customer gave her name as Phillips, sir—but we're pretty sure she's Miss le Roux all right. You did tell me to stay in the office and not go out."

"Fine. I can drop in later with a photo. But when was all this?"

"She took delivery of them three weeks ago."

Kramer whistled softly.

"So recently? Did she give any reason for wanting them?"

"She said she was a model, blue eyes were better for business purposes or something. Webber saw nothing wrong in this because she looked like a model. Anyway, he was pleased to be asked to do something so different for a change. It took him quite a bit of time to find the name of the German firm."

"I'm sure Mr. Webber was only too happy to be of assistance," Kramer said dryly. "These dollies. Tell you what, ring him and get him to come round here—it'll save some bother."

"Okay, sir."

Van Niekerk was on the telephone to Mr. Webber when Zondi returned with the food.

"Take a cup of tea and a pie down to room eighteen and then come back here," Kramer instructed him. "There's something I want you to hear."

And two minutes later he gave his subordinates a résumé of the Francis interview.

The chubby little fellow in the doorway appeared so awed by his surroundings that he could not bring himself to knock. This gave Kramer time to mop up the last of the curry before finally pushing his plate aside.

"Come in," he said.

"I'm Mr. Webber," the visitor announced, not moving an

inch. For a man of about fifty he was being very childish, but the place had this effect on some of the better class of person.

"Just the man! I'm Lieutenant Kramer and this is my assistant, Sergeant van Niekerk."

"How do you do?"

"Take a chair, Mr. Webber."

The optician scuttled across, sat, and glanced all about him.

"Not at all what I expected," he volunteered. "So bare and so ordinary; like a waiting room—not that you've had to wait long for me, mind! Ha ha."

"The torture chamber's next door," Kramer said.

"Pardon?"

"Haven't you ever been in a police station before, Mr. Webber?"

"No, not CID—not in this country."

Van Niekerk looked interested.

"Where are you from?" he asked.

"Reading, it's a place in England."

"Very nice, very nice—and you like it here? Are you going to take out your papers?"

"I'm a citizen already," Mr. Webber replied smugly.

And the momentary tension in the room was eclipsed.

"You've no idea what they say about this country at home," Mr. Webber hastened to explain. "The stories I've read in the Sunday papers."

"Well, now you know, Mr. Webber," Kramer soothed. "And someday, when we've got time, I'll tell you what I'd like to do with the people who write such rubbish without understanding our problems."

"I couldn't agree more, Lieutenant."

Kramer looked away. God knows what trouble the government was having with its immigration program if this was what was being allowed in. No guts at all.

"Here's the photograph, sir," Van Niekerk said, holding out one of the head-and-shoulders. Kramer took it and wandered around to Mr. Webber's side.

"Is this the same girl?" he asked.

"Yes, it is—that's Miss Phillips all right. I'd know her anywhere."

"Certain?"

"Yes."

But Mr. Webber still took the photograph from Kramer's hands for a close inspection.

"How did she pay for the lenses?"

"Cash. I must say she looks rather odd in this."

"She's dead."

"Good gracious."

Now he seemed entirely reluctant to give up the photograph. Kramer turned to Van Niekerk.

"Have you got the other ones handy? I think Mr. Webber would like to see one or two."

Van Niekerk frowned. This was most irregular. Nevertheless he handed them over.

Mr. Webber got to his feet for his treat and became the first man Kramer had ever seen go green.

"But—but she's been ripped right up the middle!" he gasped. "Who could have done a terrible thing like that?"

"That's what we intend to find out," Kramer said.

Mr. Webber made a very swift exit.

"Ah, well," Kramer said, pouring another cup, "that's the way the cookie crumbles. I'd like to bet that only a bloody immigrant would have lapped up her story about modeling."

"It sounds reasonable enough to me, sir."

"Maybe."

"How was she to know he was a redneck? Look at this list— she could have picked any one of them. They're not all from overseas."

"It's just that I think this Tessa was no ordinary girl. She knew what she was doing. Picked her men."

"Like who?"

"Like the doctor," Zondi suggested. "You say so yourself, boss, he is not number one."

158

"But good enough for her purposes," Kramer added. "How about that, Willie?"

The sergeant shrugged. It was a mere detail.

The outside telephone rang.

"For you," Van Niekerk told Zondi.

The conversation was very one-sided. Zondi listened in silence apart from an occasional grunt and then put his hand over the mouthpiece.

"It's Moosa," he said. "I put him onto the Lesotho car lead this morning. He's found out about it. Seems it's used by one of the fellows who fetches Gershwin his cripples from the reserves. The Lesotho plates are just so as not to make anyone suspicious of seeing it out on the dirt roads."

"Cross it off, Willie," Kramer sighed, pushing the crime sheet over to him. "There's one little theory down the drain."

"But what shall I tell him, boss?"

"Moosa, is it? Hell. I hope you know what you're doing, Kaffir."

Zondi grinned.

"He's a new man, so he tells me. Don't worry."

"Then have him wait in his place. You can go and see him later with a picture."

"Who of?"

"The brother, Lenny—now *he* worries me, and no mistake."

12

THE COLONEL WAS flattered.

"Put it this way, Lieutenant—I never allow a wog to touch my delphiniums," he said.

"Quite right, too, sir."

In another minute Frikkie Muller, the Colonel's clerk, was going to have to leave the room in a hurry. He was already putting a bend in his plastic teeth by bitting on them so hard. If only Kramer would not look so solemn.

"Take these along to the Brigadier, Frikkie," the Colonel ordered, handing over the bunch of blooms. "Say it's a thank you to his wife for that wonderful party the other night."

Frikkie departed thankfully.

"Sorry to interrupt you like that, Lieutenant; just thought I'd get them out of the way as they looked so damn silly in this office."

Not half as silly as the Brigadier would look carrying them out to his car.

"That's fine, sir. There isn't much more to tell."

"So you think this case is maybe not such a serious one after all?"

"That's right, sir. The brother has a record; not a big one but a record."

"The important thing is that it's a *criminal* record. This gives

160

us the bridge between the girl and the sort of trash who might associate with a spoke man."

"I agree, sir. And I'm pretty sure that he and his sister were mixed up in something together. She hasn't much in her post office book but then we know she wasn't shy to change her name when it suited her."

"Ah, those contact lenses—a funny business that. I don't quite see it myself."

"We've only got theories so far. Sergeant van Niekerk did some research on the notes of the case and came up with something based on what the eye specialist said about contacts."

"Oh, yes?"

"Well, she had had these lenses for three weeks but nobody saw her wearing them until after she was killed. Why wear them at all and at night? Because the specialist said that anyone using these things for the first time had to do it in easy stages, get used to them. We think she was practicing after dark."

"When was she going to wear them then?"

"She had made her move to Trekkersburg. Why not another somewhere else? Another new life?"

"I like that. If she and her brother were in trouble, they might try to run for it. The others just got to her first."

"Yes, sir, along those lines."

Kramer had to admit his admiration for the way Colonel Du Plessis had grasped the problem. He was a strange one.

"If the contacts were her big secret, Trompie, do you think she would have answered the door in them? Stop! I know what you're going to say—yes, she would, if she was expecting someone."

"Her brother."

"But it wasn't. It was the killer."

"Van Niekerk had an answer to that one, too. Trudeau said that this kind with painted irises worked best in bright daylight on account of the pupil being made small. Farthing swears that there was only one light burning in the flat and it was in her room.

"Now supposing she was in bed waiting for whoever it was—her brother. She hears a knock. She gets up just in her nightie, goes through the other room, and opens the door a little way. The light is shining from behind her and with those pupils she wouldn't be able to see a thing out there. She hears a voice she thinks she knows. She leaves the door and goes back to get into bed because it's cold—and it was cold on Sunday night."

"I've got the picture," the Colonel interrupted. "Your eyes or my eyes would open wide but hers couldn't. The opposite of the dazzle. Yes, but all this wouldn't work if she wasn't expecting a caller. If it was her brother, why didn't he show up?"

"He could have been afraid to. He could have known things had gone wrong."

"Another presumption—how would they know about his call in the first place?"

"They could have arranged it and told both of them before-hand. Or only the one."

"The girl?"

"Yes."

"Much simpler—that could be the way things happened. They tell her the brother's coming at, say, eleven. She hears the knock, opens the door, and goes back to bed. They get her. Fine."

"They could have done it the hard way, too, once that door was open."

"True, too. But we keep saying 'they.' Who are we talking about?"

"I don't know, sir. A gang."

"There are not many left who go to this sort of trouble, Trompie, man. They could have got her much easier with a car."

"She didn't go out much."

"*Ach*, man, you know what I mean."

"Yes, sir. What about a gang playing for high stakes?"

"Like the one Shoe Shoe dreamed up? I think that's a lot of bloody rubbish."

"According to Mkize's statement it was not rubbish that made him kill Shoe Shoe."

"That will be the day Shoe Shoe knows something about his VIPs that gets him the chop. I can't accept that. The Steam Pig . . . Huh! If you ask me, it's a lot of steam pudding."

After an obligatory laugh, Kramer said: "But we are agreed then, sir, that this fellow Lenny could probably give us answers to a lot of questions—including that one?"

"Agreed."

"Then I have your permission to go down to Durban with Zondi and see if we can find him?"

All along the Colonel had displayed a slight anxiety despite Kramer's unusual affability—or perhaps because of it. He was like a man expecting to have to pay for his fun. Now he knew the price.

"I'm surprised you bothered to ask me, Lieutenant," he replied heavily.

"Port Natal Division doesn't welcome intervention from our side, sir. It could lead to trouble."

"Like last time? You think I don't know that? Captain Potgeiter said he never wanted you there again. Those are big-city press boys they've got down there—they're not so easy to tame."

"I was thinking of administrative troubles, actually. You know how the Brigadier is about protocol."

"I'm sure you were."

"It's the truth, sir. No need for any rough stuff on this trip—we'll just pick him up and bring him back."

"And if Captain Potgeiter sees you? What then?"

"I'll tell him you've fixed it up at the top. He can't argue with your rank."

"If it's all so simple, why not let Potgeiter do it for you?"

"I thought it would look better in your report if it all came from this division, sir."

The Colonel blinked balefully at him from the ropes. One day he would win.

"I'll see about it, Lieutenant. In the meantime, is there anything you can give me to show the Brigadier?"

"I don't think so. It might not be wise—so much is still up in the air. But you've helped me a lot with it. Thanks."

"Don't be too cocky. What if you can't find this Lenny?"

"Then I'll pick up a photo of him and start looking elsewhere. Here, for example."

"And if you still don't find him?"

"We'll know that there's a pretty good chance he's gone the way of his sister. Better than nothing."

"Hmm, tell you what," the Colonel said, holding his paper knife by the tip. "You wrap this case up by tomorrow night or I'm going to put the whole squad on it. You seem to have overlooked the fact that my press statement, which you made so much fuss about, has been the biggest help to you so far. Without it there would have been no old woman and no brother."

It was a draw.

Van Niekerk was waiting for Kramer with a sheet of Telex in his hand. He was surprised when it was ignored, and perturbed by the expression that went with the snub.

"Trouble, sir?" he asked.

"What's Durban got to say?"

"A bit more than we know already. Leon Charles Francis got a year in Doringboom Reformatory for theft. While he was there he received a total of fourteen strokes with the heavy cane."

"Give here."

"Six for committing an indecent act and eight for serious assault."

"I said *give here!*"

Kramer snatched the paper away and glared at it. The next paragraph read:

"HELD ON SUSPICION THREE OCCASIONS SINCE RELEASE. AS-SAULTS, TWO GBH. INSUFFICIENT EVIDENCE. PROBABLE CON-NECTION WITH SOME GANG. LIVES IT UP."

And that was all.

"This the best they could do?"

"Well, he's not what you might call big stuff, sir. Even Trek-kersburg has more of them than we can keep tabs on."

"I suppose so. But this 'insufficient evidence' bit shows he's good at his work."

"Oh, yes. I wasn't saying he doesn't sound a really bad bug-ger."

"Well, we know who we mustn't show this to," Kramer said, nodding in the direction of room 18.

"Oh, she was asking for you. Wondering if she can go home now."

"Not until we get sonny boy. He warned her to keep away from here so there's no telling what he might do now."

"What's the plan then, sir? Take her to the cells?"

"I know a place; leave it to me. By the way, how are you fixed for tonight?"

"Want me to come down to Durban?"

"Actually I need a bloke here in case anyone phones in. You never know."

Van Niekerk adjusted his tie and outlook. He cleared his throat.

"Fine, sir. I'll just ring the wife."

"You do that. When Khumalo comes on, tell him to bring up the stretcher from the library—or you can have a spare bed from the barracks if you prefer."

"I'll be all right, sir. Probably have the best sleep in weeks without the kids."

Kramer wondered about that.

The cottage stood on the fringe of the sewage farm, surrounded by the most verdant vegetation Trekkersburg had to offer out-side the botanical gardens. Six blue gum trees teetered behind it and strips of pink bark lay strewn on its rusty corrugated iron roof. The setting sun put a blush on the whitewashed walls, glinted off the windows, which had glass, and gave the children in the clearing their own leaping shadows to chase.

Mrs. Francis peered at the couple waiting in the doorway to discover what brought a big flashy car their way down the rough track. You could tell she liked the look of them.

Then the man recognized Kramer up front in the passenger's seat and came running out.

"What a pleasure, Mr. Kramer," he said, opening the door for him.

"How's it, Johannes?"

"Fine! Mary's here to greet you, too, and the kids!"

Aware of Zondi's gaze, Kramer attempted a bluff manner but gave in to the children's teasing. One of their little friends edged his way into the circle to see what manner of white man could cause such excitement.

"Just a minute, I've got a visitor for you," Kramer protested, and he let Mrs. Francis out.

The atmosphere changed instantly.

"What does she want here?" Johannes demanded. "She's from a church? Sorry, we don't want your charity, madam."

Mrs. Francis's sudden smile threw him.

"Can't you recognize your own kind yet?" Kramer chided. "This is Mrs. Francis, who has come up from Claremont for a few days. I want you to look after her."

"Of course," Mary said, pushing her husband aside and taking Mrs. Francis by the hand. "Come along with me. We'll both have some tea before it's time for the children to come in."

Without a backward glance, Mrs. Francis went. And so did the children.

"No luggage?" Johannes asked thoughtfully.

"None. She came up on the bus to find out about a relative. Maybe she'll tell you about it later."

"It doesn't matter."

"How are things then, Johannes? How's Katrina?"

166

"The same."

"Uhuh."

"But she likes it better in the hospital now. They give her work to do—she makes baskets for dirty washing."

"That's good."

"You understand my sister, Mr. Kramer. Now don't you worry about this lady you brought. She'll be safe and sound with us till you want her."

"Don't throw her out before Sunday, anyway." Kramer grinned. "Bye for now."

Zondi started up and drove off as Kramer's door slammed shut.

"What was that talk about old Katrina, boss? Have they cured her of killing her babies yet?"

"Hell, no. It's just that she hasn't been raped lately. You black buggers are slacking."

Infanticide and rape, both capital offenses, were very much on Moosa's mind as he waited in his room for Zondi to appear with his next assignment. If the Pillay baby on the other side of the wall did not shut up, he would go around and strangle it. And while he was there, with the voluptuous Mrs. Pillay presumably in a dead faint, he would make a night of it.

Gogol banged open the door and confronted him, his fez wildly askew.

"Moosa!"

The Fiend of Trichaard Street cowered against the wall.

"Moosa, you just telling me what damn tricks you are up to! Five Coca-Colas and a Pepsi?"

Moosa opened one eye.

"Now don't you try denying it, man. That's three people in the shop tonight telling me that you have been sitting in Sammy's Tea Lounge all afternoon drinking Cokes. With *whose* money, I ask? Whose money? *My* money!"

"It wasn't your money."

Gogol caught his fez as it fell.

"Wasn't mine?" he said and giggled nastily. "I tell you that every cent you have in your pocket from now until the day you die is my money."

"It was expenses, not money."

"You can call it what you like. I want it, so hand over."

"Just where do you think I got money from?"

"Why should I care?"

But that stopped Gogol. It made him ponder.

"You spoke about business," he said at last. "Can it be you have something lined up?"

"Of course."

"But you had some cash even before you went out today; that is what I am not understanding. There has been nobody in this room I know."

The Pillay baby shut up.

"Wait a minute; that Zondi's been here. Am I right?"

Moosa chose to look diplomatically committal. This got the message across but only to bring a hurtful howl of laughter from Gogol.

"You—for them? That Kaffir is mad! Now I'll tell him to his face. What do you know about anything out there? Hiding behind your curtains every time Gershwin Mkize puts his foot on the pavement. You only went out today because Gershwin—"

An idea suddenly occurred to Gogol which weakened his knees and settled him apprehensively on the end of the bed. He looked at Moosa as he had never done before.

"Gershwin Mkize," he said softly.

"Yes?"

"Last night Zondi was here. Next morning . . . Were you the fellow who . . . ?"

Moosa's face gave nothing away, least of all the fact that his mind was tripping over itself trying to catch up with Gogol. It dawned on him just as Gogol spoke again.

"No, please to say nothing, Moosa. I have respect for your position."

His wide eyes showed fear, too, and that was even more gratifying.

Durban had never appealed to Kramer. She was not his kind of city. He liked his women to be big and strong and primitive, yes; but also dignified and clean. Durban was a whore.

A cheap whore who sprawled lush, legs agape at the harbor mouth, beside the warm Indian Ocean, which was not a sea but a favor that she sold. And they came in their thousands, these people who craved to pleasure their bodies, hurtling down the roads from the prim, dry veld of the interior. Some died in their eager haste—shredded by shattered windshields and buried beneath cairns of transistor radios, beach balls, teddy bears, peppermint packets, and hand luggage. But most arrived safely to wander nearly naked in the palm-lined streets and be tempted by garish signs which stood out like face paint against dirty-skinned buildings.

Of course she had lice; half a million humble parasites who knew nothing wrong in dwelling with her and sharing the take.

And crabs. Like the one they were after.

"Where do we go first, boss?"

"CID Central."

Zondi gunned the Chev over the intersection on the amber and squealed off left down a side street. He did not like Durban much either, judging from the speed at which he was driving. Or maybe he needed a piss.

Captain Potgeiter was off sick.

"Can I be of help?" his deputy asked.

"Lieutenant Kramer, Trekkersburg CID. I've come for a picture."

The deputy straightened up from the counter, his smile almost conspiratorial.

"Oh, *ja*, the Captain's friend. I've had the message. Here they are, old mate—not very recent, though."

Kramer studied the two mug shots—one full face, one profile

—which were still tacky from the print glazer. Now it was obvious why Lenny Francis had not followed his sister in trying for white: he belonged right on the borderline where only an official pen stroke could define his proper position.

"It's an easy face to remember," the deputy remarked, coming around to look over his shoulder.

That was true. The youth had an unusualy long neck with an Adam's apple like an ostrich that had swallowed a beer can. Balanced on top of it was a round head, capped in tight curls and dimpled deep in each cheek. The nose was aquiline enough, but the lips too sensuous—they dragged down a little to the left side. The eyes were sinister but this was probably because the lids had been caught in midblink by the photographer's flash.

Kramer half-closed his own eyes and saw before him a silhouette almost identical to that in the locket picture. The heavy shade had disguised a great deal.

"He can't have changed much," Kramer observed, tucking the photographs into his breast pocket. "Bit like a poof popstar."

"You could have something there," the deputy replied. "Just before you came in, one of the Indian staff was saying that Lenny learned some nasty ways in Doringboom. A tart he knows by the pie cart once told him that she wasted a whole night on the guy. No joy."

"Anything else?"

"Nothing. But I made a check with Traffic—I thought I remembered something—and he's facing a reckless charge. I've still got the papers down here."

"Let's have a look."

Kramer flipped through the docket. There was nothing remarkable in it—failure to comply with a stop sign, and a collision involving another car but nobody hurt. He noted down the registration number of Lenny's '57 Pontiac and its color, lime green.

"Ta very much, then. How's the time?"

170

"Getting on for eight."

"And how far is it over to his place?"

"Should take you about twenty minutes. I can send someone along with you."

"No, thanks. I've got my boy with me—he knows the town."

Which would have been news to Zondi, who was making his third awkward reverse out of a narrow cul-de-sac.

"Try the next one," Kramer said, cursing the Chev's nonfunctional cabin light. He held another match over the street map.

"It's okay, boss, we're here. Vista Road."

"Carry on to that fire hydrant and then stop."

There were lights burning on the front verandas of most of the houses but no one about except for a colored man across the road tinkering with the sidecar on his motorcycle. He glanced up for a moment as Kramer and Zondi got out—the latter tugging at the seat of his oversize overalls where they had become caught in the crotch.

"Not a bad area," Kramer said quietly.

Zondi nodded.

The suburb had, in fact, been white until four years before when it was redesignated under the Group Areas Act. Each bungalow had its own small garden and most had a garage. It would still have passed for a white neighborhood, if the need for new coats of paint had not been so obvious even in the moonlight. It seemed an odd address for Lenny Francis, but then again it was something like what he had been used to.

"Come on, boy," Kramer said loudly for the benefit of the curbside mechanic. "See you hold that torch nice and steady this time."

Zondi nodded and shambled after him, dragging his shoes, which had their shoelaces undone.

The owner of the first house on the even-numbered side of Vista Road responded quickly to the loud knock on his front door.

"Electricity," Kramer said.

"I've paid my bills."

"Not bloody interested. I've come to check on a power leak. Where's your meter?"

The householder sullenly admitted them and pointed to the meter board on the hall wall.

"Boy!"

Zondi leaped to it. He flicked on the torch, reached up on tiptoe, and shone the light on the main current dial. Kramer noted down a figure.

"This one's okay; let's go."

Without another word, they left the house and went into the next. And as they worked their way down to number 14, they became aware that the street was not half as deserted as it had first appeared. Kramer had anticipated this: Lenny might also be peering out between lace curtains, but he was to have no warning of what was really approaching him.

"You think he'll be by his place so early, boss?" Zondi whispered as he closed the gate to number 12.

"I reckon this is about the time he gets up," Kramer answered. "The day's just beginning for his kind."

Zondi shambled up to the front door of number 14 and tapped it with his torch.

Van Niekerk could not believe the time. It was midnight and the telephone was ringing again.

In his struggle to answer it without leaving his warm cocoon of blankets, the bloody stretcher unstretched and he rolled onto the floor.

He struggled to his feet, making a wild snatch for his pajama trousers. The night was cold.

It took two syllables to incense him.

"Look here!" he shrieked into the mouthpiece. "If you ring up one more time, coolie, I'm sending a van down for you! Understand? Zondi is not here and there are no bloody pictures for you. Now shut up!"

He slammed the receiver down and stood trembling.

172

There was a sound of laughter from through in Housebreaking, where they were working late.

Kramer was driving now and Zondi was on the back seat. They were cruising downtown Durban, thinking about what they had just learned and wondering what to do next.

The door to number 14 had been opened by an old man in braces. He said he was Willem Peterson and that his son, who owned the house, was out. The only other resident, a used-car salesman called Lenny Francis, was out, too.

Kramer had pushed him aside and searched the house. It was empty. Zondi had checked the outbuilding and garage. Nothing.

So they had taken a closer look at what Lenny's room had to offer. It was not much. The dresser and wardrobe were filled with jazzy clothing. There was a bulky pile of muscle-men magazines and a rusty chest-expander. There were some comics and a paperback on karate. There were no letters or papers of interest.

They had gone back to old Willem, who was waiting as instructed in the front room, and asked him what he knew about the lodger.

Only that he sold cars and went out a lot at night—sometimes not returning until the next day. He did not like this but his son did not mind. He had explained to Willem that salesmen often worked such hours as they could hardly expect men to leave their jobs to buy a car during the day. It was natural for the lodger to be out after hours and on Sundays.

The old man's patent disapproval of Lenny was a great help. By pandering to it, Kramer was able to extract a reasonable account of his movements over the past few days.

Lenny had got back very late on Sunday, the night Tessa had been killed.

On Monday he had remained in his room until about seven in the evening before going out for about three hours.

On Tuesday he had gone out very early, no doubt to break

173

the news of his sister's death to his mother. (How odd that he knew in advance that it would be worth his while to go to the station and buy a copy of the *Gazette*.) Lenny had returned at lunchtime to pick something up. The son had asked for a lift into town but Lenny had said he was going upcountry. He could have been meaning Trekkersburg.

And on Wednesday evening—twenty-four hours before—he had left in his car at about six after spending all day in bed. He had not come back.

"It's a pity this isn't last night," Kramer remarked.

"Too true, boss."

Zondi's voice was tired; he had not slept in two days. It was very late and very pointless to track a man down in a strange city.

"Man, if we only knew one place this Lenny goes to," Kramer sighed, reluctantly turning the Chev around to head for Central CID and the helpful deputy.

"Just a minute; my stomach he says we do," Zondi replied, leaning forward over the seat. "What about the pie cart?"

Kramer held the lock on the wheel until the Chev had completed its 360-degree turn and then he opened it up down West Street. Three blocks farther on they saw the lights of the mobile diner where it had been trundled out into the car park.

"Two pies, boss?"

"Two each."

They drew in with a screech of brakes and killed the lights. A bunch of teen-agers in a hot rod beside them raised a small cheer and two tramps—who had been pestering an elderly couple in a Mercedes—scuttled into the shadows.

But Kramer was aware only of the lime green '57 Pontiac parked near the exit. One front fender was crumpled and the number plates were those registered in the name of Leon Charles Francis.

"I go, boss," Zondi hissed. And he slipped out of the car.

Kramer watched him in his rear-view mirror as he moved

174

swiftly back toward the entrance. He was going to come in again at the other gate and have a look in the Pontiac as he went by. He moved out of sight.

Kramer flashed his lights for service. An old Indian in a filthy waiter's jacket clamped his tray under one arm and advanced like a somnambulist.

As he gave his order, Kramer could see out of the corner of his eye that Zondi had reached the Pontiac and was giving the thumbs-down. Stuff it.

But the waiter was not as dopey as he looked. He was halfway back to the pie cart when he returned to Kramer's window.

"Sorry to be troubling you, master."

"What's the matter?"

"You come by this place with a native man in your car, master. That man by the other side."

"What of it?"

"He is working for you?"

"None of your bloody business."

"For police, maybe, master?"

So it was not that the man wanted to know whether he should bring half the order on a piece of newspaper.

"CID."

"That car he belong to Lenny Francis. You look for him?"

"Could be."

The waiter made his quota of change jingle in a pocket. Kramer gave him some money of his own.

"God bless you, master. Lenny leave that car here last night. He go with many chums in black stationary wagon. Along eight o'clock time."

"Sammy, you're a bright boy."

"Chums they come from same place as you, master. Also got Trekkersburg numbering plate."

Kramer winced. He had overlooked this in their elaborate plans for casing 14 Vista Road. Still, Lenny had not been there to care. And he could stay wherever he was at least until day-break.

Durban had one virtue. The nights were warm. Kramer and Zondi slept in the car on the beach and were quite comfortable.

A HIGH WHINE came from the print glazer in a corner of Photographic. Prinsloo slouched over and spat on the revolving chrome-plated drum. His saliva jittered into steam.

"Hot enough—we can begin," he said.

Van Niekerk took a handful of small prints from the sink and handed it over.

"Not too many at once, Willie; I've got to lay them out on this cloth belt and it moves slowly."

"Going to take a long time?"

"*Ja.*"

"He wants them by ten."

"So? Your Lieutenant bloody Kramer is going to learn he can't do everything in a hurry. And next time he'll ask the blokes with the original negative for his prints."

Van Niekerk took a snack from his left nostril unnoticed.

"Zondi's the one who gets on my wick," he grumbled. "What's this with him and Kramer?"

Prinsloo shrugged.

"I can let you have them in batches if that's any good," he said, pulling over the guillotine ready to trim off the excess paper.

"Fine."

"You can let me have some more now."

"I slept here last night."

"Oh, yes? He works you hard, does he?"

"Nonstop. And you should see him this morning; you would think he was up against the clock."

"His nerves must be shot to hell."

"Dead jumpy."

Kramer cleared his throat two feet behind them.

Moosa was almost inconsolable. But Zondi managed it in the end.

"Where should I go, Sergeant?" he asked, accepting the photograph of Lenny.

"You can forget about Trichaard Street; Gershwin's given it a bad name for a while. I've got some people at the market, the station, the beer halls. I don't know—where you like."

"I see. It's all hands to the wheel."

"What's that?"

"You're calling in all of us."

"Sure, you've got it."

"Then I might take a little stroll over toward the river. I've not seen that part for some time."

"You won't see much either. It's white now."

"Oh, dear."

"But go where you like, man. Just keep your eye on the cars —that's the important thing. If you see him in one, get the number and ring in."

"But will that rude Boer master answer me?"

"I'll be there."

"And the name? I meant to write it down."

"Leon Francis—they call him Lenny. He was seen leaving his place in a blue suit. Five foot six."

"Thank you."

"So long then."

Moosa got up to open the door for him.

"One minute, Moosa, another thing. You haven't gone talking big all over the place, have you? Nobody knows?"

178

"Indeed to goodness, no! Allah forbid."

But Zondi left still pondering the very different reception he had had from Gogol—and the knowing little wink.

Kramer was waiting for him in the Chev at the corner.

"Get in, man, we haven't got all day. I want you for a job." They drove off.

"Moosa's talked."

"Let him. It's a good idea to let them think we have to use Moosa."

"We'll still pay him, boss?"

"Why not? People may tell him things, revenge or some crap like that. Make it piece rates."

"I'm sorry, boss."

"I tell you Moosa was a good idea. But didn't you pick up anything from the others?"

"Nothing."

"Or weren't they saying?"

"They are very worried about something, but I do not think they have ever seen this Lenny before."

"Man, this is strange, Zondi. It was the same with mine. They would tell me if they knew—even just for protection."

"Quite so, boss. A bad spirit is hiding here; it is like when the birds in the bush go quiet and yet there has been no sound."

"Of course I don't think Lenny operated in Trekkersburg and we didn't give them the link-up. So that leaves us with trying the pie-cart trick again. Remember his mother said that she had asked him to put flowers for her at the crematorium?"

"Mr. Abbott he said no flowers."

"That was only while he was there, man. Lenny could have come by later."

Zondi put a Lucky in Kramer's mouth and lit it. He took one for himself.

"So that is why we go this road?"

"Yes, I want you to have a word with the boys there. The ones who work in the garden. *Ach*, what's the matter, man?"

"That fellow would not put flowers for his mother—he's a bad one."

"It would be hard for him not to do it if she asked him."

"But I thought he was frightened to come here."

"You've got to be careful, Zondi, you're mixing up what we think with what we know."

"But, boss—"

Kramer thumped the steering wheel with his fist.

"Listen, Kaffir," he bellowed. "We've got nothing on this case worth a potful of snot and we've got until tonight to get somewhere or I'm in trouble. You, too."

Zondi immersed himself in his fingernails until they arrived at the crematorium.

"Wait," Kramer said, and went into the building.

He found the white-coated superintendent coming out of his office.

"Good morning, I'm Mr. Byers. Can I help you?"

"CID, Mr. Byers. Can my boy ask yours some questions?"

"He's not going to upset them, is he? They're hard enough to get out here on the hill."

"No, the inquiry has nothing to do with them."

"Go ahead then. I was just going to ask where the tea had got to—would you like some while he's busy?"

Kramer hesitated. He was still angry, but angry now at himself.

"Ta, I'd like some. I'm Lieutenant Kramer, by the way."

"Ah! Just the chap I want to see, I'm told. But you go and get rid of the boy first."

Kramer went over to the big plate-glass doors and beckoned Zondi over.

"Round the back here, there's a bloke making tea. Chat him up for a start."

He winked. Zondi smiled back.

"Then trot over to that place with the wall around it. There's a garden inside with nameplates and flowers in the middle.

Look them over and talk to whoever works there. The boss wants to speak to me."

"Thanks, boss."

Kramer went into the office. Byers was taking a cardboard box out of a cupboard.

"There you are, Lieutenant. The tea's coming—so's Christmas. Now what do we do about this?"

The box was much lighter than Kramer had expected. He shook it.

"What is it?" he asked.

"The old dear that Georgie Abbott sent us by mistake."

"Hell, I'd forgotten about her. Can't you—er—?"

"Sprinkle her about a bit? Oh, a little more wouldn't hurt, but I'm afraid I must abide by the old bylaws. No papers, no last resting place here."

"Then I suppose I'd better take it back with me meantime."

"Good chap. Just sign this receipt, would you? Thanks."

"Now I'm here, Mr. Byers, perhaps I could ask you a few questions?"

"Certainly, delighted. But first I must ask you to come with me through to the control room. I've Maxwell and Flynn arriving any minute now. Friday is our busy day."

Kramer followed him across.

"Please just go ahead. I'm going to fiddle about a bit but I can listen," Byers said, closing the door.

Kramer sat down. He tapped the box in his lap.

"You know then, Mr. Byers, that this lady was not intended for you. We're interested in the one that was."

"Naturally."

"Mr. Abbott has given us a statement in which he said that there was nobody attending this funeral and no flowers."

"Well, he got that right anyway."

"How would you know?"

"You've been here for a funeral, I suppose? You will then have noticed the officiating clergy presses a floor switch at the appropriate moment. That lights this up and I know when to start the music and get it rolling. Right?"

Kramer nodded. He had not asked for a detailed lecture but he should have realized the control panel had the look of a fancy toy about it.

"Now what if that bulb in there should go? There would be no red flash for me and what could happen then?"

"You'd hear the slow clapping begin."

That was a mistake.

"I believe in a little levity at times, Lieutenant, but never in respect of the living. This is an important service we provide. It is not as simple as it looks. Timing is vital. And remember, the slightest hitch can cause immense distress to the bereaved, who are already suffering enough."

It took Kramer a moment or two to recover.

"I'm sorry, sir. Go on, please."

"It wasn't anything, really. I was just going to point out to you this peephole gadget I've had installed for just such a contingency. I make a practice of regular inspections and can assure you that at no time did I see anyone present at that funeral besides the clergy and the funeral directors."

"Is it one of those wide-angle lens things?"

"It is. Rather neat, I think."

Kramer put his eye to it.

"You didn't see anyone hanging about before or afterwards?"

"No. Not that there's really anywhere for them to hang, as you put it."

There was a tap at the door and a sulky Zulu man entered with a tea tray.

"It's taken you long enough, Philemon. Got your girl friend in there, have you?"

Philemon kept his eyes on the brimming milk jug.

"All right; put it down over there and then go and give the front steps another wipe over. There's been a dog sniffing about, leaving dust marks."

"Yes, my boss. The policeman he wants to talk to his master."

"I say, old boy—don't go, have your tea first. I'm sorry I snapped like that; you just touched on rather a sore point."

"I'll come back," Kramer said.

He returned in less than a minute.

"Any luck?"

"None at all."

And Kramer's face showed it.

"I'm just letting it stew a bit. Old Philemon never bothers to warm the pot first. Any more questions?"

"I can't think of any, Mr. Byers. Can you? Did anything unusual happen at all on Tuesday?"

"Hmmm. Why, it did, come to think of it."

"What?"

"Oh, nothing you chappies want to know about. Milk?"

"Ta."

"Oops, not ready yet. We'll give it another minute."

Claustrophobia had never been one of Kramer's problems but now he began to exhibit signs of susceptibility. He disregarded the *No Smoking* sign and lit a Lucky.

"Now where had we got to? Oh, yes. Seeing as we've got a moment or two, I may as well tell you. Quite the nicest thing happened; the chairman of the Parks Committee, no less, paid a call on me. He is nominally in charge of us, you see, and we are, in turn, responsible to him. Yet despite this I've never known a chairman before take the slightest notice of us personally. Milk, you said?"

Kramer poured his own.

"Some of these councillors have no right to be in office, if you ask me. They give you a job and expect you to get on with it. The only time you hear from them is when things go wrong. But Councillor Trenshaw not only called on me in my office, he also asked to see over the whole establishment. It was the end of the afternoon so I was happy to oblige him."

"Why did he decide to come at that time? Did he know your hours?"

Kramer felt he had to say something.

"That was the most heartening aspect of it all, Lieutenant. He had been a mourner at the last funeral of this day but, as he said, he'd not let that make him forget the backroom boys."

Councillor Trenshaw sounded a bit of a ghoul. Kramer's interest picked up.

"And you showed him all over the place, you said? What about his dead friend?"

"More of a family acquaintance, I gathered."

"Still, it seems a funny moment to pick. Do you mean he was there when the oven was going?"

"Of course."

"Christ."

"Good heavens! I see what you're getting at, old boy. They were still taking the handles off in the preparation room when we went through to the incinerator. It was the girl who was being done—or so we thought at the time. We even discussed her case."

"Really?"

"Councillor Trenshaw was very interested in her. He had arrived early for his friend's funeral, which was immediately after hers, and had noticed how sad it was there were no people or flowers. That's why he asked me who it was."

"You have her name?"

"Well, that's all I knew—wasn't it? And I told him her age because Farthing had mentioned it to me in passing."

"I see. Well, it takes all kinds. I don't think I'd have stayed around in that room. Too morbid for me."

"I'm surprised to hear you say that with your job. Councillor Trenshaw wasn't the least troubled. Why, he waited there to see the procedure when we opened the doors again. It gave me an excellent opportunity to press for some more up-to-date equipment."

"You could say then, Mr. Byers—and don't get me wrong—that Councillor Trenshaw enjoyed his visit?"

"I would rather say that he seemed very satisfied with everything he saw. He congratulated us all."

Mr. Byers glanced up at the clock.

"I must be mad. Here am I, gabbling away about nothing, and I've got the new tapes to put on. You must excuse me."

Suddenly there were a lot of questions that Kramer wanted to ask. Far more than he knew would be prudent. So he left.

And all the way back to town he remained silent.

Zondi was changing down for the turn into De Wet Street toward the office when Kramer ordered him to carry straight on. He did so without question. He understood.

Presently they arrived at Trekkersburg Bird Sanctuary. Apart from the waterfowl on the lake, and a giant tortoise, it was deserted. The thousands of egrets which also lived there commuted to the countryside during the day—returning at dusk to shriek and squabble deafeningly in the trees. This was what brought the crowds; no show, no humans.

It was quiet.

The tortoise ignored Zondi. After one hundred and nine years, or so claimed the brass plate bolted to its shell, there was nothing new in the world.

Zondi dropped a burning cigarette stub in front of its head to see what would happen. Nothing.

But Kramer had to react to smoke when he sniffed it.

"Zondi!"

"I come, boss."

The door was already open for him.

A black Oldsmobile made its way swiftly along De Wet Street. The driver, a tough, red-faced man with oiled gray hair, handled it well—braking neatly out of the flow of traffic and slipping into the parking-prohibited area in front of the main branch of Barclays Bank. A freckled youth in shirtsleeves sat chewing beside him.

Van Niekerk paused to watch them.

The driver took a careful look around. Then he nodded to the youth and they got out. Both were armed.

185

A passing stenographer, hurrying back from a hair appointment, heard Van Niekerk's sigh and half-turned. But his eyes were on the men.

The driver had tucked his revolver into his waistband and was unlocking the trunk of the Oldsmobile. His young companion stood self-consciously over him, the automatic in his hand really far too large to dangle casually by the trigger guard.

"You'd better look out how you handle that thing," Van Niekerk reprimanded. "The safety's off and there could be trouble if it dropped."

"Mind your own bloody business," the driver said, heaving two bulky briefcases out of the car.

The youth insolently blew a bubble with his gum. It burst and stuck to the embryo ginger mustache.

Van Niekerk had to laugh.

"We'd soon change your ways in the force," he said mildly, turning his back on an outburst of apologies.

And then he sighed again.

Of all days, the Lieutenant had to pick a Friday to send him on a check of the banks. Friday, when money was pouring in by the bagful, struggling out by the walletful, and every teller in the town had a queue long enough to buy the *Mona Lisa*.

Van Niekerk had been shrewd enough to ask the managers to accompany him to the counters in each case, but even this was not much help. They were harassed, too, and as impatient as their staff in trying to identify a customer from a photograph. Computers had made faces redundant.

"If only you could let us have an account number," they repeated.

"Miss Theresa le Roux?"

"No."

"Miss Phillips?"

"Not any of our Miss Phillipses."

And so a long, tedious, fruitless task had come to an end. The main branch of Barclays had not been able to help either.

Van Niekerk stepped back into the sun.

186

"I'm buggered if I know why people use banks," he muttered to himself. "I wouldn't if I didn't have to."

Then he realized there was no reason why the girl should use a bank—she didn't have a wife like his who enjoyed flashing a check book around.

He walked quickly down to the building society branch nearest to Barnato Street and went in. There were the usual three or four customers trying to make the tethered pens write.

"Can I help you?"

"Yes, miss. CID. Just look at this snap, please."

"Not her surely?"

"Who?"

"That funny Miss What's-her-name. Beryl, come over here a minute."

There were times when Van Niekerk felt that his church was quite wrong in what it said about the miniskirt. The pleasure he experienced was supremely innocent and so, he felt sure, was Beryl.

"That's Miss Phillips," she said firmly. "She always pays in ten-rand notes. But she took them all out again last week and hasn't been in since."

"Oh, Beryl, you can't say that without asking Mr. Fowlie first!"

"Never mind; I just wanted to know if you knew her," Van Niekerk soothed. "I'll see Mr. Fowlie now, please, but I won't tell, girls."

Beryl smiled and walked very innocently across to fetch Mr. Fowlie from his office.

A lone egret flapped slowly overhead. They watched it bank, identify a particular nest, and come in with its flaps down hard.

"Must have got the sack," Kramer murmured.

Zondi frowned.

"Forget it, man. Just tell me what you're thinking now about what I said."

"Hau, it can mean big, big trouble."

187

"And even bigger trouble if we're wrong, Zondi. That's the bugger of it. One mistake and it'll be the Brigadier for us this time. And the bloody chop."

"Maybe it is best that this time you talk with Colonel Dupe."

"It'd give him a miscarriage."

"You whites." Zondi shook his head. "Why is it when a man becomes a big boss like with the council you think he can do no wrong? With my people we make our chiefs by the blood, this way we do not get the skelms telling us what to do. No man does all this work for nothing, like you say this boss Trenshaw does."

"It's called democracy, man. They don't do it for nothing though; many of them like to help."

"By telling other persons what to do?"

"All right then, they're after the power it gives them."

"You can like that thing too much, boss."

"True."

"There have been other gangs with a white boss, like the one robbing the stores in Zululand."

"Joey Allen's mob? But he was white rubbish, not a bloody city councillor."

"That's why they catch him so easy, I think. Could be this boss Trenshaw is a clever one. He is white—he knows the white people must respect him."

"Okay, man, okay. So what do I tell the Colonel?"

"He knows what Shoe Shoe's telling Gershwin about the bosses."

"He doesn't believe it."

"Tell him the other thing then."

"Fine; I just walk into his office and say I've linked Councillor Trenshaw with the murdered girl. How? Oh, easy, sir. You see he did a strange thing. Right after going to a friend's funeral he went round the back and saw what he thought was the girl in question being burned up to nothing. He waited until she was nothing, sir, and then said how pleased he was with how things were going."

"You're talking a silly way, boss."

Kramer shared out the remainder of the meal they had bought in Durban at the pie cart. Zondi took his portion gratefully.

"Let me try again, then. I'll say I have reason to believe that Councillor Trenshaw was seen and heard acting suspiciously at the crematorium on Tuesday this week. Asked to give an explanation for this allegation, I will state that whatever a man's sense of responsibility, there is a time and a place. I will point out that this girl's funeral was advertised in the press that morning and that, according to information received from the superintendent of the crematorium, the aforesaid Councillor Trenshaw did not admit to a close relationship with the deceased party involved in the funeral which followed."

He paused to take a bite from his fragment of pie.

"I will then add that, in my opinion, Councillor Trenshaw displayed an unnatural interest in the workings of the establishment—and an unnatural interest in the incineration of a body, believed to be that of the girl in the funeral advertisement.

"I will state that his interest went beyond the casual interest of a normal person observing such proceedings in that he insisted on staying until the body was totally destroyed.

"And at this point I will ask permission to introduce a hypothesis which may shed some light on the matter."

Zondi snorted, showering crust flakes all over his suit.

"What's the matter? Do I sound like Sam Safrinsky?"

"Supreme court, boss! Not just Jewboy lawyer."

"Thanks. Do you know what a hypothesis is?"

"Very dirty talk that, boss."

The laughter did a lot for both of them.

"Listen and learn then, Kaffir. My hypothesis is that Councillor Trenshaw is taking part in some illegal enterprise of a nature so serious that it involves the liquidation of certain of its members when they prove difficult or of no further use. Furthermore, I suggest that a man of Councillor Trenshaw's education and intelligence could well be the head of this enterprise. This is improbable but not, with respect, impossible.

"And on this basis, I suggest that Councillor Trenshaw went to the crematorium with the express purpose of reassuring himself that certain evidence had been satisfactorily destroyed.

"Furthermore, there is the question of the method used. If we allow this hypothesis to include the death of Bantu male Shoe Shoe, we will note that this was carried out by proxy. It was done badly but did not in any way provide an obvious link to this alleged enterprise. You could say that whoever ordered the killing was satisfied that the victim could not reveal anything specific—from this we deduce the victim had already been interrogated—and that it was much safer to have it done in this way.

"But then we come to the girl. There need be no scruples in killing her for she is a colored and they know her position. But as far as the world is concerned, she is a white. The gang, if I may call it that, takes the precaution of importing an assassin from the Rand. All goes according to plan but Councillor Trenshaw is understandably anxious there will be no hitches. How very natural for him to display such an interest in her final disposal."

It was still very quiet beside the lake.

"You are right, it is no good, boss," Zondi said after dusting himself down. "This 'high' thing you are talking about does not put Tessa with Boss Trenshaw before she gets killed."

"I know it doesn't, Zondi. It's all bloody bull probably. And we can't risk our necks on that. I'm not even sure that Byers bloke was telling the exact truth. He could have been building up his story to make it sound even better for him. Look, it's half-past twelve now. Take me up there again quickly and then we'll get back to see what Sergeant van Niekerk has found out."

14

THE DOOR OPENED cautiously. The Colonel put his head around it and beamed when he saw Van Niekerk was alone in the office.

"Ah, Sergeant, it is good to find a man who likes his work." Van Niekerk shot to his feet.

"Good morning—I mean good afternoon, sir."

"I'm not disturbing you, am I?"

"No, sir. I was just bringing the crime sheet up to date."

"Very good. Do you mind if I see it? This is excellent. So clear. I must try and introduce this method to other members of the squad."

"Thank you, sir."

"And what were you writing on it?"

"That entry there, sir, in green. I've just been doing a check on Miss Phil—er—Miss le Roux's finances. I found that she had over two hundred rand in a building society under a false name."

"Had? In what sense?"

"She took it all out last week."

"That's good. It ties in with Lieutenant Kramer's theory that she was about to leave us when it happened. But where is he now?"

"Out with Zondi—they've been gone all morning."

"Hmm. No idea where, I suppose?"

"Round the informers. He also said they might call at the crematorium."

The Colonel bent over the crime sheet.

"What happened in Durban to make him want to go there? I see they didn't get this Lenny bloke after all."

"No, sir."

"Well, I won't ask any more questions until I see him tonight." The Colonel chuckled.

"Tonight, sir?"

"Hasn't he told you? About my little plan? That's the Lieutenant for you."

And the Colonel was gone, leaving Van Niekerk looking very vexed indeed.

There were a number of vehicles in the car park near the entrance to the crematorium building but no sign of a hearse anywhere.

"What's going on?" Kramer muttered as Zondi backed the Chev up beside them. "Must be it's all over and they're just coming out. The undertaker's boys have already burnt it home for lunch."

He looked at his watch. It was almost one o'clock.

Then Zondi switched off the engine and they could hear the sound of organ music dimly through the thick stone walls of the chapel. There was a rapid fade on the last verse and Kramer smiled.

"Mr. Byers is in a hurry for his lunch, too," he said.

They waited for the mourners to emerge. Nothing happened. Then the organ started up again.

"This priest's got a lot to say for himself, hey, Zondi?"

"It is their way, boss."

When next the music stopped and again nobody came out, Kramer had had enough.

"We'll be here all day waiting for this lot," he said. "Look, I'm going inside to see Byers in his control room. We haven't the time to mess around."

192

He strode rapidly over to the entrance, pushed through the doors, and headed for the small door at the far end of the hallway. But on his way down he paused for a quick glance through the windows of the chapel door.

It was empty.

"Back again so soon, old boy? Did you leave something?"

Kramer turned slowly to face Byers.

"I thought there was a funeral on," he said.

"Oh, no; the people outside are here for some dedication service or other down in the Garden of Remembrance. A plaque, I think."

"It was the music."

"Don't tell me. I've had endless trouble ever since you left. You know those new tapes I mentioned? With a choral effect to help the singers along? I just couldn't get the balance right. That's what you must have heard; I've been juggling about with them in the lunch break."

"You must think I'm a proper fool."

"Not at all, old boy. But didn't you notice you couldn't hear the devil dodger's voice in between?"

"Who?"

"The clergy."

"No, I wasn't expecting to."

"Quite so—music carries much better than voices and it's louder for a start. Do you know anything about tapes, by the way?"

An odd look came over Kramer's face. He suddenly felt he knew something about one tape in particular—but he had to be sure.

The librarian at the *Trekkersburg Gazette* gave the impression of an irritable man with right-wing views. Those that knew him well, however, realized that this was only his way of keeping the left-wing editorial staff at bay. Given half a chance they would be yelling for files all day and never allow him time to bring his clippings up to date.

In fact he was the sort of man who gave the African school-master all the help he could possibly need in compiling potted biographies of the city councillors.

"I am most grateful," Zondi told him. "My pupils will be delighted to make better acquaintance with the leaders of our fair city."

And with that he opened the file on Councillor Terence Derek Trenshaw.

Kramer believed in expedience. It was expedient to put Zondi onto collecting background details, expedient to have the increasingly truculent Van Niekerk confined to the office, and expedient to have Mrs. Perkins wake her dear little Bobby although he did not get up until three.

Bob Perkins was delighted.

"So the tape's important after all?" he asked, hunting about for it. "I didn't think so, with your leaving it with me."

"Have you got a portable?"

"Oh, this thing can plug in anywhere; I'll take an adapter. Here you are."

He handed Kramer the tape.

"Fine, then let's go."

Mrs. Perkins went out to the garden gate to wave them off. She flinched nervously when Kramer let out the clutch and left some tire tread behind with her. "Going far?"

"Just around the corner."

"Barnato Street?"

"Ja."

"Smashing. What do you want me to do?"

"Play the tape."

It was Bob's turn to flinch as Kramer began braking outside number 223 and then changed his mind so abruptly that the delivery boy ahead of them owed his life to a decimal point. The Chev finally stopped four houses down on the far side of the old night-cart lane.

"How about some real detective stuff then, Bob?"

194

"Great! What must I do?"

"You see that lane there? It leads up the side of the property we're interested in. All we have to do is go up it very quietly until we get to a gate in the wall. On the other side is a cottage —I'll go first and open the door. Then you come. Nobody can see you until you are right by the door because there are some high bushes. Step across that part smartly and I'll tell you the rest."

"Check."

Kramer hid a smile as they got out.

And it all went exactly as planned, with Bob making the leap into the cottage like a true Springbok.

Kramer looked through the lace curtains at the kitchen windows on the far side of the garden. Miss Henry was hovering about the maid Rebecca. They were sharing the washing-up.

"Okay, now all you've got to do is get that recorder of yours going and we're away."

"Over here?"

"Just push the sofa from the wall if the plug's hard to reach."

Bob gave it a shove with his knee and it rolled aside on well-oiled casters. Then he knelt down to fit the reel.

Miss Henry was pouring water from a kettle into a teapot over the sink.

"Hurry it, if you can, Bob."

"Won't be a sec. I suppose you noticed someone else has had a deck here before?"

Kramer spun from the windows.

"Where?"

Bob pointed to an area of the carpet which had been covered by the sofa. There were four slight impressions in it like those made by the rubber cushions at each corner of a tape recorder.

"Run it to the last piece, where there isn't so much missing."

"Right. Fast forward wind coming up."

Miss Henry was still in the kitchen.

"One more thing, Bob: can you play it loud as a piano?"

"If you like. I've got one hell of a wattage on this."

"Like a piano."

"That's set. I made a note about volume on the box."

He talked too much. Miss Henry had gone. Kramer swore silently.

"Countdown?"

"Zero. Let's have it, Bob."

Kramer started as the first faltering notes of "Greensleeves" plunked out. Then he sat down on the carpet beside Bob to listen.

The sound he had expected began very softly in a very high key. It gradually built in strength and then started wavering from one side of the scale to the other. It did not come from the amplifier.

Rebecca was having the shrieks in the kitchen.

The pianist's fingers tripped over a chord and there was a pause. The chord was repeated slowly and then the tune went on.

Rebecca was in the garden now and so was Miss Henry, almost crushed in the Zulu maid's terrified embrace.

The tape snapped.

"Hell, I'm sorry. That was a lousy splicing."

"Perfect, my friend."

Kramer rose and opened a window on the two women edging compulsively toward the cottage.

"Good afternoon, ladies," he said cheerfully.

Rebecca covered her head and ran, squealing like a black sow.

Miss Henry was made of sterner stuff.

"I knew it couldn't really be her," she said.

"Why not, Miss Henry?"

"Because she's with the Lord—and *He* doesn't allow it."

That brought Kramer's head back through the lace curtains. He pressed a fist to his lips and then went outside.

"I'm sorry that we've upset your servant. It was just a little test we had to carry out."

"All I can say is that it's just as well the old lady is in the front room. A shock like this could have done terrible things to her. I must admit I don't feel quite myself either."

"I'm sorry about that, too."

Miss Henry subsided into the garden seat conveniently behind her.

"It was uncanny, you know," she said.

"The music?"

"Dear old 'Greensleeves.' The number of times we've heard that in the past. Always the same mistakes, too, the silly things. And the way it goes boomp-boomp-boomp like a train coming out of the station. Who was playing? One of her nice gentleman pupils?"

"Which exactly do you mean, Miss Henry?"

"Oh, they all looked about the same from where we were. Two were on the tall side, one middling, and there was rather a stout gentleman, too. None was any better than the other at it. A shame, too, because an hour's lesson isn't cheap."

"They always stayed an hour?"

"From eight to nine. You could set your watch by it."

"I know I've probably asked you some of these things before, Miss Henry—you don't mind?"

"It's only you're always on about my poor gentlemen. They haven't done anything wrong, have they?"

"Why do you keep calling them gentlemen?"

"Because of their clothes and the way they held themselves. I can always spot one; it's my upbringing, you know."

"Last time you said there were five of them."

"Gracious, did I? Perhaps I was counting that gentleman who called about her life insurance."

"Really?"

"Yes. I almost bumped into him one night as he was coming out of the lane and I was coming back from a late meeting at church. He said 'excuse me' so politely I had to mention it to her."

"Why didn't you mention it to me then?"

Miss Henry caught the change of tone and her brows quivered in an anxious arch.

"You did ask about regular callers, sir. He only came the few times."

"Did she say what insurance company?"

"I think it was—Trinity? Does that sound right?"

"Is this the man, Miss Henry?"

"I haven't got my specs with me; if—"

"Just take a look."

"Goodness, that's him. I know by the shape of the head. A Mr.—?"

"Francis, Leon Francis."

This went down well with Miss Henry. She put her head to one side and whispered it over.

"That is a nice name. Now you aren't being nasty to him, are you?"

"Come on, Miss Henry, I've told you how sorry I am we gave you a fright. We didn't do it on purpose, you know."

"Now you've gone and reminded me again. The awfulest part was when the music stopped. Rebecca and me both thought we could hear the poor thing talking."

"We weren't making a sound in there."

"How silly! You never could hear her anyway, even from up close, and she always pulled the big velvet curtains for our sakes."

"We all make mistakes, Miss Henry," Kramer said, taking her arm.

And he led her, just like a real lady, all the way down to the kitchen door.

There was nothing like a stroll by the river, especially in the spring. Love was everywhere you looked if your ears were sharp enough.

Then Moosa made the mistake of uttering an emphatic gasp and the big black lover spotted him from his position in the tall grass.

198

"Churra! You wait!"

Moosa could not bring himself to—he fled. And stumbled right into another unhappy circumstance.

"What do you want, coolie?" the hobo snarled, looking up from the suitcase of new shirts he was packing.

Moosa lifted his shoe delicately off the open lid.

"A thousand, two thousand pardons! My stomach is giving me hell, master."

He nodded toward a clump of bushes right down at the river's edge.

"Got the runs, have you?"

The hobo laughed nastily and his companion, who had been urinating behind a tree, came round grinning.

"You know what, Clivey boy? I'd say the churra's been putting some of that hair grease of his in the curry."

This joke went down even better. Moosa joined in the laughter with a will.

"What's so funny, coolie?"

"He's being cheeky, Clivey boy. Shall we?"

"Please, my masters. It was the big grass hiding you beneath."

The first hobo closed the suitcase with a double snap of the catches.

"I don't want to touch the dirty bastard in his condition, Steve."

Another good laugh.

Steve picked up a stone.

"Go on, run then, churra!"

It missed Moosa by a good yard but he kept zigzagging until he reached the bushes. There he was sick.

For a long while he just sat listlessly. Then he dragged out his handkerchief and the police photograph came with it. Moosa scrambled to his feet. For the past hour he had quite forgotten that he was being paid to fight crime in Trekkersburg. Any crime. Those shirts in the suitcase had been in their cellophane wrappers. Unopened.

When Zondi arrived at the cottage in Barnato Street he was still wearing his chauffeur's coat. Bob Perkins was just leaving.

"I've really enjoyed myself," he said, as he backed along the veranda with the tape recorder in his arms. "Of course I don't mind walking, Lieutenant, it's not far. And thanks a lot, hey?"

Kramer waved a dismissal.

"Did you get what I sent you for, boy?" he said.

Zondi stepped into the cottage after him and laughed.

"That driver of Boss Trenshaw is a proper fool. He thought I was trying to take his job away from him."

"So you didn't get anything?"

"Oh, yes. I told him my master was a number one doctor and that I had a flat over the garage. Then he talked without worry."

"Good. And the newspaper files?"

"First class."

"We've been busy, too."

"It worked well, boss?"

"Spot on. It ties up right down the line. Miss le Roux was in a vice racket all right. Sit down and I'll tell you."

Zondi chose the sofa and it fitted his length perfectly.

"We'll start with the tape. We tried it out on Miss Henry and on the girl. They definitely thought it was ghosts at work up here."

He paused for the chuckle.

"This tape is what they heard at night when those men came here. Another point: it runs exactly one hour, Mr. Perkins tells me. The men stayed here for exactly an hour each time."

"She works like a factory man, boss."

"Piecework? Ten rand an hour, according to Sergeant van Niekerk. He also said on the phone he was going to finish that list of organ sales, but there isn't much point now."

"Boss?"

"No lessons; not in music, Zondi. How could they say to their wives they were going to their music teacher and then not be able to play any better?"

200

"This driver I talked with said that his boss took his car by himself two nights a week."

"Did he say why?"

"Yes. Boss Trenshaw tells him he goes to long meetings but he likes to drive himself a little, too. He believe him, boss."

"And the way I see it, there is no real reason why he shouldn't. I don't mean meetings here though. Oh, no, he would be too clever to use the girl himself. How big is he?"

"Five foot eight inches."

"Uhuh. Middling but average—so is Sergeant van Niekerk and Mr. Perkins. I think we can say his meetings are with the lot behind all this. They've probably got quite a ring of girls like this one. It's the type that Trenshaw mixes with who go for this sort of thing. They've got the money and the troubles with their women. You should see their wives at the races on Saturday— very posh, yes, but when they stand by a stallion they go all bloody twitchy."

A sense of shock was registered by the clicking of Zondi's tongue.

"Yes, I'm sure there are probably more girls than one because this gang is on the ball. They went to a lot of trouble setting up this tape. I think we'll have to look around at some more music teachers in Trekkersburg—it's like the massage game but not so likely to make you think twice."

"You know what this Boss Trenshaw does for his work?"

"Give me the stuff now."

Kramer read rapidly down the itemized information. He whistled.

"Protea Electronics! There's where the tape came from for a start. And he's worked as a youngster in the Prison Service!"

Zondi did his memory trick.

"The newspaper it says: 'Councillor Trenshaw has come a long way since his first job as a civilian instructor in radio repairs at Pretoria Central. He was only nineteen at the time and had studied at night school.' "

"A long way? I'll say, and he's brought some of his old contacts along, too, for the ride."

"But why kill this girl, boss? That is what I do not understand. It is taking a big chance."

"You forget, Zondi: not the way they did it. If it hadn't been for Mr. Abbott there would have been no trouble."

"Still I ask why, boss."

"Because she could have caused them a lot of trouble if she had wanted to. She was colored, remember? The chances are they did not know this."

"Lenny knew."

"I've been changing my mind about his position with this gang. I'm beginning to think he was what started the trouble for them. He found out what his sister was doing and tried to blackmail them with the Act."

"He did not belong. I see."

"I think it's an all-white arrangement. That's why our blokes haven't picked anything up. Mine are too low class and yours —well!"

"And maybe this is why we can't find Lenny. They have done things to him, too."

"Yes, that's it."

"Shoe Shoe?"

"The same. He knew something and he tried to get money for it. How easy it would be for him to talk to Trenshaw on the city hall steps. I think we know what the Steam Pig is now."

There was a tinkle of crockery and Miss Henry appeared at the door with a tray.

"Just thought you might be needing a little something about now," she said and gaped at the recumbent Zondi.

"My boy's sick," he explained, taking the tray.

"Poor thing, he doesn't look very strong, being such a mite. Can I get you anything for him?"

"He'll be all right. He eats too much. Thanks for the tea."

Miss Henry bobbed a curtsy and went away.

"Boss Kramer," Zondi said, "I have one more thing to ask you."

"Go on."

"Why is it that you are so sure that you must catch Trenshaw but you just sit and talk all afternoon? My watch says it is four o'clock."

"Just going," Kramer replied from the door. "You take the Chev and wait with Sergeant van Niekerk. This is not a job for Kaffirs."

Zondi had tea first.

Protea Electronics was in a new building in the old quarter of central Trekkersburg. The sign outside was small enough to indicate that it did big business.

Kramer could smell there was still sawdust about, left by the shopfitters who had constructed the very smart paneled reception counter. He rang the bell. Immediately a middle-aged woman with belligerent chins appeared through a door marked MANAGER'S SECRETARY. She did not ask him what he wanted but simply stared like a laser beam in the apparent hope he would disintegrate.

"I want to see Mr. Trenshaw."

"Who are you?"

"Mr. Kramer."

"Of?"

"Trekkersburg."

She thought about it.

"Of?"

"I'm from the city hall."

"Then why come here?"

"Because I want to see Mr. Trenshaw."

"That sounds very stupid."

Kramer had had enough.

"Tell me where your boss is and make it snappy!"

The electronic bitch robot switched wavelengths.

"I'm very sorry, sir, but he's at the city hall at present for a cocktail party."

"What cocktail party?"

"It's in the Assembly Room—just off the council chamber."

"I know the bloody plan of the place. I want to know what party this is."

"Councillor Trenshaw told me it was to mark the signing of a contract, I think. The one for the big new native township they're going to build out the other side of Peacehaven."

"Oh, the five-million-rand one."

"It's ten as far as I can remember."

"Well, you're wrong, madam."

Kramer turned and stalked out.

He had not the slightest idea of what the township was going to cost the city. But he did know that he had given his name to her and set the ball rolling.

Talking of balls, it was party time.

Moosa felt relatively safe on this side of the frontier in the front window of his friend Mohammed Singh's tailoring shop.

The Salvation Army Men's Hostel stood across the road, representing the last outpost of white civilization. If there had not been so many potholes in the tarmac there would have been a white line to divide the lanes and that would have marked where the two group areas met.

Singh had been most instructive. Having sat in his window for more than twenty years, cranking away at his Singer and swallowing pins, he had picked up a lot about the establishment over the way.

The small, neglected-looking bungalow, with its wire baskets of tired ferns hanging from the veranda rafters, was where Ensign Roberts lived with his family of eight. It was said that they had less than thirty rand a week and Mrs. Roberts did most of her shopping in Indian stores.

Ensign Roberts was in sole charge of the hostel adjacent to his garden but surrounded by a high corrugated iron fence. The only access was through a pair of large wooden doors hung on brick columns. They were wide open at present but would close firmly at ten o'clock. They would part before seven only if the police dropped off some bum they had taken pity on. Even then Ensign Roberts had been heard to vehemently refuse admittance.

The good man—for he was a good man as well as a Christian —had his problems. The wing coming down toward the gate was the least of them. This was where the old-age pensioners on about twenty rand a month lived. They were quiet and sleepy and only occasionally caused trouble by stealing old newspapers from each other. Next, in the first two rooms of the wing to the right at the far end, were the ex-prisoners. Getting them settled down into jobs and keeping them off drink was more complicated, but in general the failures never stayed long. The real troublemakers filled the rest of the L-shaped building with their stink and their hell-raising. These were the gentlemen of the road, the tramps, the hobos, the drunks, the *dagga* smokers, the surgeons and lawyers who had said what-the-hell and walked out in patent leather shoes. You could not trust them for a moment—not even in their sleep. Ensign Roberts bore scars on his face to prove it, having had his spectacles smashed trying to calm a prodigal who encountered Jesus Christ in his dreams.

These were the men in whom Moosa was interested. They would be along at five to claim a bed before going out again to beg and, perhaps, take some shirts to be sold. He had Singh's permission to use the telephone the moment he saw the riverbank comedians.

Suddenly there they were: right outside the shop window, looking in. Moosa froze. He was the only dummy with a head but the suitcase was gone and they were too drunk to notice.

Then Moosa suffered a second, far greater, shock.

15

KRAMER HATED PARTIES. Parties of any description. And cocktail parties more than any other kind, although they were seldom his lot. Having admitted a prejudice, he was still able to say that this particular party was the worst ever held.

Most of the eighty guests seemed to think so, too. You could see their charming faces ached to get away.

Precisely what was wrong with it was another matter. There were no cocktails, of course, but there was plenty of drink. The mayor's personal staff met the heavy demand for free civic Scotch recklessly, without benefit of tot measure. And there was plenty of food spread over a long trestle table disguised by a tablecloth bearing the Trekkersburg coat of arms. The sly matronly glutton could help herself to anything ranging from salmon roe on toast to a green onion on a stick. The sandwiches were to be avoided, however, as the brittle bread had lost its grip on the cucumber.

It had all the makings of a successful function—and the added attraction of a four-piece band.

At first Kramer had suspected that Mannie Hendriks and his Cococabana Trio were primarily responsible for the strange gloom which pervaded the assembly. He had slipped in through the side entrance just as they began a soulful number which described, in musical terms, the plight of a wretched Peruvian

206

peasant who had lost his beloved donkey; that was what Mannie said and you had to believe him. But even when the drummer introduced a medley from *South Pacific* the mood had not improved.

Then Kramer remembered a dance to which he had gone with some fellow recruits from the police college. They shared an adolescent belief that all nurses were promiscuous and it was in the dining room of a mental hospital just outside Pretoria. He had drawn sweaty-palmed Student Nurse Bekker, who wanted to talk psychology all night. When, to get into the garden, he had mumbled how much he detested parties, she informed him that he was suffering feelings of sexual inadequacy. This had been a surprise.

But now he realized that Miss Bekker might have had something there. He *was* feeling inadequate—and, to use her phrase, probably projecting this into what he saw.

Everything had been so clear-cut up to the moment Councillor Trenshaw appeared briefly through a gap in the crowd. He had been holding his wife's handbag while she demonstrated an exercise from her keep-fit class. Then their friends laughed ambiguously and closed in about them again.

Kramer had not had time for a proper assessment, but it was clear that Councillor Trenshaw was a cool customer. So cool that thoughts of a disastrous misapprehension chilled Kramer's brain. Yet he had to do something.

The music stopped.

And about the only person who was thoroughly enjoying herself, the society columnist from the *Gazette*, zeroed in on the new face she spotted beside the bust of Theophilus Shepstone.

"I'm Felicity Painter—and who are you, my dear? I won't let you budge from there until you tell me!"

She was very much bigger than Kramer and twirled the end of her long string of beads like a lariat.

"Security, madam."

"Really?"

"Yes, madam."

"Oh, dear, what a pity."

And she went yodeling off after a couple who immediately stampeded for the exit.

The party was beginning to fold. The band had stopped.

Kramer looked anxiously across but the musicians had just paused to top up their drinks. Thank God, they had a bit to go yet, and that committee chairman never left early because it was rude.

Then he had it. The idea that would cost him nothing if he was wrong—and bring him the jackpot if he was right.

Mannie was an old acquaintance, after all.

"Request, Trompie? This isn't that sort of do, you know."

"I'd count it a big favor, man."

"Tell me what it is."

" 'Greensleeves.' "

"That oldie! We can't play it on this kind of gig. They want show stuff, Latin Am. It'll sound all wrong."

"They won't mind it that much. Most of them probably won't even notice. For old time's sake."

"The things I do for people."

"Make it short, if you like."

"Okay. Don't ask me why. You hear that, you blokes? My friend here wants a few bars of 'Greensleeves.' Let's take it from the top."

And as Mannie gave the downbeat, Kramer stepped upon the bandstand beside him to look over the heads at Councillor Trenshaw, who stood against the doors to the council chamber at the far end of the room.

"Greensleeves": the simple melody had an effect on Trenshaw which its regal composer never contemplated. It hit him right between the ears. It lifted him on his toes. It brought blood to his face. It fixed his startled eyes on Kramer.

Kramer looked back.

The Cococabana Trio got carried away. With maracas and

guitar they soon had the sweet English maiden stamping in the dust of a Mexican square along with the best of them.

Then it was Kramer's turn to gape.

Three other men were staring up at him, their faces registering alarm. One by one they turned to push their way toward Councillor Trenshaw.

In their wake came Kramer. They reached the council chamber doors and so did he.

"Please go straight through, gentlemen," he said softly.

The group swung on him. A short, plump man took a pace forward.

"Let's not worry the ladies, gentlemen."

They nodded and went in ahead of Kramer, who closed the doors on the party and then crossed the chamber to the light switches. Night had fallen unnoticed.

"Now will you all please take a seat."

The four men advanced slowly, as in someone else's dream, on the large crescent table that seated the council in full session. They did not sit together but went automatically to their places.

Christ, they all had places.

For a moment Kramer hesitated, and then he mounted the platform and took the mayor's chair. He looked down on the table and saw each council member was provided with a blotter and a wooden wedge bearing his name.

"Councillor Ferguson, Councillor Da Silva, Councillor Trenshaw, Councillor Ford," he read out, from left to right.

He knew what the next words would be.

"What's the meaning of all this?" demanded Da Silva.

Kramer did not know himself—a vice racket run by a fifth of the city council was inconceivable. And what made it all most puzzling was the way they were all glaring at him. They were not frightened; they were angry.

"We have a right to know!" Ford barked.

Kramer took a deep breath. It was critically important that he say the right thing.

209

"The Steam Pig, gentlemen."

Something registered all right: Da Silva shot to his feet, furious.

"You've had the contracts off us! You people promised it was all finished and done with."

"What was, Councillor?"

"You know very well."

"The business about the girl," Trenshaw mumbled.

"But it isn't finished."

"Look—"

Trenshaw extended a hand to restrain his colleague.

"Steady now, Irving. We don't know this one. He could be trying to work something for himself on the side."

Kramer remained passive as they stared intently at him, and they found no clue to his internal turmoil. But it was not good, he could not go on: he did not know what role he was supposed to be playing, or the words that went with it.

"I am a police officer. Lieutenant Kramer of Trekkersburg CID. I am investigating the murder of a colored female going by the name of Theresa le Roux. I have reason to suspect that you know something to our advantage."

They let him say it all. And then they just sat. A bomb would not have shifted them. They would have welcomed it.

Da Silva began to sob.

"Well, thank God, it's over," Trenshaw sighed and the others nodded.

Kramer came down from the dais.

"If one of you would like to make a statement, I will just remind you that it is possible for a witness to give state's evidence. This means proceedings will not be taken against you. Murder is a capital offense."

"We haven't murdered anyone!"

"No, Councillor Trenshaw? Then you tell me what it was you did to the girl—or had done for you?"

"Nothing!"

210

A giggle emerged from Ferguson. He had begun to crack back in the Assembly Room.

"What if we all talk?" Trenshaw suggested, a slight smile finding its place out of long habit in a twist of his lips.

"Go ahead, sir, I'm listening."

Van Niekerk had given Zondi the typewriter to clean. To his surprise it was being done very thoroughly.

"What are you using—meths?" he asked.

"Carbon tetrachloride, Sergeant."

"Why can't you just say car. tet., man? Where did you get it?"

"Photographic."

"Was Sergeant Prinsloo there?"

"Yes, Sergeant."

Van Niekerk went back to his list of people who had bought electronic organs in Trekkersburg. Some addresses were still missing.

"Where did you put the directory?"

"Beside you, Sergeant."

"Trying to be funny, Zondi?"

"No, sir."

The directory flopped open and Van Niekerk had to move the outside telephone to make room.

"You say that the Lieutenant rang when I was speaking to the Colonel?"

"Yes. He has gone to a cocktail party at the city hall, Sergeant."

"I like that!"

"He said that we must ring him if there is important news, but not otherwise."

"I see."

Van Niekerk smiled to himself.

Kramer had been right about two things: Trenshaw was the leader of a gang and it had been mixed up in a vice racket.

Only the racket belonged to somebody else. To judge from the response to his opening remark, none other than that elusive but menacing specter the Steam Pig. But he had not pressed the point.

Time was relative and he had relatively little of it. Back at headquarters, the brotherhood of Arsecreepers Anonymous would be already plotting his downfall. They knew where to find him. They would not know what to do with what they found.

It was expedient, then, simply to let the four talk, cross-talk, sob, and express. The whole of their story was emerging very quickly. One question from him would have destroyed the pace, even given time for second thoughts and for lawyers.

And while he listened, Kramer made a number of astute deductions based on obscure references—perception being relative, too.

Trenshaw had been the leader of a gang formed in childhood, forgotten in the acned years of night classes, fondly remembered in the decades of profitable sophistication, and re-formed when worldly success finally opened the doors to the stifling confines of the Albert Club.

Not that it had been the same gang all along. Trenshaw himself was a stranger to Trekkersburg until his fortieth year, and the other three had never met during their early lives in the city. Each, however, had once belonged to a gang and every gang has its component parts: Trenshaw, the slightly soft-looking boy who nevertheless dared to put red pepper in the crotch piece of his aunt's drawers as they hung on the line; Da Silva, the fat boy who liked to make thin boys cry with twists of his surprisingly strong fingers; Ford, the jovial boy who collected dirty words and stories—even made some up; Ferguson, the boy whose parents were never at home and who timorously insisted he always came along for the ride. None of them bad boys—and what fun they had had.

The Albert Club had looked over its half-moon spectacles as they each made their entrance, rustled an airmail copy of *The*

Times, and wished to God that old Brigadier Pinkie Thomas had not faded away. The new secretary, an upstart who had never seen action, was allowing the tone to go to pieces in a damnable fashion. Once the black ball had dealt summarily with counter-jumpers, Jews, and Nationalist party wallahs—now, alas, there were increasingly few men of honor left to do their duty at membership meetings. The whole world was going to hell—look at what had happened to the Seaforths, and to the Camerons. And that was in the UK.

For their part, the four new members had tried very hard to meet the exacting standards which still permeated the vast, paneled rooms. They learned to speak to the sashed Indian waiters with due courtesy, as if to a fellow countryman. They cheerfully endured campaigns which had left thousands staining the map red where it was losing its color. They even learned a compassion for the fierce old bachelors who had lived in an officers' mess all their lives and wished to die in one; there was an almost irresistible attraction in such firm concepts of good, in articulate English spoken slowly round a sip of Cape brandy, in killers who had the innocence of children.

In the end, though, they had moved to the far extreme of the long bar to where their charcoal-suited generation pompously discussed share prices and the effects of cholesterol on the cardiac tissues. This was less of a strain but incredibly boring. Especially when you knew the form of every hobbyhorse in every race to closing time.

In short, the adult world proved a grievous disappointment and their regression to covert childhood was natural enough. It began with a secret wink that Trenshaw had meant for his fellow councillor Da Silva but which they had all returned. And secret signs are the very foundation of gangs.

Soon the four of them were happier than they had been for years. If their excesses caused damage, their wealth could provide compensation and buy silence. Nothing they did, even with claymores that bizarre night in the billiard room, could be regarded by adults as anything but childish. Best of all, they learned that rumors of their antics—they had only forgotten themselves that once at the club—were earning them reputations formerly the prerogative of devil-may-care subalterns.

Then something happened.

Trenshaw expanded Protea Electronics and went to Japan to arrange a hard-bargained contract for transistors. He spent many long days on factory floors and in board rooms. And yet all he told the others about on his return were the nights. The use of sex as a means of persuasion by the lesser Japanese exporter beggared the imagination. When it was used competitively, very little else was left intact.

Trenshaw was a changed man—and so, vicariously, were his companions. The gang had started to grow up again. They began to titillate each other with fantasies about their respective secretaries. Wartime issues of *Lilliput* and *Men Only* were discovered in their garages and laughingly passed between them. A *Playboy* magazine somehow evaded the customs and postal authorities to go the rounds, despite the risk of a fine or imprisonment for possession. Widows and divorcées soon became the brunt of many a subliminal joke.

But these were grown men, not teen-agers, still curious and a little afraid. They all had wives. They had all bedded a woman calculated to do wonders for them socially. That she had proved disappointing in other respects had, up till then, been part of the price.

A price, that was it. These were cautious men, these city councillors; an affair with all its unpredictable and sordid risks was unthinkable. A straightforward business arrangement was not, when you came to think about it.

Now Durban was a port, an acknowledged place for trade and barter, and an obvious place to begin. Yet, in the final analysis, only a fool would walk in off the street to strike a deal with a stranger. You had to know your woman first. You needed at least one satisfied customer, and you needed to trust him.

Trenshaw met Jackson on what was to have been their final visit. The others were out on the veranda of the Edward, talking

214

themselves into a self-righteous puritanism as they watched the night's bikini girls return their ogles with full-bodied contempt. Jackson had mistaken Trenshaw for the manager—after all, he was in his best suit. And by the time Trenshaw had convinced him of his mistake, they had reached the bar. Jackson had insisted on making his apology a large one and Trenshaw, who was feeling low, accepted it. Then he insisted on negating Jackson's gesture by buying him a double, too. Jackson said he would have to get it down rather quickly as he was off to a party in a nearby block of flats. It was plain he was afraid he might miss something. Trenshaw was intrigued.

His clumsy probing amused Jackson. Yes, there were going to be girls. Young girls. He did not know their names—names were not ever used at his sort of parties. It was just going to be all clean dirty fun. He was sorry he could not invite Trenshaw to join him. Very sorry, indeed. But you had to be so very careful.

Trenshaw was sorry, too, when he returned to the others and told them what had happened. He had no need to embellish what he had learned. They all recognized the irony that for once their role of civic dignitary would not be voiced as proof of their integrity. It would sound very strange in the ears of a man like Jackson and not worth the risk. He could take it as a measure of what they had at stake—he could also see their position as posing a danger for everyone concerned.

But he had accepted Trenshaw's business card and had made a promise to pop in on him any time he was in Trékkersburg.

Understandably the corporate life of the frolicsome four had gone into a decline on their return home. Sensing something, their wives resorted to a measure of dutiful abandon which ill became their years. This was only embarrassing and thankfully short-lived. Three secretaries were replaced by mature women, a fourth resigned independently in enormous shame to marry at the mouth of a twelve-bore. It was a bad time.

And then one night Trenshaw had appeared at the long bar in the Albert with a curious smile on his face. Jackson had been to see him. Jackson was in town for the one thing that would bring him all those miles from Durban. It had to be special.

That was why he had telephoned them to meet—they were going to hear it from the horse's mouth. Trenshaw had already been to the hall porter to sign Jackson on as a visitor. He would come right through the minute he arrived. They chose a remote corner, creaked down into their cane chairs, and waited.

Jackson never arrived.

He telephoned next day and apologized effusively to Trenshaw. Things had got a little out of hand. It had been too incredible for words and only ten rand, for God's sake. What had been most impressive, however, were the safeguards. To be quite frank with Trenshaw, sixty minutes was all you were allowed but it left him so—well, he had not been able to face the idea of booze-up on top of it.

Trenshaw was adamant: Jackson had to see him when he called again in Trekkersburg; they would lunch together.

Which they did. And when the others gathered beneath the painting of General Buller, they did not need Jackson to tell them what an hour with Theresa le Roux entailed, music and all. Trenshaw spoke with the tongue of a fallen angel. At the end of it, he declared that Jackson had confessed to having made a check on his background. He had been given the address and an introduction. He was also permitted, after very careful consideration, to allow no more than three others to share his good fortune.

For nobody wanted to kill the golden goose.

But somebody had. And this was not so long after Jackson had dropped the sky on them all, as they played five-up around the Trekkersburg Country Club course, by airily stating he had films and tapes recording acts of unlawful intercourse with a person of another race. He produced a document to prove Theresa was colored. Finally, he advised his fellow golfers to use their influence as best they could to see certain contracts for the new Bantu township went to the list of firms he had had typed out.

As soon as they had seen the names, they knew that Jackson was a man of infinite resource. He could not only search for and find the corruptible, he could also foresee the outraged reaction of the incorruptible being coerced into awarding major contracts to the wrong people. All he asked was that the lesser jobs be passed to a specific group of the multitude of small companies competing for them. There was going to be such a squabble among them anyway, like urchins tossed a handful of pennies, that no one would take much notice of who were the victors. The total sum divided would not amount to much, but if it all went into a single pocket, the figures would move into the millions. The work itself could be subcontracted out.

It was a masterpiece, providing the four elected members of the council could swing it the right way. Even if they could not, it had not been a vast investment, no considerable loss—except to themselves, and there would be other times. The lasting qualities of film and tape were almost unlimited.

And it was no use being silly and committing suicide. They had their families to think of. Once the contracts were signed, the tapes, the films, and the girl would be destroyed. It was well known that a tape or a film, being a copy, could be copied. A coaccused—or at the very least, state witness—could not. By destroying Miss le Roux, it was proof positive that no copies of the records would remain, as it would be incriminatory evidence.

And, after all, gentlemen, she was only a colored. It was not quite the same thing as killing a white. Look how she deceived you, shamed you, humiliated you in the name of eroticism yet really because she hated you for something you could not help —being white.

Desperation gives an edge to men's minds, a ring to their voices, a ruthlessness to their actions, which can be mistaken for conviction. The other members of the Bantu Affairs Committee were only too pleased to have some of the more petty decisions taken for them.

As promised, the girl died in a manner unspecified but sworn to be undetectable. Her funeral notice on Tuesday, the day of the signing, was premature but, as Jackson pointed out on the telephone that morning, an act of good faith made possible by the full council's approval of the committee's recommendations the Friday before.

Trenshaw had still not been able to believe it. He had borne the brunt of what had happened. The others had blamed him entirely, most unfairly. Especially after Jackson admitted that the orgy in that beachfront flat down in Durban had never taken place. They were infuriated to learn, too, that Trenshaw's overwhelming anxiety to see the matter safely to its conclusion had compelled him to claim an acquaintance with some old fool of a captain who was cremated on Wednesday afternoon.

They had stopped talking.

16

CONFESSION DID a lot for the soul but little for the prosecution.
It could not proceed without evidence and there was none.
Everything had been arranged too thoughtfully for that. All
Kramer could offer the court so far was an earful of hearsay.
There had to be a link.

"I want Jackson."

Trenshaw smiled. In the short lull he had been thinking.

"I suppose you must."

"But you don't?"

Trenshaw looked across at his companions. Ferguson had
been apparently taken ill suddenly and the other two were
adjusting his clothing in an attempt to lessen the lividity of his
face. They were totally preoccupied.

"Speaking for myself this time, no."

"Why's that? You don't want to be the only ones who get it."

"Ah. Get what?"

So this was the obverse side to Trenshaw, this was the electronics manufacturer who had set the company geishas such a
formidable task. All he ever needed was a chance to clear his
head.

"You know."

"Don't you find, officer, that speaking to someone about your
problems is often such a help? There they are, all bottled up

inside you, and nothing seems to go right. So you spread them out—"

"What's all this bull about, Trenshaw?"

"Perspective. That, together with the little law I know, tells me you're on rather shaky ground. You see, all you've heard from us is something we could quite easily forget by tomorrow. And then again, we did take all those precautions—that wonderful little tape of the music lesson, for example."

"Tape? There are other tapes, and the films."

"But Jackson has them. While I could once see them reaching you in an anonymous parcel, I don't think he would consider such a move prudent at this stage."

"Who would tell him? How would he know about this?"

"Jackson is not alone in this world, officer. He made that quite clear."

"Where is he?"

"I haven't the faintest."

"You're not going to help me?"

"Sorry. It's a bit much to ask."

"Then you're making one hell of a mistake, man, let me tell you that."

Trenshaw raised a black caterpillar eyebrow. He was surprised by the way Kramer spoke, lightly and almost with regret.

"I can't see it."

"Well, the fact is we've got you and your mates already," Kramer said softly. "Certain tapes and film material came into our possession this afternoon. Your face—your voice with 'Greensleeves' playing in the background. What do you think gave me the idea of coming here in the first place?"

"Jesus Christ! But Jackson—"

"Is not alone in this world, as you said yourself only a moment ago."

Down he went. Practically fracturing his spine in an uncontrolled descent onto the carved teak chair. The groan was a trifle theatrical.

And the best part of it all was that Kramer was more than

220

certain that the audio and visual recordings had never existed. They simply had not been necessary—any more than a real orgy in Durban had been necessary. It just was not Jackson's way of doing things. He always cut his risks to a minimum to achieve the desired result. Having the equipment in the Barnato Street cottage could have caused quite an embarrassment if there had been a blaze and gallant firemen had extracted it together with the reluctant couple—neighbors lived for the night they could dial Emergency. Film had to be processed and with movies this was not a job you could do in the bathroom. Besides which, such evidence could cut both ways and the girl would have taken rather a lot of persuasion. Jackson had been aware all along he would never need to use it. His secret was knowing his man—all down the line from the avaricious Shoe Shoe to the bumbling Dr. Matthews. However, Jackson had deviated from his policy of caution in one respect: he had killed the girl. Now this had been most unnecessary—she could only jeopardize her own freedom by a rash act in the name of justice. Something must have gone seriously wrong somewhere. He meant to find out what.

"Look, Fergy's in a desperate way—we must get a doctor!"

Da Silva was tugging at Kramer's elbow. He shook him off.

"Come on, Trenshaw. We've got one of them, we've got you lot—where's Jackson?"

"He—"

"Yes?"

"He was going to meet me."

"Where?"

"Here, tonight. After the party."

"Jesus—when?"

Trenshaw tried to focus on his watch. His whole arm was shaking.

"About ten minutes from now."

"Description?"

"What?"

"Tall? Fat? Clothes?"

"A bow tie. He always wore a bow tie. With spots."

Da Silva was making for the Assembly Room doors. Kramer vaulted the table and shoved him back against the wall.

"You bloody brute! That man's dying!"

Kramer parried the blow and hit him. Official cautions took time, so he hit him again.

And then he said one word: "Phone."

It was Ford who looked up from gazing at his friend Ferguson's protruding tongue to point to the town clerk's podium beside the mayoral seat.

Kramer found the instrument hidden underneath the writing surface on a shelf.

"Switchboard? Call an ambulance—there's a critical heart case in the—just a moment."

He covered the mouthpiece with his hand.

"I want you all out of this top floor before Jackson gets here. Where can you go?"

"You can't move Fergy in this condition!" protested Da Silva, who was much tougher than he felt to the knuckles. "Besides, he's too heavy."

"I've seen you in action on film, Fat Boy—you've got the strength. Now, where to?"

Trenshaw stood up shakily.

"Say the gents' at the rear of the stage. There's a service lift."

"Hello, switch? The heart case is in the men's lavatories behind the stage. That's right. Police. So—what's that? Urgent? Are you sure? Please, and put it through on this number."

Da Silva and Ford already had Ferguson supported between them.

"Better take his feet," Ford said to Trenshaw.

"I'll open the door first."

"Not that one, Trenshaw. The side door into the passage. I'll see to the ladies. Just you stay with him until the ambo comes."

"What then?"

"Hurry, man!"

His call came through.

The general run of conversations conducted on the twenty-eight lines connecting the Trekkersburg city hall with the telephone exchange were not worth putting down *Women's Own* to listen to. They were polysyllabic marathons about main drainage which could have been curtailed considerably by the appropriate use of four-letter words.

This one, however, warranted plugging in an extra set of headphones for Mavis, the caretaker's wife, who always saw the late shift had a nice hot cup of tea.

"Kramer here."

"Lieutenant?"

"Make it snappy, Van Niekerk."

"Hell, how did you know it was me straight off, sir? Having a nice party?"

"I said snappy!"

"Just a minute, sir—the Colonel wants to say something. Oh, it's just he hopes you're not giving the ladies too much—"

"Shut up and get on with it—they said it was urgent."

"Did they, sir? It wasn't as urgent as all that. I hope I haven't taken you away from something important."

"Sergeant, I'll give you ten seconds to give me the message or I'll come round and kick your bloody balls off. Now speak!"

"Yes, sir. Well, it's that coolie making trouble again."

"What coolie?"

"Zondi's mate—Moosa."

"So?"

"He rang up three times jabbering all kinds of rubbish about some shirts that were stolen and this bloke Lenny."

"Where from?"

"The call, sir, or the shirts?"

"Two seconds—"

"I thought you'd like to know, sir. Anyway, I've sent Zondi down to investigate. I got sick of it."

There was a long pause.

"Sergeant, did I hear right? You get a tip-off regards Lenny and you send Zondi down? By himself?"

"*Ach*, it was real churra talk—maybe it was a tip-off. I don't think so."

"Did Zondi speak to him?"

"I was detailed to handle the calls, Lieutenant."

There was a long pause.

Kramer's next seven words whipped off two pairs of headphones and spilled the tea. But the eavesdroppers made miraculous recoveries.

"Yes, Sergeant van Niekerk, that's exactly what I mean. I'll do it personally."

"What for?"

"Because you've not only probably buggered up this entire investigation, you've also sent—"

"Yes?"

A receiver was replaced.

"Sir?"

What a pity; a moment's pretended prudery had made them miss what had obviously been the best bit.

Kramer walked slowly around the table to the double doors leading back into the Assembly Room. He listened for the sound of women's voices from the other side and heard nothing. But then the doors were specially made to prevent civic secrets from leaking out, and like everything else, it worked both ways.

He turned suddenly right and headed for the side door into the passage: the hell with Jackson. He turned about: the hell with Zondi.

As Kramer slipped out of the council chamber into the Assembly Room, immediately closing the door behind him, he realized that ccuncillors' wives had a rough deal. And that they

224

grew very used to being left high and dry without explanation and only their delinquent servants to talk about.

The hen party broke up with a great clucking of mild recrimination.

"Whatever have you boys been doing in there?" Mrs. Trenshaw chided. "Did you sneak dear Phyllis van Reenen in there without our knowing?"

So they were not altogether as stupid as they seemed to their husbands.

"Sorry; not tonight, ladies."

It helped to get them laughing. Paved the way, so to speak.

"I'm afraid something very important has cropped up," Kramer said, "None of your hubbies had the courage to ask you so they sent me: do you think you could all make your own way home? They said take the cars."

"I should hope so!" snorted a peroxided shrew with long nails who was strangling her silver fox. And her companions echoed the lack of sentiment.

Kramer smiled charmingly as they walked to the exit—he had one minute to go.

Then Mrs. Trenshaw swung around.

"Oh, you might tell my husband," she said, "that there was a man looking for him a little while ago. We told him where you were but he just took a peep through that big keyhole and said it looked a long business and he couldn't wait."

"What man?"

Kramer stepped forward.

"Pardon? Oh, he didn't give his name. Said it wasn't important."

"I *still* say bow ties suit some men," the shrew added firmly, as if having the final word in an argument.

Then she and the other women gasped, for they have never seen a man move so fast.

Van Niekerk was right; the Salvation Army Men's Hostel had

seemed a most unlikely place to find Lenny. It was almost enough to convince you that Moosa had run amok. But as Kramer pressed his foot to the floorboards, it all suddenly made very good sense. The sort of sense that Jackson had displayed on other occasions.

Going back to what the waiter at the pie cart had said, Lenny had been picked up by several men in a Trekkersburg car. Point two: he had not been back to his flat since then. Conclusion: Lenny was staying in Trekkersburg. If he had moved into any nonwhite area, however, the presence of a stranger would have been noted, and particularly so by police informers. The alternative was a white area, and that would also have attracted attention anywhere but in the hostel. Ensign Roberts was always pointedly indifferent as to where a man came from or why. Nor would his suspicions be aroused by a man claiming the rights of a white while looking very much on the borderline: an accident of pigmentation was a common reason for men taking to the road rather than spend lives producing written evidence of their statutory status.

The hostel was, in fact, the ideal place for Lenny to lie low within Jackson's call.

And this meant that Zondi could now be in far greater peril than it appeared when the call from headquarters came through beside the mayoral seat. That area of the chamber had been right opposite the keyhole. If the mysterious Jackson had known a policeman when he saw one, or conceivably recognized Kramer, then he would have immediately set about destroying whatever evidence there was. This just might include Lenny Francis—and Zondi would doubtless try to prevent that from happening.

Unlike Jackson, he would be all alone in the world at the time.

The hostel was around the next corner to the right, coming up fast.

Moosa had the shakes. And a suspicion that he had wet himself, ever so slightly. But Moosa was not afraid.

226

He had never felt such curious excitement; it tickled its way right down him, even into his loins. His eyes felt fat with their looking. It was simply that to maintain his watch on the hostel he had been forced to stand on his toes for well over an hour, enough to give any mature man of sedentary habits quivering muscles. Singh had been adamant about putting up his steel window guards after nightfall as he always did to protect his property. He offered Moosa a box but it had proved too high and exposed too much of the watcher. So Moosa had no choice but to put a cruel strain on his legs and back.

Despite the discomfort, he had left his post only four times and then to make brief telephone calls. As it was, he missed the arrival of a big black car with dirty number plates that now stood parked right outside the hostel gates.

At first Moosa had mistaken the white man seated over on the far side in the passenger seat for Zondi's boss. The trouble was he kept his back turned as he stared into the yard. But the lights of a passing bus had shown he had dark hair after all. Obviously he was waiting for the driver to return from calling on Ensign Roberts. Well, he would have to be very patient. This was the hour during which Bible reading took place and Ensign Roberts permitted no interruptions—nor would he allow anyone who had supper in the hostel to leave until it was over. Moosa wondered if it was significant that he had not seen Leon Francis leave the rehabilitation dormitory when the meal bell rang.

This brought him back to that fourth and last call he had made to the CID headquarters. It had been surprisingly cordial. He had been assured most politely that Bantu Detective Sergeant Zondi was already on his way down, and that Lieutenant Kramer himself was taking an interest in his information.

What was beginning to bother Moosa was that he had been back at the window for another twenty minutes and yet had seen no sign of either of them.

It took Kramer more time than he had supposed to slink through the gardens that backed onto the hostel. There had been dogs and rosebushes and hard-arsed gnomes to contend with. His shins were a mess but luckily nobody heard or saw him.

The corrugated iron fence had also posed a problem, being very difficult to climb quietly if at all. Finally, however, he came across an avocado tree with branches as orderly as the rungs of a ladder. And up he went.

Better and better—right in front of him now was some scaffolding that carried on around a chapel which was being built in the hostel yard behind Ensign Roberts' house. Kramer swung over to it with little trouble.

The builders, presumably drawn from the rehabilitation group, had reached the eaves, and so the scaffolding afforded a good high vantage point. Only there was nothing to see. The yard was completely deserted. All the dormitories were in darkness, as the regulations required when not in use. The sole light came from the dining room—and with it the sound of someone reading Scripture in a deep monotone.

Kramer rose slowly to his feet and looked over the last course of bricks to the road. He drew in his breath sharply.

There was a big black car at the hostel gates, with a white man seated at the passenger window. The traffic's lights did not reach around to his face, and anyway from that distance it would have been impossible to distinguish the features, or even the type of clothing he wore. Except that whereas a conventional tie would have made a vertical blur, a bow tie made a dark blob under the chin.

Jackson.

Kramer was sure of it. He was searching for the way down to the ground when he thought again. According to the councillors' wives, Jackson had left in a hurry. Now he was sitting there as if he had all the time in the world. This was so eccentric it was dangerous. More than that: potentially lethal.

There had to be a reason. Kramer forced himself to ponder it although his whole body strained on a poodle leash. Logic demanded that he begin with what was known: Jackson was a cautious man; Jackson kept himself out of trouble; Jackson was not alone; Jackson had sent a man in for Lenny Francis.

Kramer started to crawl on all fours along the scaffolding to look down into the yard again. He had been on the property for perhaps two minutes—in itself more than long enough for a messenger to fetch Lenny to the car. It was no messenger that Jackson had dispatched but a killer.

The yard, fifteen feet below and in deep shadow, still appeared empty. To his left, flanking one side of the chapel, was the corrugated iron fence behind Ensign Roberts' back garden. Directly in front of him, the bare earth stretched away for twenty yards until it met the old-age pensioners' wing running across at right angles. On his right the wing housing the rehabilitation and hobo section protruded to within a few feet of the chapel. He could almost reach out to touch it.

Then he heard a sound. It came from two doors down.

"Christ. Oh, bloody hell. What's happening?" the voice was soggy with sleep.

Click.

"You Kaffir bastard!"

The answering laugh was one Kramer would recognize anywhere.

"How long have you been sitting there?"

"Shh! CID."

Zondi was in his playful mood.

But this was no time for games. He would lead his prisoner only a matter of ten yards before they could be seen from the gate. Jackson would be off like a flash. Or he might fire first and then flee.

Kramer had to stop that door from opening, and there was no longer the time to look for ladders. He calculated that by swinging from the edge of the scaffolding, he would be left with a drop of nine feet. He could make it safely.

But before he could move, someone else did. The figure slipped out of the door nearest to him and began to edge toward

229

the next one up the line—the one from which Zondi would emerge at any second.

The .38 Smith & Wesson was in Kramer's hand and leveled when it struck him that Jackson would react to a shot like an Olympic sprinter to a starting pistol.

The figure stopped moving. Like Jackson, it was waiting.

Cramp bit Kramer in the left calf. He rocked on his haunches, putting out his free hand to steady himself. It touched something hard and cold: the blade of a trowel honed sharp by coarse mortar. He grasped it tightly by the handle.

The door opened, a fraction too soon.

Lenny Francis stepped out into the night with a gun in his back and Zondi behind it. They took three paces. The figure sprang. There was a glint. A small cry came from Zondi. He sprawled, tripping Lenny.

Then as the figure raised its knife hand again, Kramer sprang. Not feet first but in a long dive with the trowel held at the apex of his arrowed body.

There was nothing calculated about it. Pure chance provided the perfect trajectory that tore open the throat of the hired killer. Gravity did the rest of the damage.

Kramer landed badly and Zondi's skull, so hard against the ground, drove the wind from him. He curled up, gasping, retching, helpless.

Lenny, untouched, recovered Zondi's automatic and trained it on them.

The engine of the big black was running. The man had slid across and started it a minute ago. Now he was revving it gently.

Moosa had lost all patience. If this was how the CID responded to two good tip-offs, they were not worth his time and trouble. He would tender his account and sell cabbages.

Then the car was switched off again. The white man with a bow tie got out and stood on the pavement, his right hand closed over something in his trousers pocket.

Just a minute; this could be a detective after all. Moosa decided to keep watch for one minute longer.

Van Niekerk slammed down the receiver and turned to Colonel Du Plessis.

"It was just that churra bastard to say there's nothing doing down at the hostel."

"Moosa?"

"He wanted to bugger off home."

"Why tell him to stay on then?"

"Why *not*, sir?"

The Colonel dearly loved a dry wit. Their relationship deepened.

"He took a hell of a time to get that out, Sergeant."

"Oh, he also talked a lot of crap about us having a bloke down there."

"And so?"

"I didn't say anything. Two seconds later he's changed his mind and thinks it's someone paying a visit."

"He was sure it wasn't the Lieutenant?"

"Positive."

"But where is he then? And Zondi?"

Van Niekerk shrugged. The movement could not have been made more expressive by Don Quixote's mother-in-law.

"*Ach*, it can wait, Van. We'll give him until eight and then take over the case; meantime let's get your complaint about his conduct on the telephone down in writing. I can't have my officers speaking like that. Paper?"

Van Niekerk had an idea as he drew the foolscap from its appointed place.

"I suppose there's not a chance he's in trouble, sir?"

"Some bloody hope," the Colonel muttered.

Kramer laughed and found it personally reassuring.

But it disconcerted Lenny.

"What's so bloody funny?" he demanded in a hoarse whisper, jabbing at him with the automatic.

For a start, Lenny was. His actions were absurd. Only a fool would handle a loaded firearm like an interviewer's mike. Only a fool would dither around instead of getting the hell out while the going was good.

And then there was that soft trickle coming from Zondi's mouth down there in the dust—each obscure Zulu obscenity a delight in itself, although the joke was really on Jackson.

"I was thinking of Jackson," Kramer said.

"Don't worry; I've seen him."

So that was it. Lenny must have stepped back a couple of paces and caught a glimpse of the watcher by the gate. Yet this should not have deterred him. He could have got out the back way. Better still, he could have shot from the shadows at close range and made off for the wide blue yonder in the big black car. There had been more than enough time for all this.

As it was, Kramer had already recovered both wit and wind and made a cursory review of the proceedings. There was a fine irony in the fact that Jackson had finally revealed himself to be a man cautious to a fault. If only he had taken a chance and hired an amateur to deal with Lenny, things might have been so different. The thing was that every killer—however deprived his childhood—had his qualms. The novice suffered most in this respect, being inclined to overreact out of a sense of insecurity. But what had happened was no accident and Jackson would have made sure of hiring a true professional. In this he had overlooked that while an expert virtually ensured a proper job being done, he was also confident enough to employ one of his lesser skills when assailed by some inner misgivings. The *tsotsi*, now languidly losing body heat beside them, had clearly balked at something—in all probability the very human dread of a bad name. And there was certainly no surer way of getting one than by needlessly killing a policeman; it inevitably brought out the very worst in the forces of law and order, who would then disrupt the entire twilight fraternity, implicated or otherwise, with a process of elimination which was often just that. If at the end of it the dead officer's colleagues failed to get their man, the private sector would. It was enough to give any psychopath a social conscience—and make him twist a knife to strike an artful blow with the hilt.

Zondi sat up, shook his head, and felt behind his ear for blood. There was none.

"What now, boss?" he said.

Kramer shrugged and then looked expectantly at Lenny. He saw a changed man.

"Get up slowly," Lenny ordered, as though he had been waiting for just this moment to assert himself. "Put your hands on your head and go round to the kitchen."

Kramer and Zondi set off immediately. When a hypersensitive young thug held your life in the curl of his trigger finger, it paid to humor him until a realistic alternative suggested itself. Even if you were somewhat vague about the kitchen's exact location.

"The next one along," Lenny corrected them.

The kitchen door was slightly ajar. Kramer pushed it wide open with his foot and stepped inside.

Only a fool would accompany him and Zondi into a darkened room and so, having new regard for Lenny's character, he was not surprised to find it relatively well lit. He was taken aback, however, to note that the light which passed through the big window came from the street and that he could see what had to be Jackson down there leaning on a gatepost. He had certainly got his mental plan of the hostel a little confused.

"Over there," Lenny said, pointing.

Again they obeyed without hesitation and found themselves boxed into the far corner with the window wall on their right, another wall behind them, an Aga stove to their left, and the end of a double-sink unit before them. The latter had been pressed out of a single sheet of stainless steel so that when Lenny heaved himself up on the far drainboard, they felt the vibrations carry through to their end.

Ordinarily the drainboard might have seemed a somewhat eccentric place to sit, but in the circumstances it was nothing more than strategically sound: it allowed Lenny to keep one eye on Jackson and the other on the pair in the corner, it was too far for a quick rush and too near for a bullet to miss.

But this on its own fell short of explaining precisely what Lenny had in mind by bringing them there in the first place—or indeed why he felt it necessary to prolong the association. Kramer realized now that he had been more seriously affected by his fall than he had so far conceded; his thoughts had been engaged on all manner of frivolities and, like the prisoner debating his final menu in the death cell, had been avoiding the real issue. It had to stop.

"Your arse is getting wet," he cautioned politely.

Lenny frowned.

"Those splashes of water on the sink—they're seeping up into your pants."

"You don't say."

"Just thought you ought to know."

"Thanks."

"Can we talk then? You don't mind?"

"If you like, Mr. Detective. Just keep your voice down."

"Why?"

"I don't want you to frighten him away."

"Jackson's coming here?"

"He will, by and by."

"To see what happened to the *tsotsi?*"

"That's the idea."

"Uhuh. What then?"

"I'll shoot him."

The raw stupidity implicit in this statement gave Kramer mental indigestion. There was simply no place for it alongside the obvious fact that Jackson could have been dropped at the gate with the minimum of fuss. He could take no more.

So it was left to Zondi to get down to brass tacks.

"You're going to shoot us, too?" he asked.

"Police? Don't make me laugh!"

But Lenny should have delivered the line with more conviction. Such patent insincerity worked faster than a double dose of fruit salts—Kramer's blood fizzed and his brain burped. Suddenly he was thinking clearly again.

Of course; the little bastard had had it all worked out from the start. And what hurt now was that he had used some of Kramer's own logic to perfect his plan; a shot ringing from the yard would have Jackson sprinting for the border, two shots would have him hurdling the customs post, but three shots all coming together would wrap things up very nicely—the three shots he would fire as Jackson came poking around the kitchen area looking for his missing employee. Why he wanted to kill them, too, was academic at this stage.

And here was the inevitable flaw: Lenny was banking on their cooperation by pretending he meant them no harm.

Zondi must have come to a similar conclusion simultaneously, for he inquired: "And if we start to make a noise now? What then?"

The muzzle of the pistol lifted to meet his eyes.

"Let's not talk about what won't happen," Lenny said.

It was not such a flaw after all: a score of two out of three was not bad.

So the only hope now lay in a chance diversion. There was some likelihood of this in the direction of the door leading to the dining hall but not while the sound of an accordion continued to come from behind it. Ensign Roberts, squeezing the good life into his errant singers with the application of an anesthetist using bellows-resuscitation, was indeed a versatile man—further evidence of this stood within reach on the drainboard: an old-fashioned electric toaster with flap-down sides having new elements fitted.

Lenny had noticed the sequence of Kramer's eye movements.

"Roberts never finishes his sing-song before eight," he said.

"That's twenty minutes from now and nobody will make a move until then."

"You think Jackson won't wait that long?"

"He knows about Roberts' habits, too. He'll come before then."

Kramer shrugged and picked up a screwdriver.

"Watch it," Lenny warned.

"Christ, I'm not likely to try anything with this! Anyway—"

"Yes?"

"We haven't any proper evidence on Jackson, so you may be doing us a favor."

That threw Lenny—and so did the next move.

"What the hell do you think you're doing?" he snapped.

"Mending a toaster."

"Hey?"

"Here, boy, gimma ama-pliers."

"Yes, my baas."

Lenny could not watch dumbfounded as Kramer and Zondi slipped whimsically into their old routine of electrician and electrician's mate, an act perfected in dozens of unsuspecting homes. Within seconds the illusion was complete—right down to the feeling that the black man, obsequiously responding to gruff requests for tools within easy reach, could have done the job much better himself.

"You bastards are mad," Lenny muttered.

"Ama—screwdrife."

"Here, my baas."

"Where's the ee-element, you stupid Kaffir?"

"By your hand, my baas."

"Don't bugger around; how am I supposed to see it there? Hey?"

It had its touches of comedy, too, but Lenny could not be totally distracted from the window. This was a pity because it meant that Jackson had little chance of taking the initiative and saving more than his own life.

"My baas is sure the wire he going by that bottom side?"

236

"You know a better way of doing it?"

"No, my baas."

"Then shut your flaming trap and use your brain, if you've got one."

Zondi looked in surprise at Kramer, as if the line was not in the script he knew. Then he scratched his head, thought hard, and grinned sheepishly.

"Hau, sorry, my baas."

"Okay, cut it out—that's enough," Lenny said.

"Bloody hell, we've just finished the job," Kramer protested, closing the side flaps. "Can't we at least see if the thing works now?"

And he reached casually for the wall switch, flicking it on before Lenny could raise an objection. Nothing happened. Kramer tugged at the plastic knob on the near side of the toaster and opened the flap slightly to inspect the elements. They remained dull.

Lenny could not help a small smile. It showed his dimples.

"What's your next trick?" he asked.

A good question—especially as Kramer had quietly turned the tables and was now armed with a weapon more swift and certain than the Walther PPK. And a question of choice: knowing that there would be no escape from the room without killing Lenny, he had to decide whether to do it immediately, while the little bastard was still unsuspecting, or to take a chance on getting a number of things cleared up first. He opted for the latter, although it made the speed of his reactions to any sudden move a critical factor.

That settled, all he had to do was unsettle Lenny and see how much he could learn from him in the time remaining.

So he said: "Aren't you frightened, son?"

"Me? Why should I be?"

"Because your little plan isn't going to work, you know. It's a proper balls-up."

"Oh, really?"

"Yes. You should have got us while you could out in the yard."

"I've told you both, I don't want to hurt you."

"Come on, man! You were just too scared to get in close enough for a knife. You didn't know how much we were putting on and you'd heard of our judo tricks."

"That'll be the day."

"Admit it. You're going to blow holes in us straight after Jackson."

"Crap."

"Even waited for old Zondi here to come round so there'd be no problems getting him into this room."

"It was only a minute at most. Anyway, give me one good reason."

"Simple. The way things are going now we'll be witnesses to a murder—Jackson's. I'm sure you don't want that."

"True."

"My point is that your first shot will bring the buggers flying through the door over there. You haven't a chance of getting away."

"True also—if you weren't going with me when I leave. That's why I waited for the Kaffir to stand up."

"Well, well. Hear that, Zondi? Sonny boy here's been reading the papers; he wants us as hostages. What are his chances?"

"I think bad, boss."

Lenny began to look very agitated, as well he might. Time was running out and Jackson still had not budged. Granted, there were about ten minutes to go before Our Father broke up the meeting, but now a hint of mutiny was stirring in the corner. His two captives were finding the loopholes in hastily improvised explanations for their continued existence and soon there would be no accounting for their actions. The suggestion he was holding them as hostages had been too obvious a fabrication—he could quite easily shoot whom he liked and then escape by holding the rescue party at gunpoint until he reached the door. His dilemma was very similar to that faced by Kramer and would force him to the same conclusion: somehow he had to keep the chat going long enough for him to achieve his ends. It would have to be one hell of an engaging topic.

Kramer nudged Zondi.

"Well, I'm buggered if I'm going to stand around here all night," he said. "This kiddo's been too clever by half and it's time he realized it. In fact, I bet he has already. So what do you say to our giving a little yell for the boys next door?"

Zondi opened his mouth.

"Want to know who did it?" Lenny blurted out desperately.

"Kill your sister? As if we didn't already. Come on, Kaffir, together now."

"It wasn't Jackson."

"We know—he hired a spoke, but he did it all the same, legally."

"No, he didn't!"

"Someone did."

"Sure. But how did you lot—"

"We all make mistakes."

"Hey?"

"I suppose you must know or Jackson wouldn't be trying to get you. He hates evidence lying about."

"So that's what you think?"

Zondi broke wind.

"He's trying to waste time, boss," he added.

"You're right, man."

Lenny made a quick check on Jackson's position.

"For Jesus' sake, I did it!" he said.

And Kramer sighed. Honest to God, his sense of timing was inspired.

"I sodding did, you know!"

"Oh, piss off. Don't try and act tough; it's too late."

"You don't believe me?"

"How did you get the spoke man down here—smuggled him in a bike?"

"He got a job for the weekend in a furniture van."

"You don't say; that was clever."

"Long-distance removal, a whole house of things, Pretoria to Trekkersburg and back early Monday morning. The firm gets them the passes."

"Name?"

"I don't know. The wogs I fixed it up with didn't say."

"Description?"

"Never saw him. Wrote her address in the phone box by the city hall."

"Shoe Shoe saw you do this?"

Lenny faltered.

"No, he'd copped it before."

"Why?"

"He tried to get money off Trenshaw—blackmail. He didn't know what he was talking about but he was a security risk. We got Gershwin—"

"I know, but go on, I'm interested. How come a brother murders his own sister? Even for a *gamaat*, that's pretty low."

"I'm not a bloody—"

Lenny stopped short of his denial and in that moment Kramer knew he was winning: the poor bastard was going to any lengths to keep things going until Jackson appeared.

"She was a bitch, a whoring filthy bitch who thought she had a right to get out of this sodding country and leave us."

"You and your mum?"

"Yes. Oh, she'd be okay anywhere with her bloody music and junk. That's all she cared about."

"But it seems you were helping her, sonny. Were you her ponce?"

Lenny laughed.

"I was her ponce all right. Knew Jackson wanted a dolly for the township job and lined her up. I never said who she was, mind."

"But how did you find her in the first place?"

"She found me, man. Contacted me through an old school-mate—"

Lenny paused.

"Durban High?" Kramer asked softly.

"Never you bloody mind. Anyway, she said she wanted my help to get a passport."

"A forged one?"

"Natch—only I didn't tell her that was out of my class."

"And that's why she did it? Not just for the money?"

"*Ja,* lay there on her back thinking of Merrie stuffing England."

Whatever the Race Board said, Lenny didn't talk like a colored, or think like one either.

"The contact lenses were for the passport then?"

"Some bull I slung her to keep her happy. Make it more authentic."

"Why kill her, though? Jackson must have been pretty pleased with the setup. And with you."

"I'll say."

Then Lenny stiffened.

"The bastard's just taken something out of his pocket," he whispered.

"Boss!" Zondi said urgently.

"No, man, not now. I want to hear—"

"But, boss . . ."

"He hasn't started walking yet," Lenny said, keeping his voice very low. "It went wrong, you see. I got a big kick out of what those creepy council freaks did to her for their ten rand and then, when it was all over, I checked in at Barnato Street one night when we had them, and said no go on the passport. Hell, that bloody backfired all right. She did her nut—weeping and yelling and saying she'd go straight round and tell you buggers all about it and take us all inside with her. I started to make promises, I promised a passport for Sunday night—then I fixed up with the spoke. I had to do something. Christ, I *had* to!"

"But I thought this was all Jackson's idea? A bonus for the contracts was having her knocked off?"

"Huh! That's a joke. Who said this?"

"Trenshaw."

"No, man, that was Jackson trying to keep them happy. Got the bloody shock of his life when he saw it in the paper that she had died. He planned to have her around for years to pressure them. And then when he saw the article, he really went mad. He sussed it was something to do with me, me being the contact, and sent his boys down to Durban. They gave me the business but I saved it up for the end. I told him she was my sister."

"But he'd have known that already from the papers he showed the councillors."

"Passports I can't fix—those things I can. They had Le Roux on them."

"So Jackson didn't see you doing your own sister?"

"He said he couldn't, but he wasn't sure. He told me to stick around, sent me to this place. I had to or it would have been suspicious. Something must have happened for him to twig."

"I told you: we got Trenshaw—and the others."

But Lenny was not really listening any longer. He was taking aim through the window.

"Lenny, is Jackson the big shot in all this?" Kramer asked softly.

There was an almost imperceptible shake of the head.

"Then who *is* the bloody Steam Pig?"

Too late—Lenny's finger was already tightening in the steady squeeze he had been taught as a cadet on Durban High's rifle range.

Any second . . .

So Kramer let go of the plastic knob, which allowed the side of the toaster to drop and make contact with the stainless steel sink unit.

The spark was unexpectedly small. But the effect of the 220-volt charge on Lenny was as anticipated; he gasped mightily, his body arched back, and his fingers—thank God—stiffened out nice and straight. For an instant longer the current passed

242

down the wire to the toaster perched on its little insulated feet, through the crude connection improvised on the hinged side flap, out along the draining board, and up through the highly conductive wet trouser seat. Then the kitchen's fuse blew in a box over near the dining-hall door.

Kramer heard the pop and abandoned caution as he scrambled to catch Lenny before he could topple into a pile of dishes. He just made it.

A moment later Zondi was at his side. Together they gently lowered Lenny's upper half sideways so that his head dipped beneath the washing-up water and his curious little sounds became innocuous bubbling.

That done, they looked out of the window.

It was rather shocking to see Jackson carrying on out there in the yard as if nothing had happened. He had his back turned and was stooping to examine the *tsotsi*. But they would get to see his face soon enough.

Kramer and Zondi spun and started for the outside door, going up on their toes ready to sprint around and make the most of an attack from the rear.

Then it happened. Lenny died. And his own body current was discharged totally, blowing his mind and causing a sinew-snapping spasm that put a bullet into Mrs. Beeton.

The shot did not echo but everyone seemed to listen to it for a very long time.

At least that was how it seemed until the door to the dining room crashed open. Ensign Roberts, who had the advantage of having the light coming from behind him, took one glance at the slumped form on the sink. The fight was spectacular.

But Jackson did not stay to watch.

Kramer's right elbow hurt like hell, worse than his groin. He flinched.

"So you think this is bad?" Strydom murmured, removing another fragment of spectacle lens.

Kramer made no reply. He had said nothing about his injuries

243

except to use them as an excuse to get him into the hospital without attracting undue attention. It was just that the District Surgeon always made a point of cheering up his patients by comparing their sufferings favorably with those of others.

"Christ, you should take a look at Ensign Roberts in D ward," he said. "He's got a right eye like a squashed guava."

"Stupid bastard."

"*Ach*, no, Lieutenant, that's not the attitude. He was trying to help. He thought—"

"We'll never bloody get Jackson now."

"The Colonel seems to think different."

"He would. Him and Van Niekerk dancing round at HQ, organizing their ruddy roadblocks and slapping each other's bum. They haven't a hope."

"Why not?"

"They don't know what he looks like."

"What about his car?"

"Moosa chucked a brick through the back window—he'll have it changed anyway."

"Who?"

"Just a churra we know."

"Pity it wasn't the windshield. But that's coolies for you—no guts."

"Uhuh."

"Anyhow, you should have no worries. You got the brother —and a few others besides, I hear."

"Oh, yes?"

"No, I'm not trying to get anything out of you. The Colonel said it was hush-hush but he was very pleased."

"Big deal. He won't have a scrap of evidence when that little lot he's questioning see their lawyers and lose their memories."

"Look, what more can you do?"

"Get the bastards behind it."

"Oh, so there's not just Jackson?"

The sister in charge of the casualty department came over and cleared her throat in A minor.

"Excuse me, doctor," she said, "but there's a boy outside who wants to see this patient."

"Zondi?" Kramer asked.

"He says he's from the CID."

"Fine, send him in, Sister. I'm almost finished."

"Thank you, doctor."

Zondi entered with his eyes respectfully averted and handed Kramer a slip of paper. On it he had scrawled: "Colonel telling Van that Ferguson can die soon. 2100 hrs."

This was just what Kramer had been waiting for—and his only way of getting the information without arousing suspicion. Now that Lenny was dead and Jackson had fled, he knew of only five men remaining who had plainly registered something when he had mentioned the Steam Pig. Four already disclaimed any knowledge of the phrase but they had their lives to live. The fifth had not.

Kramer winked his gratitude at a good and faithful servant and then dismissed him.

The drag of the next five minutes was a greater agony than anything Strydom's clumsy fingers could inflict. In fact it seemed a full hour of missed opportunity before Kramer arrived in the side ward and began to browbeat the nurse at Ferguson's bedside into allowing them to be alone. As an only son, he claimed that right.

She was touched and left. There was only the one bed in the room.

"I'm dying," Ferguson said, looking awed, then giggled.

Kramer could just catch his words by bending low over him. Actually Ferguson did not look all that bad, but he had the right idea if he was going to be of any assistance.

"Remember me?" Kramer asked.

"Hmmmm?"

"Any ideas?"

"Specialish?"

"Try again."

"Brother—Jack?"

245

"Shall I tell you?"

Ferguson nodded with the eagerness of a child anticipating avuncular delights.

"I'm from the Steam Pig. Remember?"

This brought a strange smile to the candle-wax lips. It broadened jerkily into a leery grin.

"Give her. My love."

"*Who?*"

"Her. Little piggy."

"I said Steam Pig."

Ferguson brightened.

"She's dead," he observed with satisfaction.

"Who? Peggy is it?"

"You are a bit thick," Ferguson scoffed, becoming lucid all of a sudden. "We all called her the Pig after Derek said it first. What a laugh! A dirty pig all right—the things she'd let you do. Oh, my."

"Holy Jesus."

"Nobody knew who the Pig was, you see. We could talk about her in the club and nobody knew."

"But *steam?*"

"Very clever. I said *Steam* Pig. Chuff, chuff, chuff. It was like a steam engine. Chuff-chuff-chuff she'd go in time to the music. We added Steam just for fun. Like a code."

And Ferguson began to hum "Greensleeves" with a distinctive locomotive rhythm that Kramer recognized instantly.

"You poor bloody sod," he said.

"Steam Piggy thought it such a joke!"

"I bet."

Kramer left abruptly.

"Holy Jesus," he said again, in the passage. The nurse, returning with her cup of tea, stared after him with the utmost sympathy. He looked ill.

He was sick to the stomach to think that of all the types of names he had considered, not once had the idea of a nickname occurred to him. No wonder nobody had ever stopped to ex-

246

plain it before—the topic had always been the girl and they must have supposed he understood what such a trifling thing meant. It had never been important.

Except to Shoe Shoe, and he had missed the point as well. Look where that had got him. God, the consequences could be almost as devastating if this ever got into the Colonel's after-dinner joke book.

Oh, sod him. He'd never catch Jackson and so he'd sodding well never know. The sod.

Kramer stepped out into the night heading briskly on foot for the Trekkersburg Tudor Tavern. It had been a lot of trouble to go to for a whore, a steam-driven colored whore from Durban at that, but it bought steak.